T0041578

SUPERNATURAL™

THE OFFICIAL COLORING BOOK

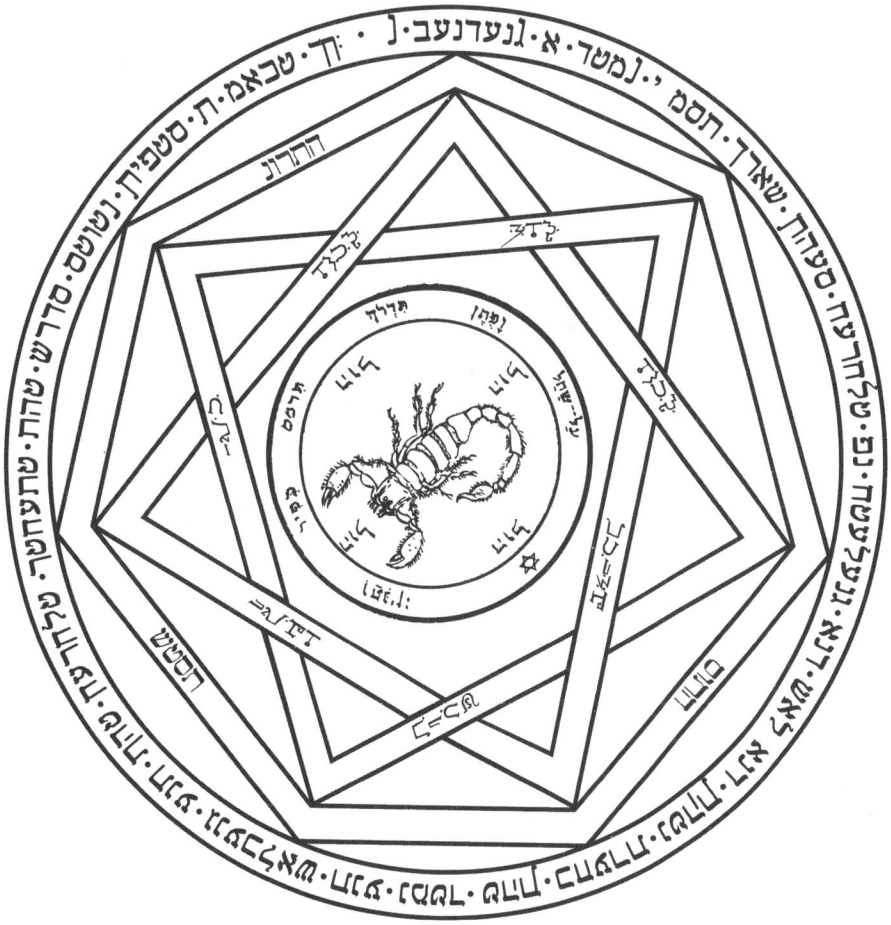

INSIGHT
EDITIONS

San Rafael, California

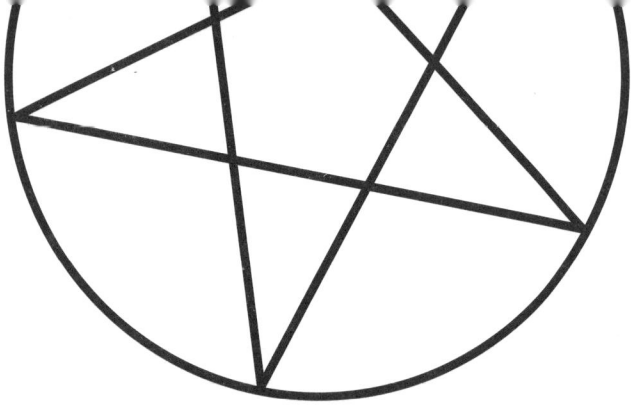

Ever since their mother was killed by the Yellow-Eyed Demon, Sam and Dean Winchester have literally gone to Hell and back hunting supernatural creatures. From killer clowns and hex bags to creepy one-star motel rooms, *Supernatural* is packed with otherworldly color and intricate sigils to explore. So grab your rock salt and pencils, and get to know everything from the Devil's Trap to angel blades up close and personal as you color your way through the world of the Winchester brothers.

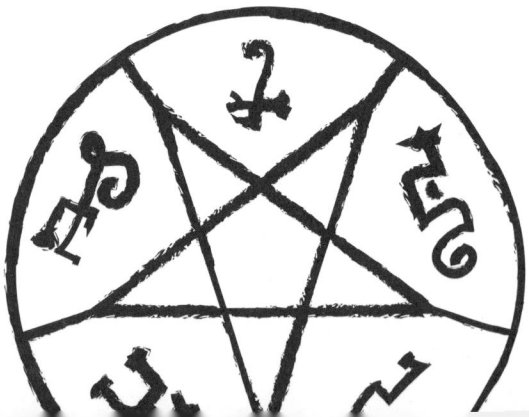

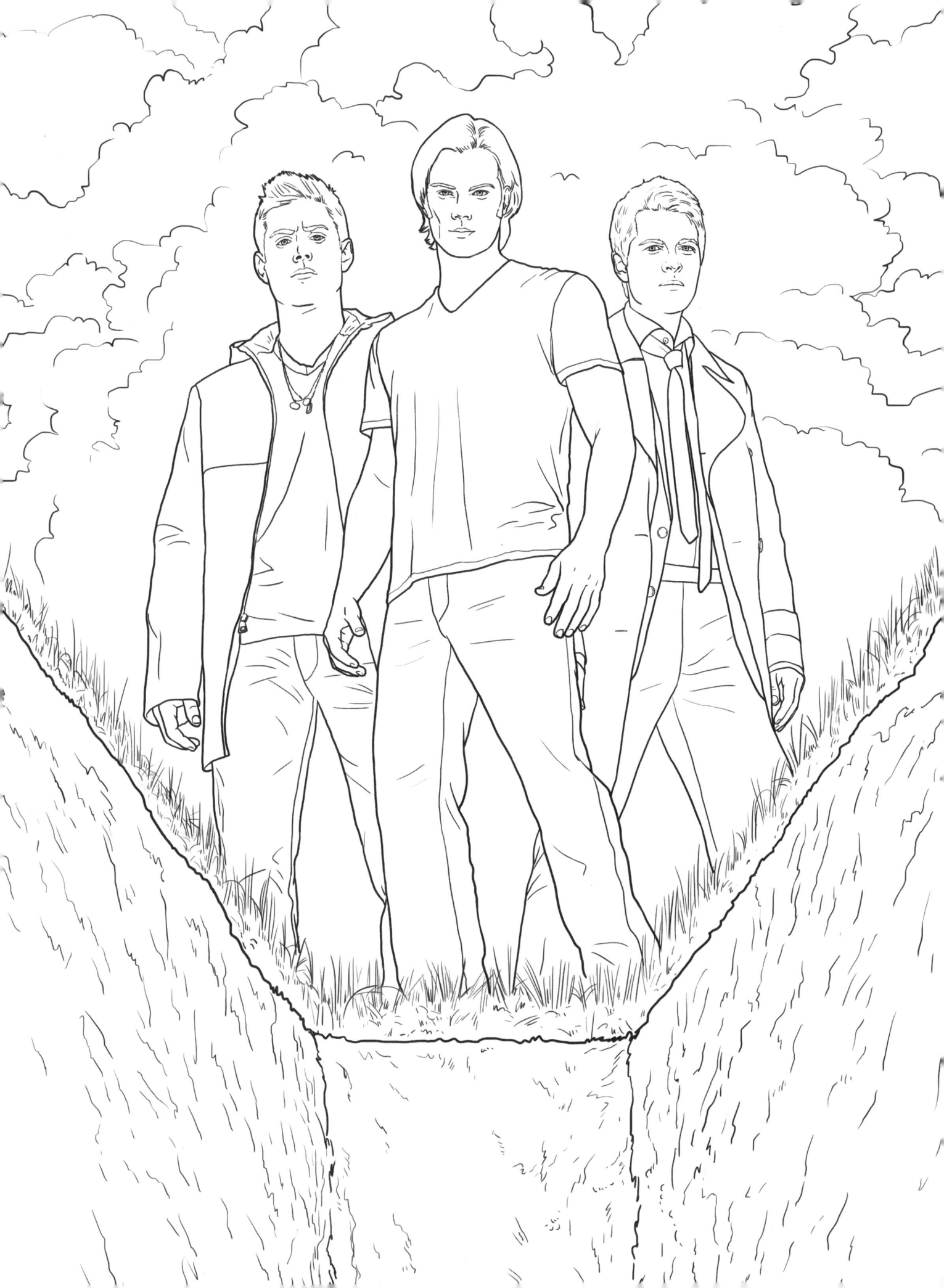

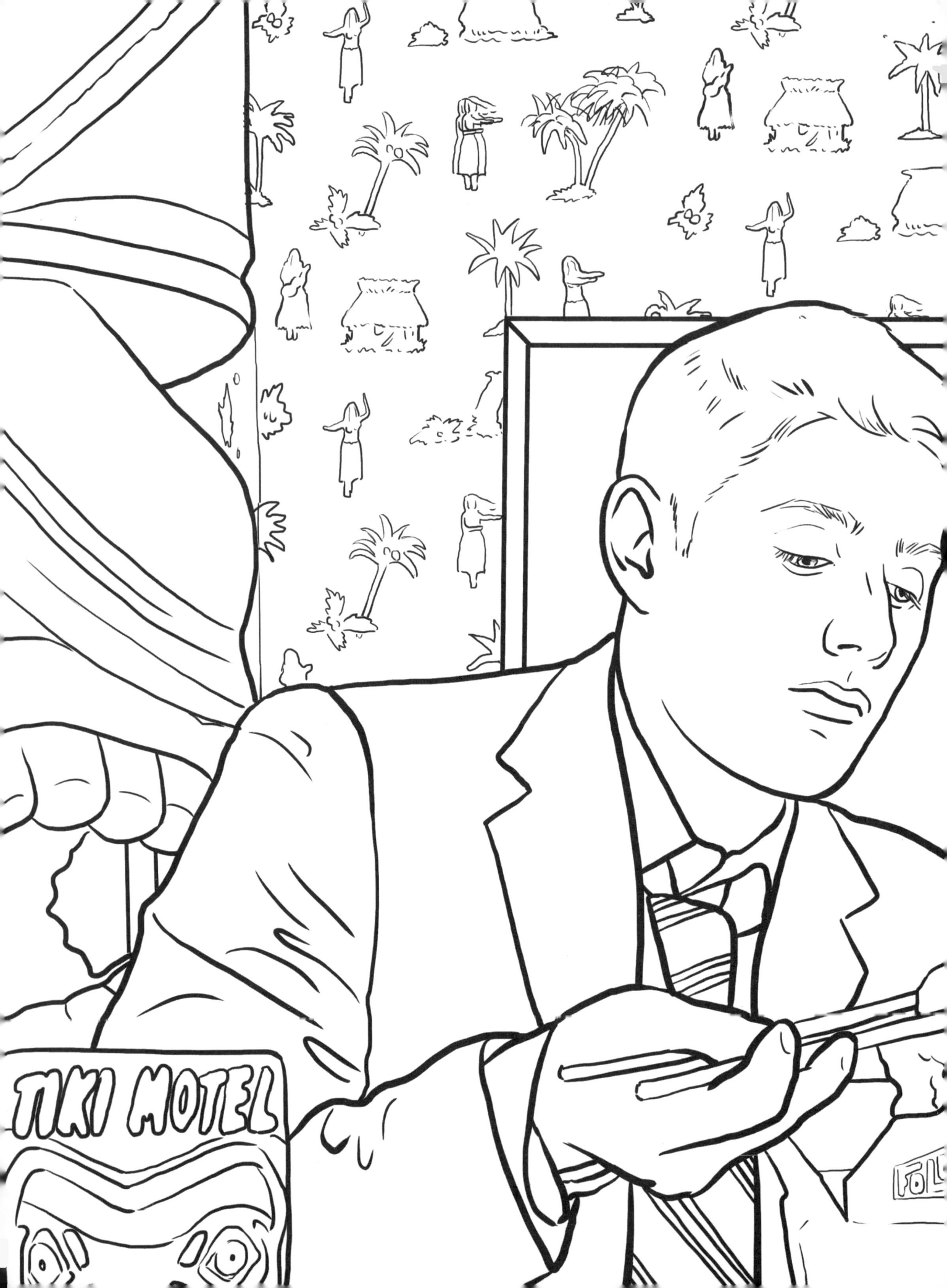
TIKI MOTEL

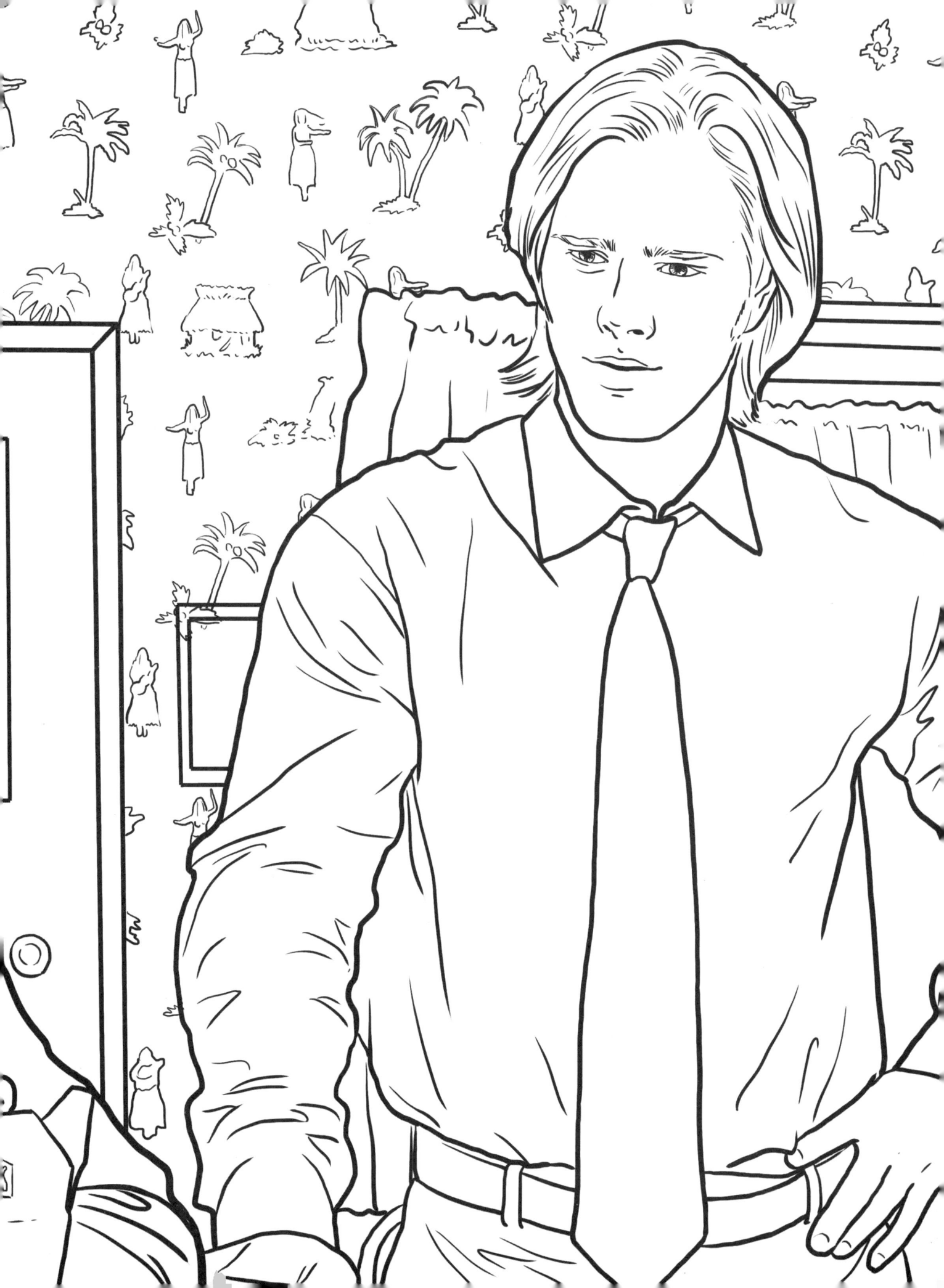

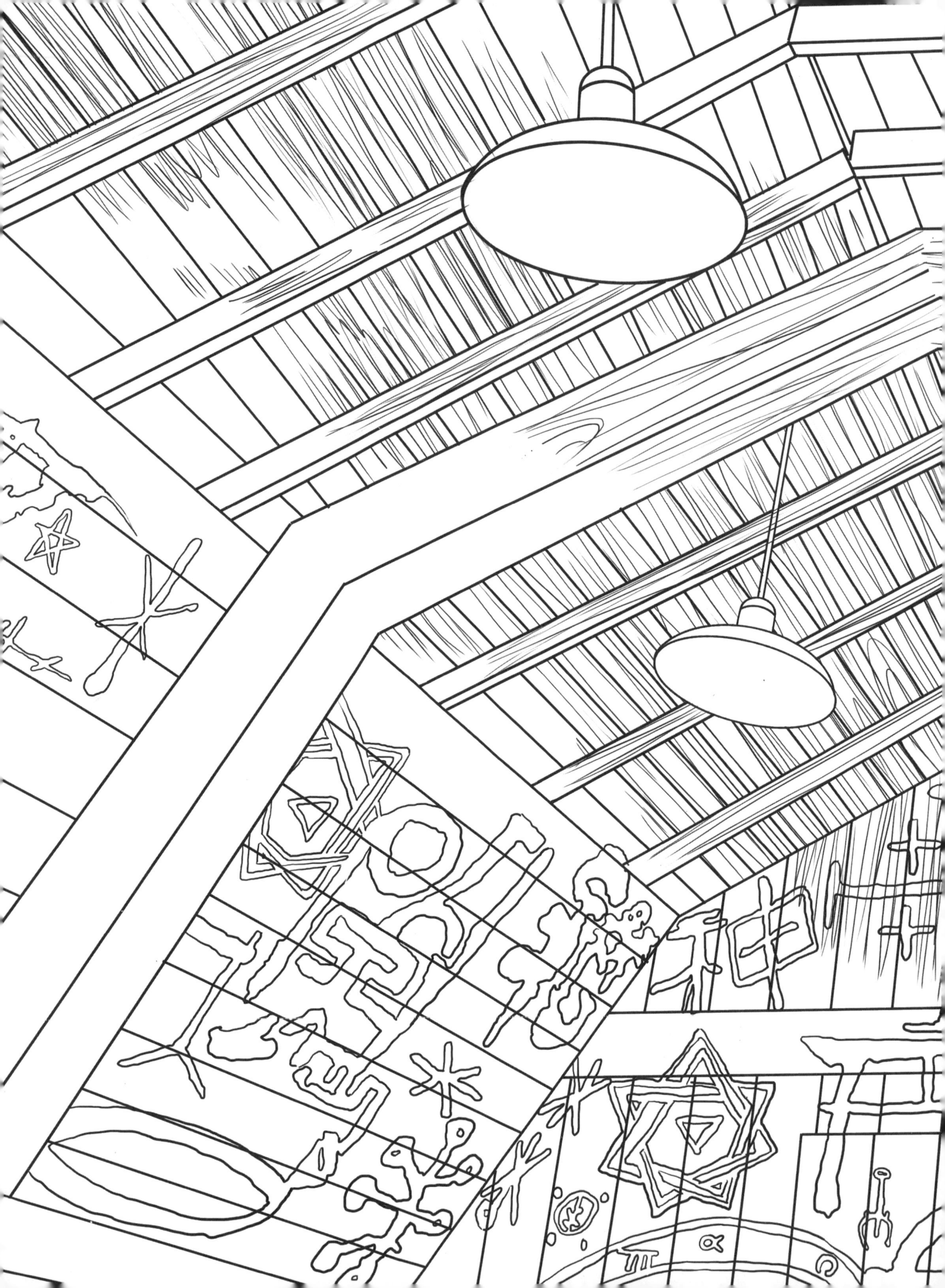

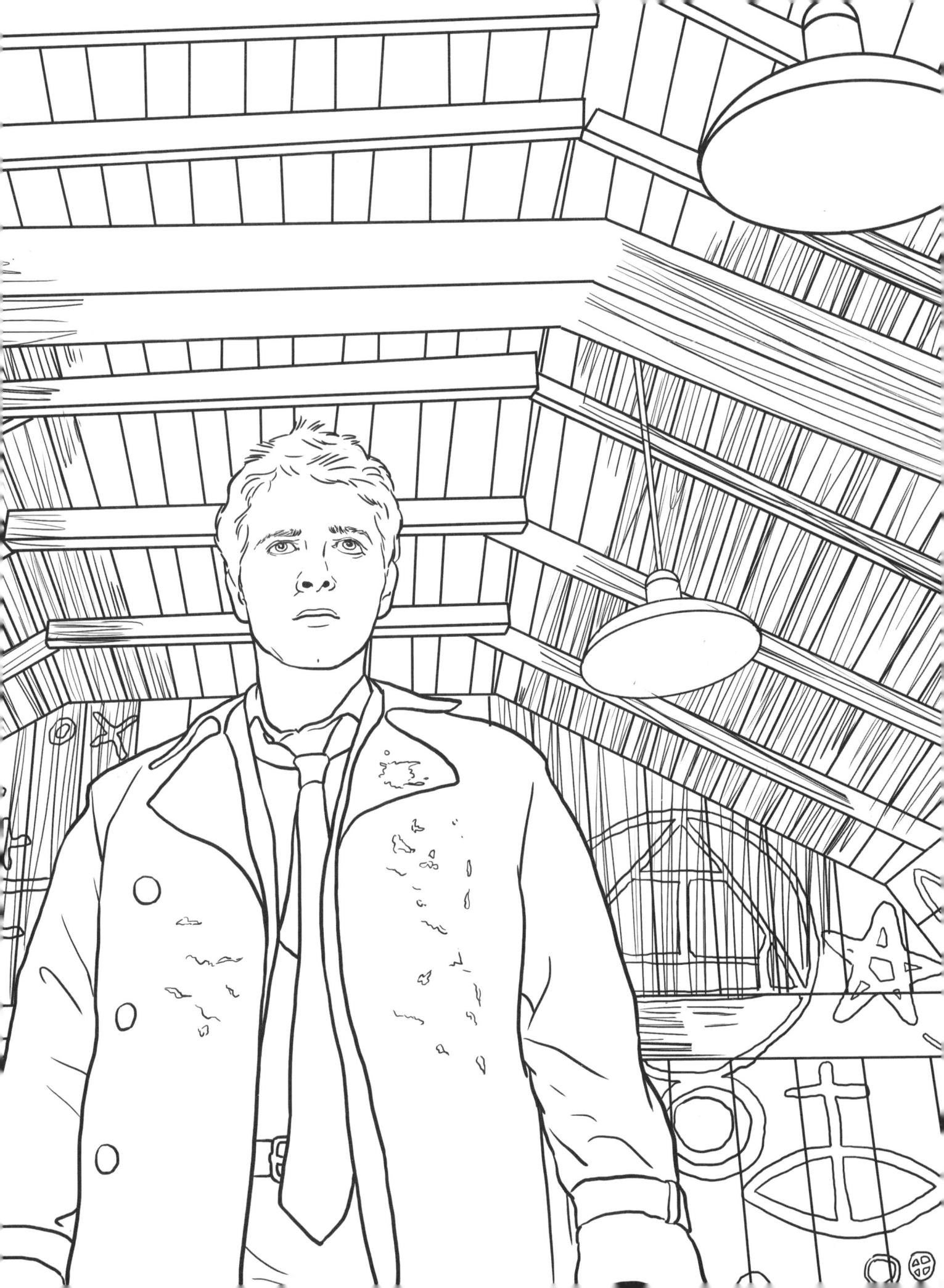

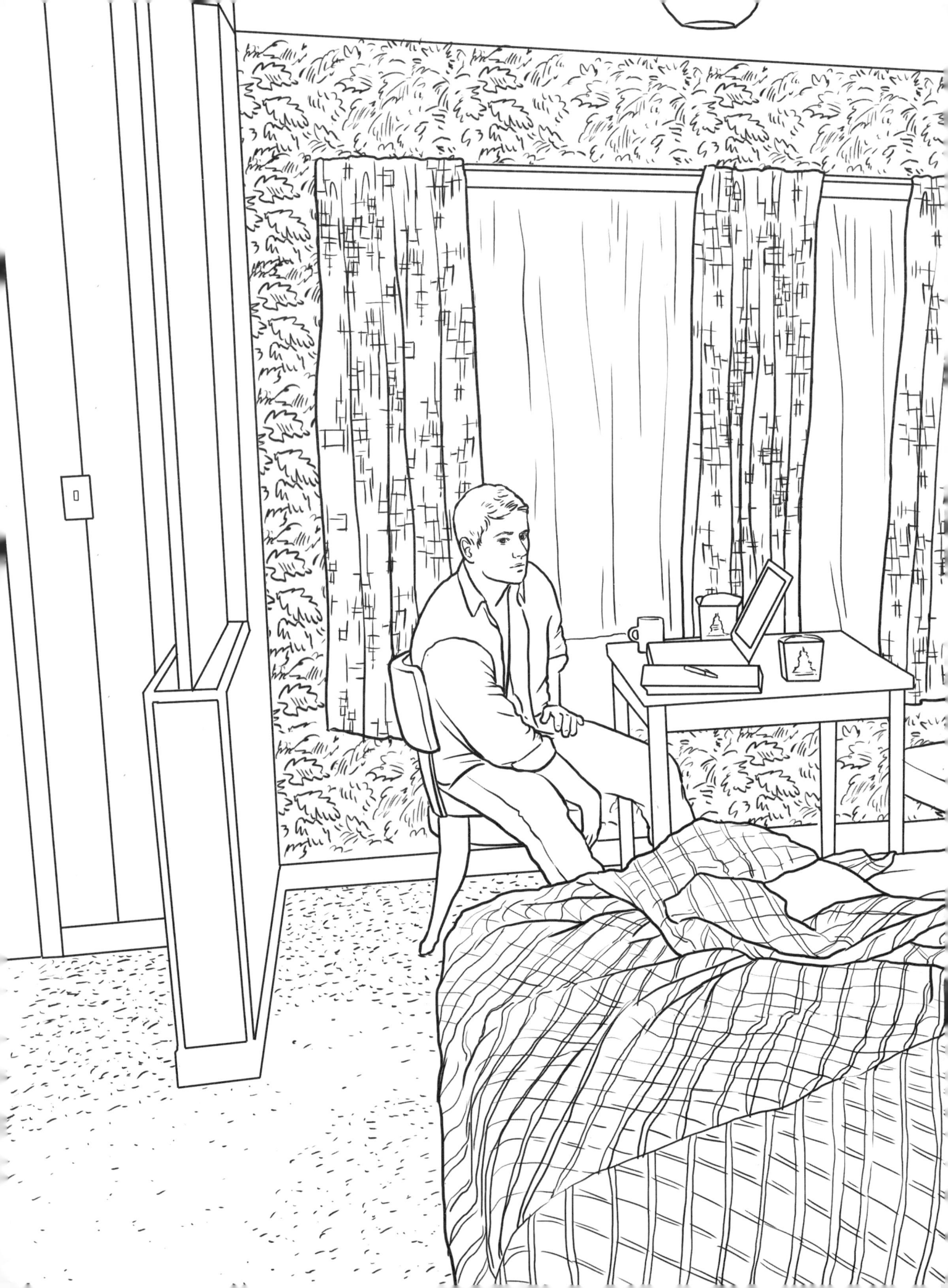

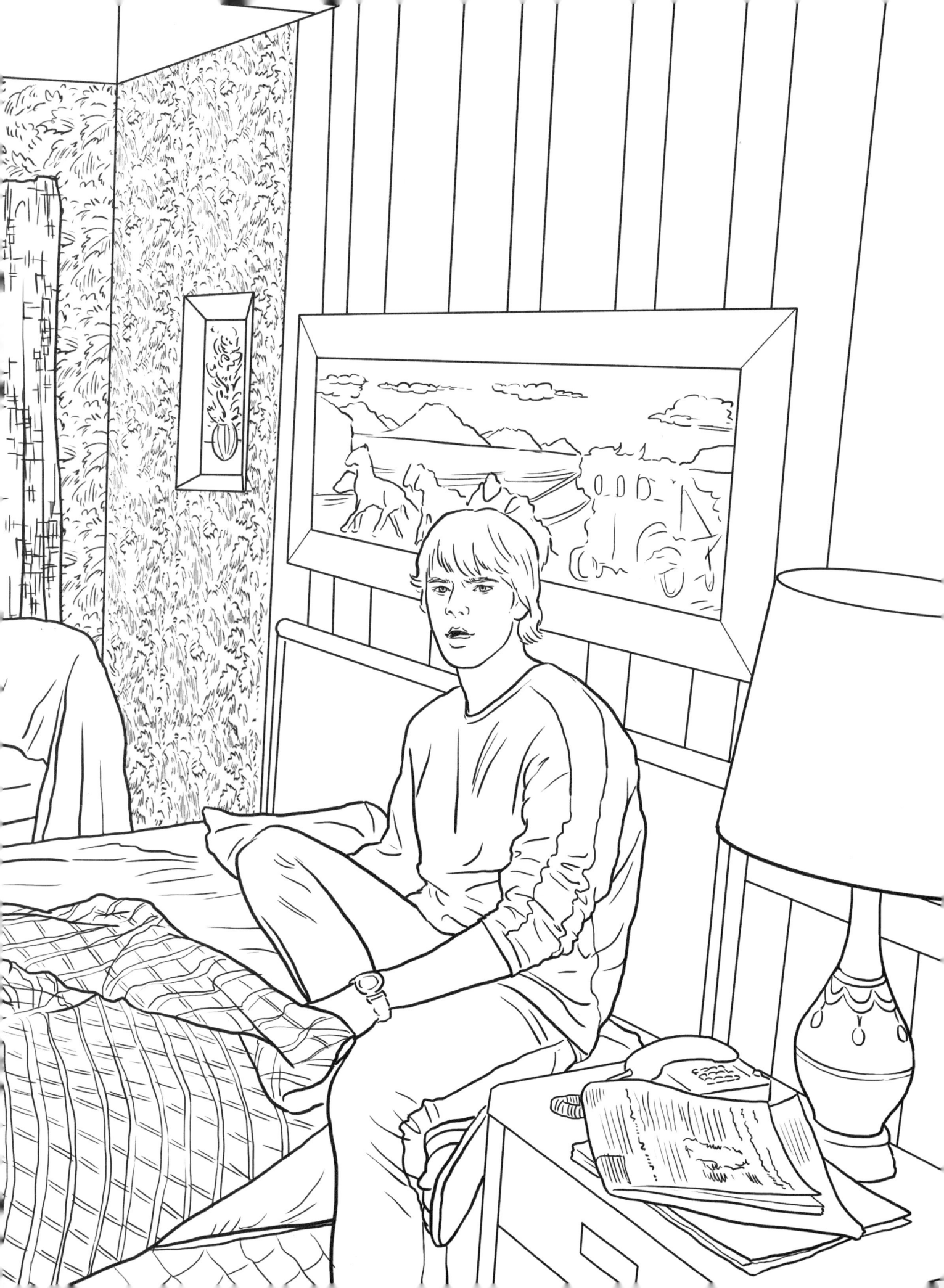

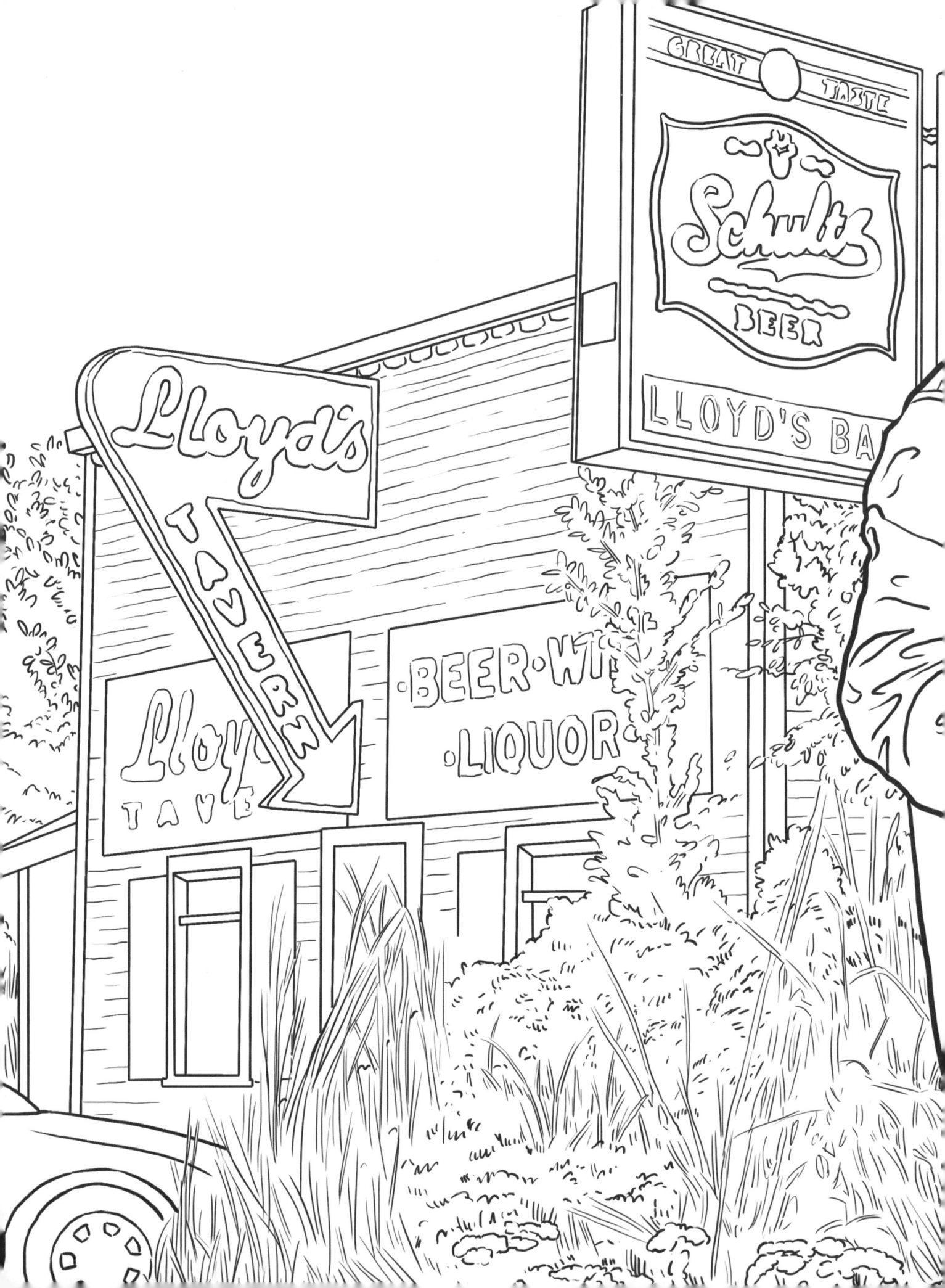
GREAT TASTE
Schultz
BEER
LLOYD'S BA
Lloyd's
TAVERN
Lloyd
TAVE
·BEER·WI
·LIQUOR

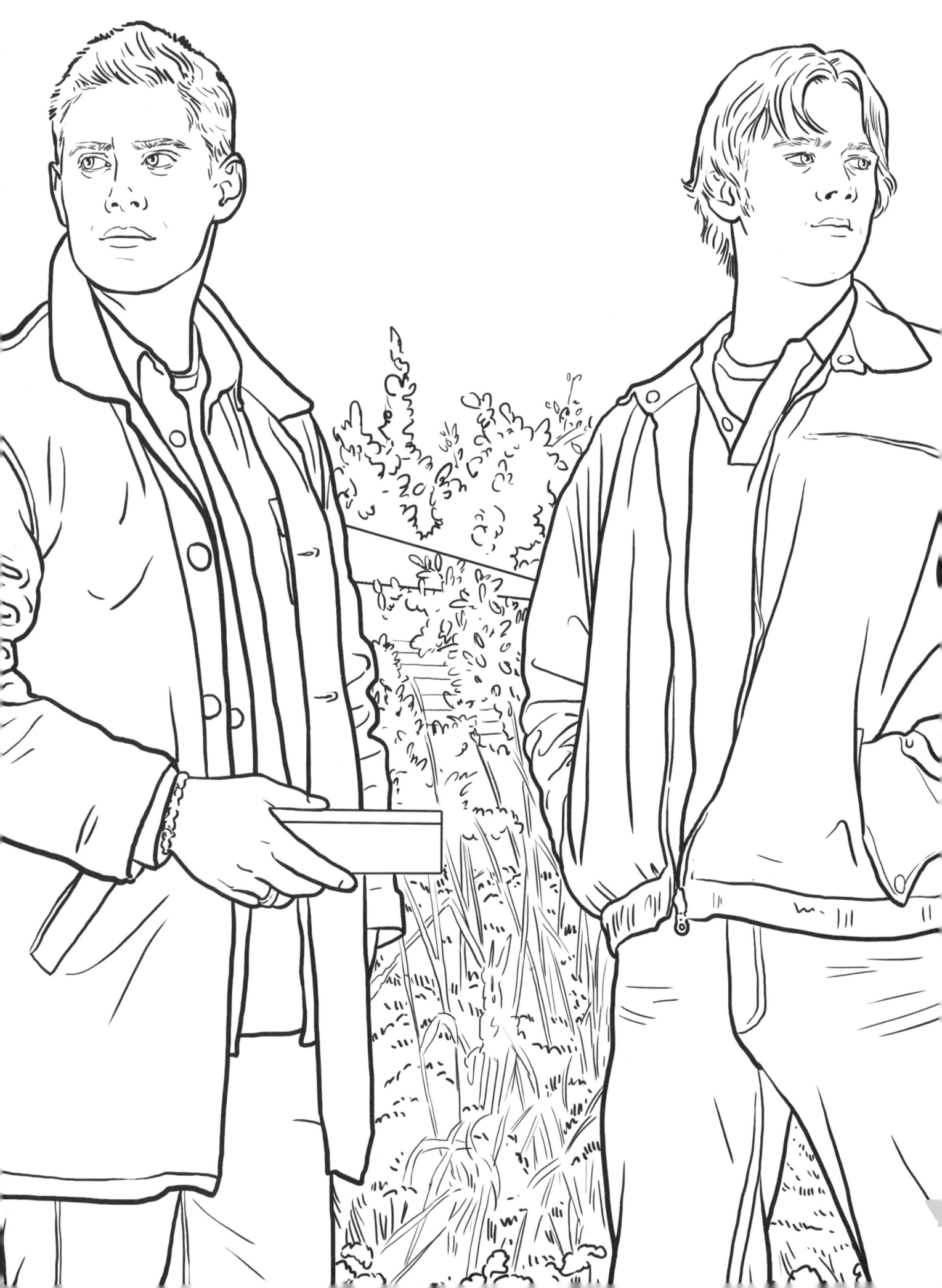

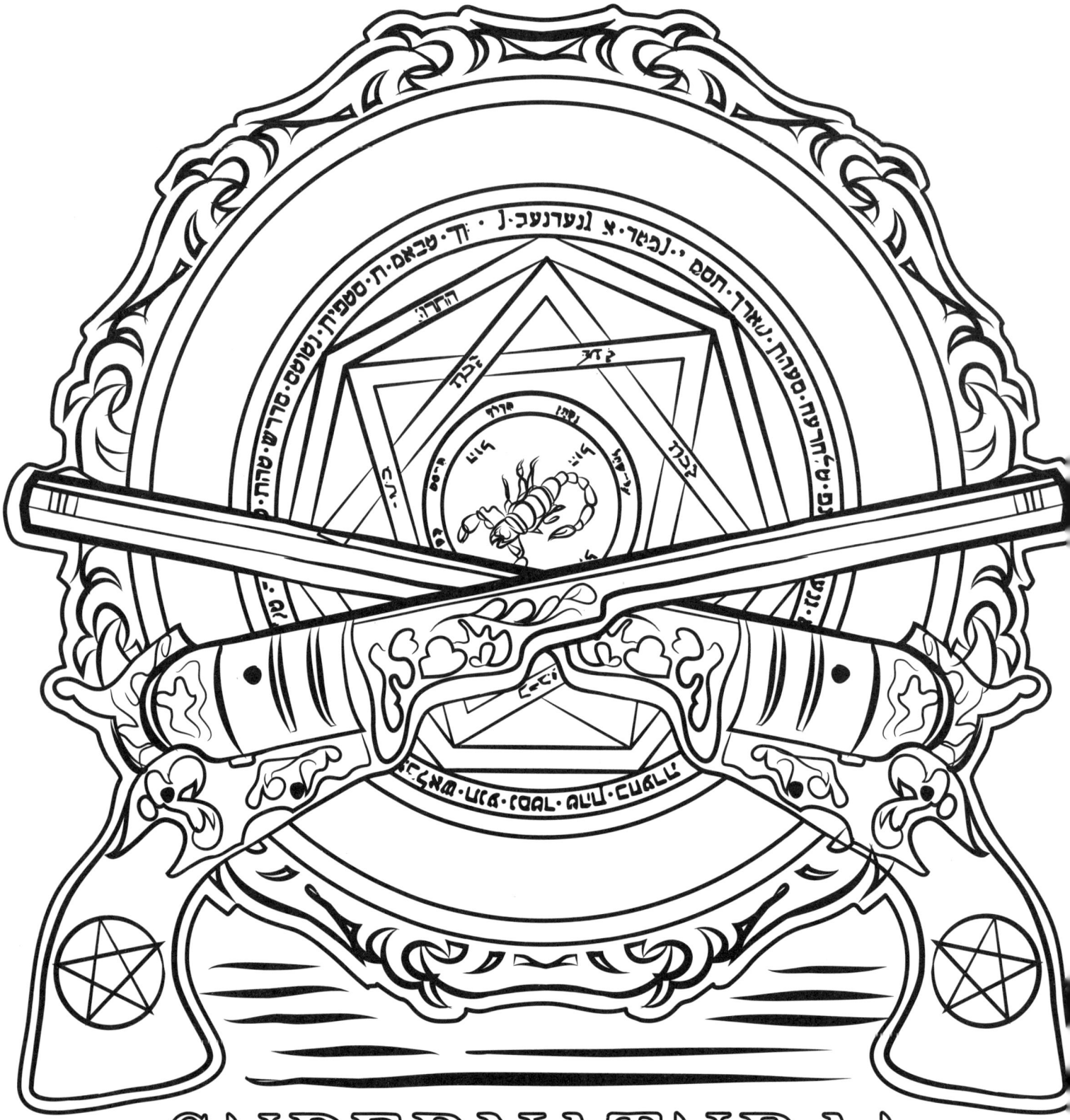

SUPERNATURAL

JOIN THE HUNT

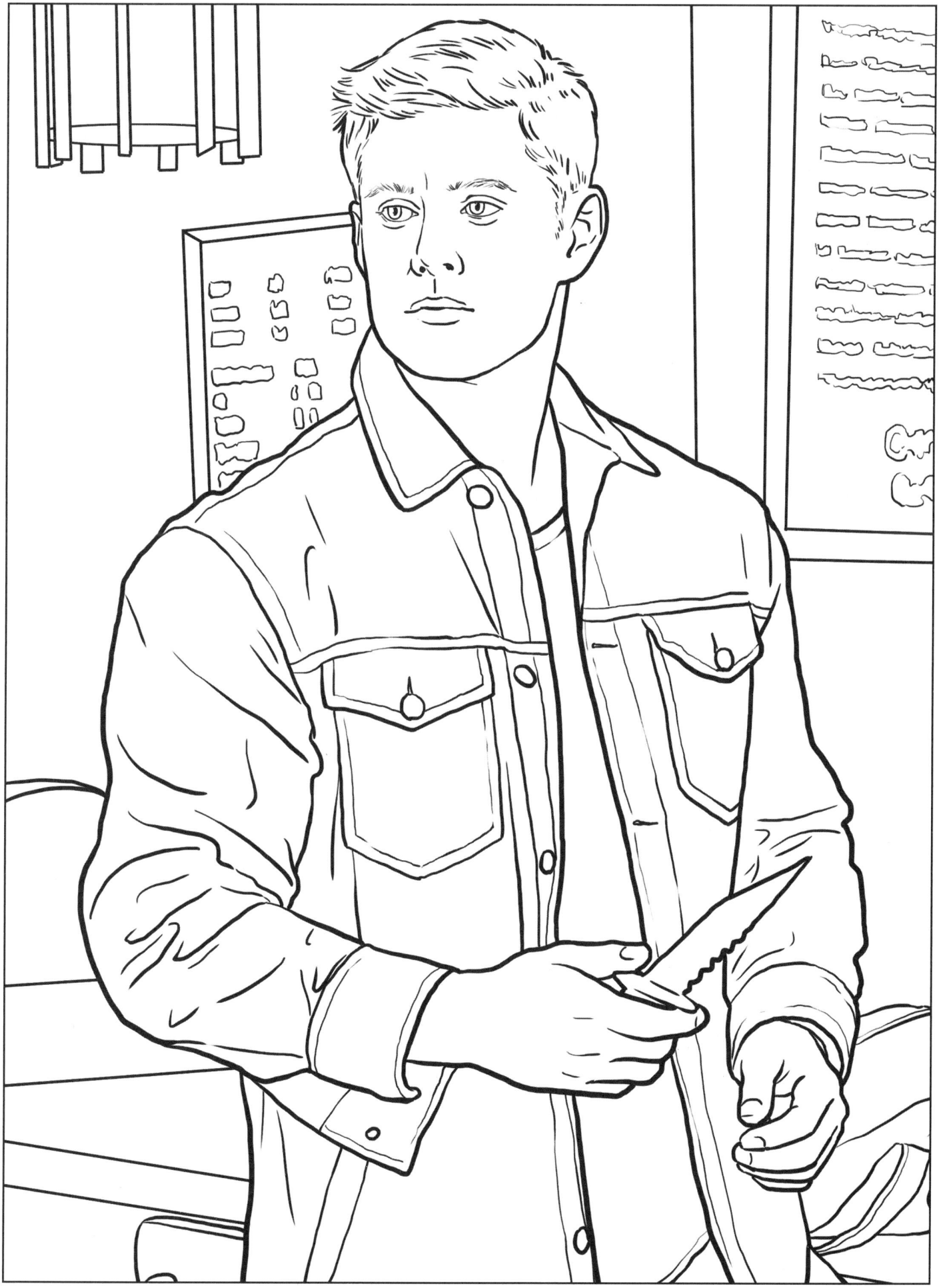

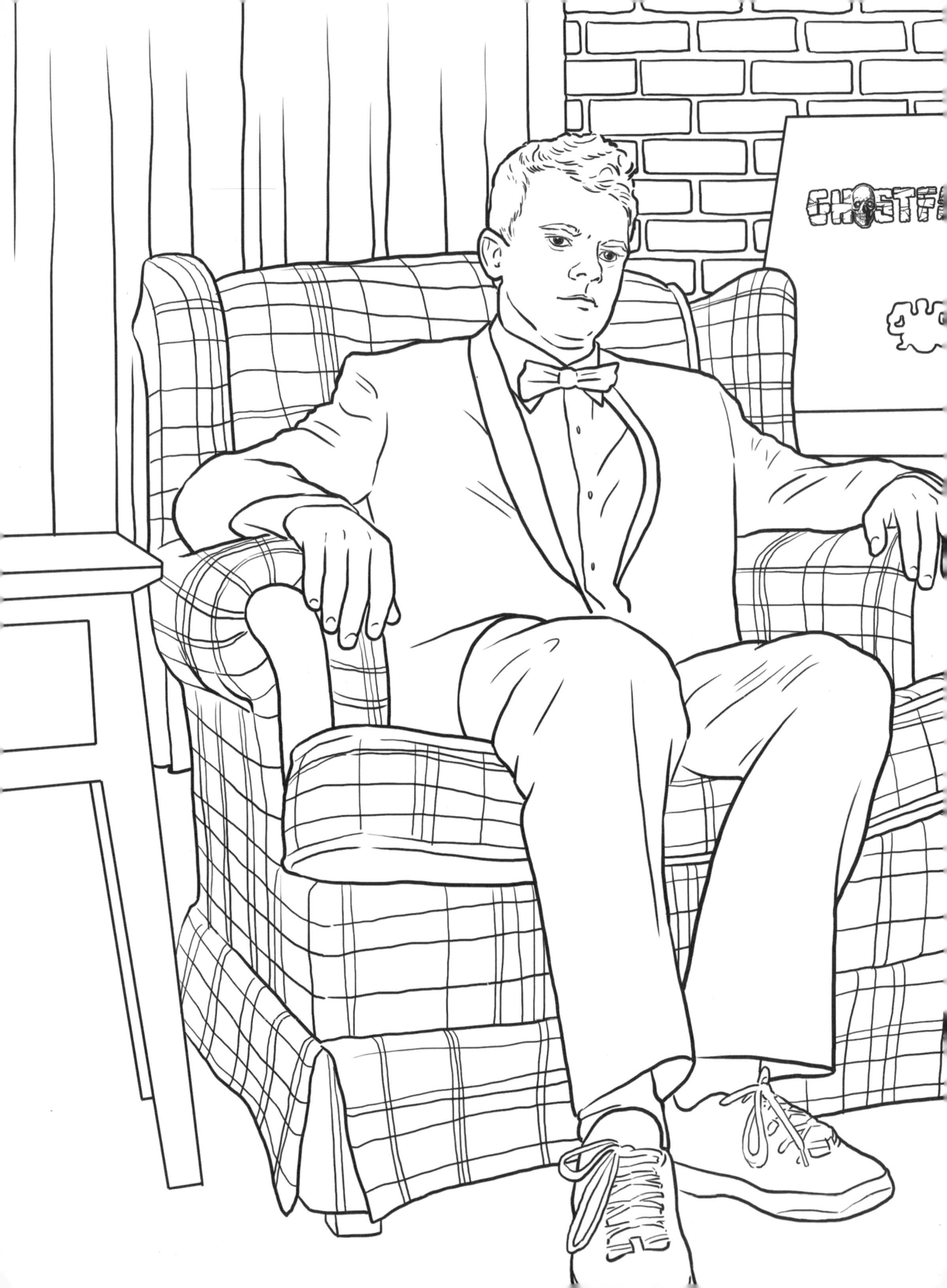

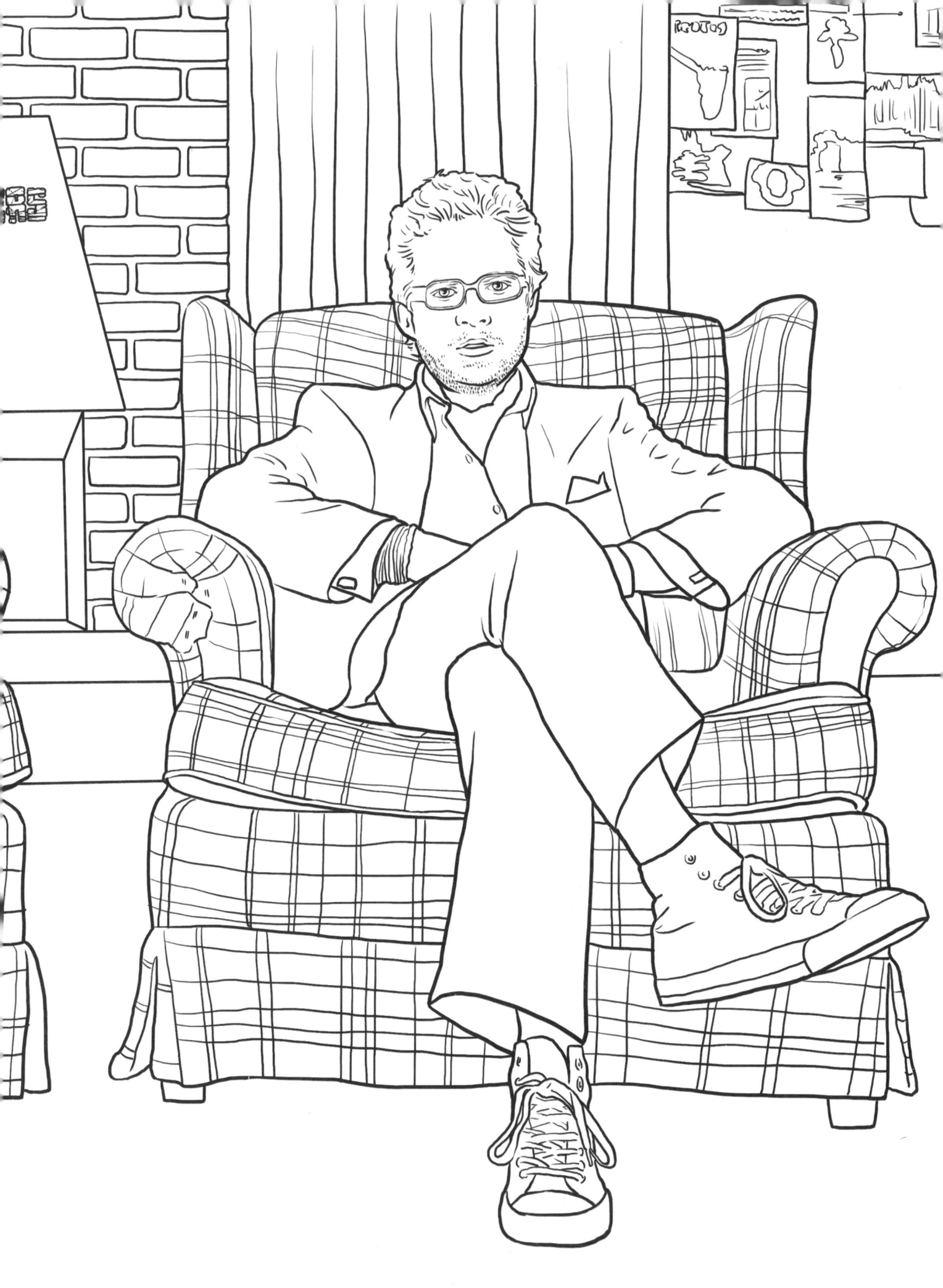

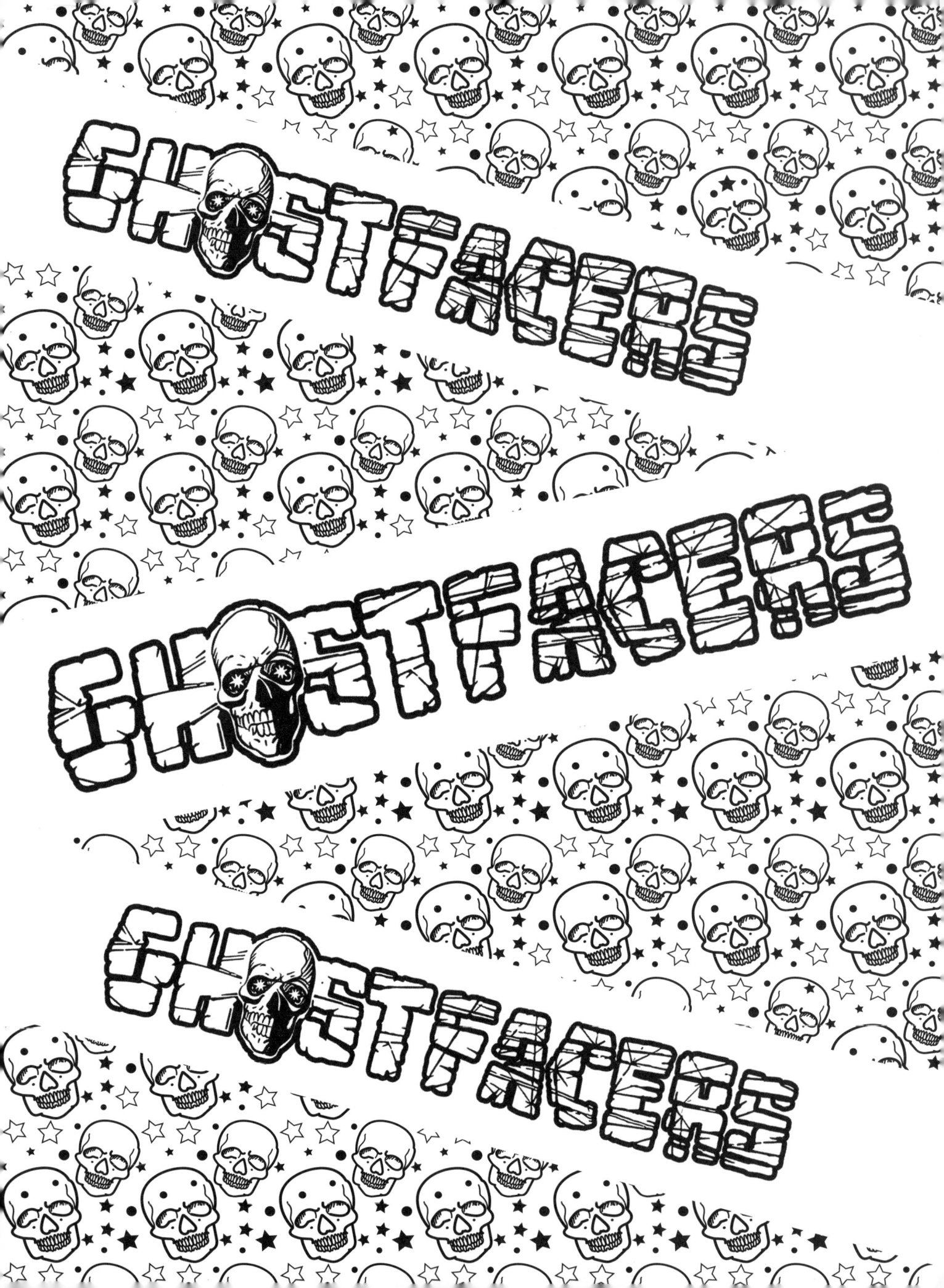
GHOSTFACERS
GHOSTFACERS
GHOSTFACERS

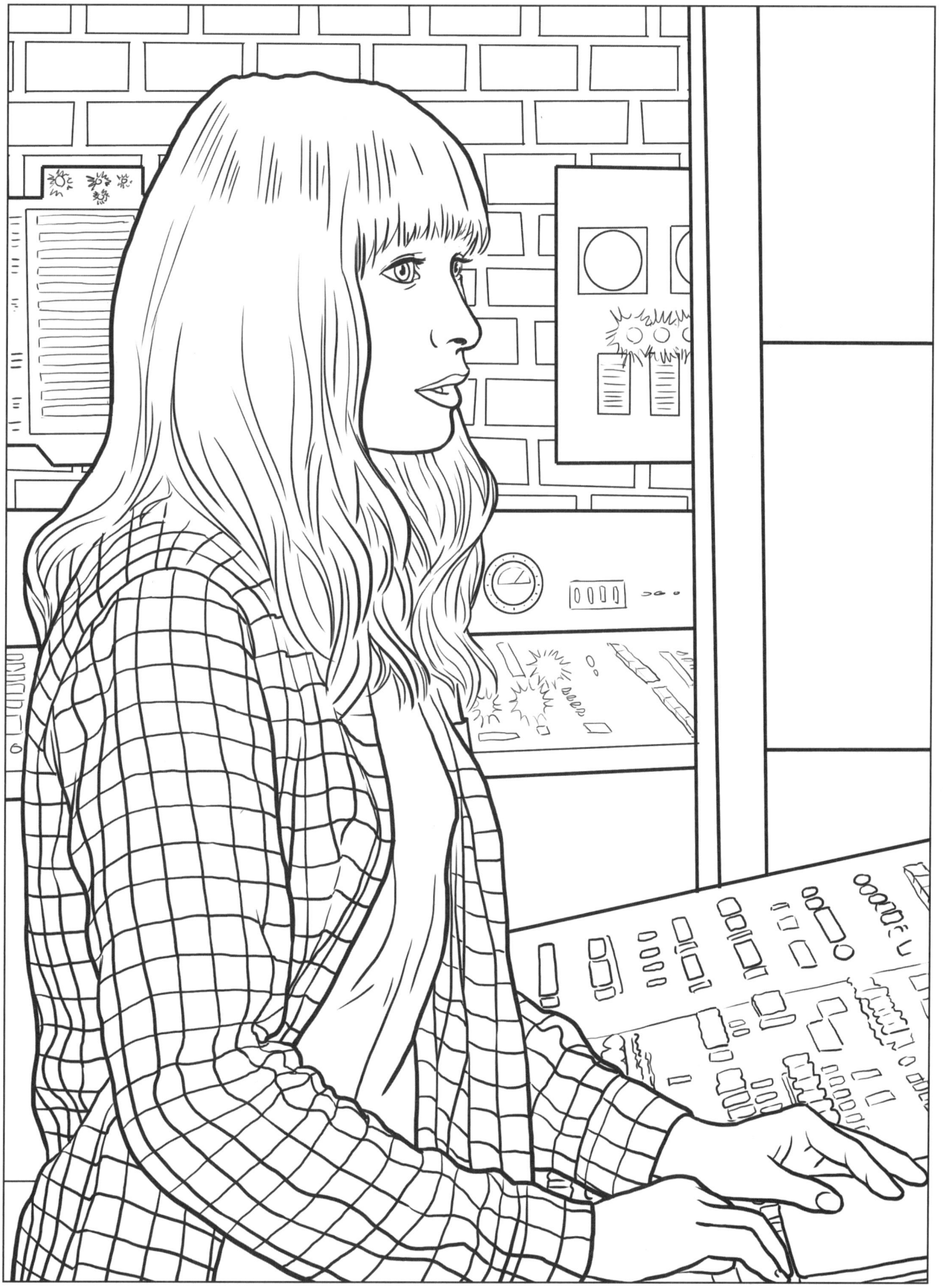
beep

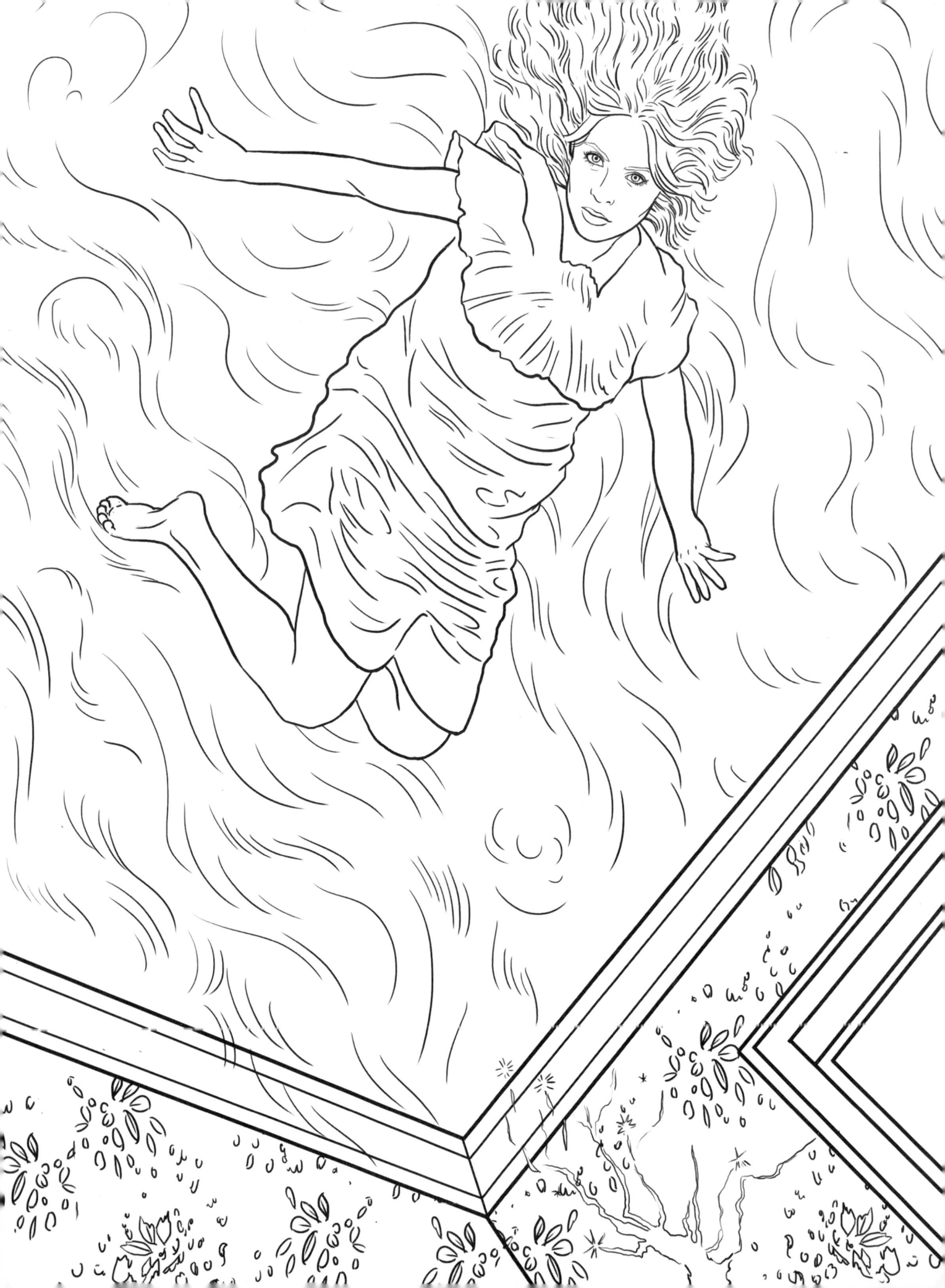

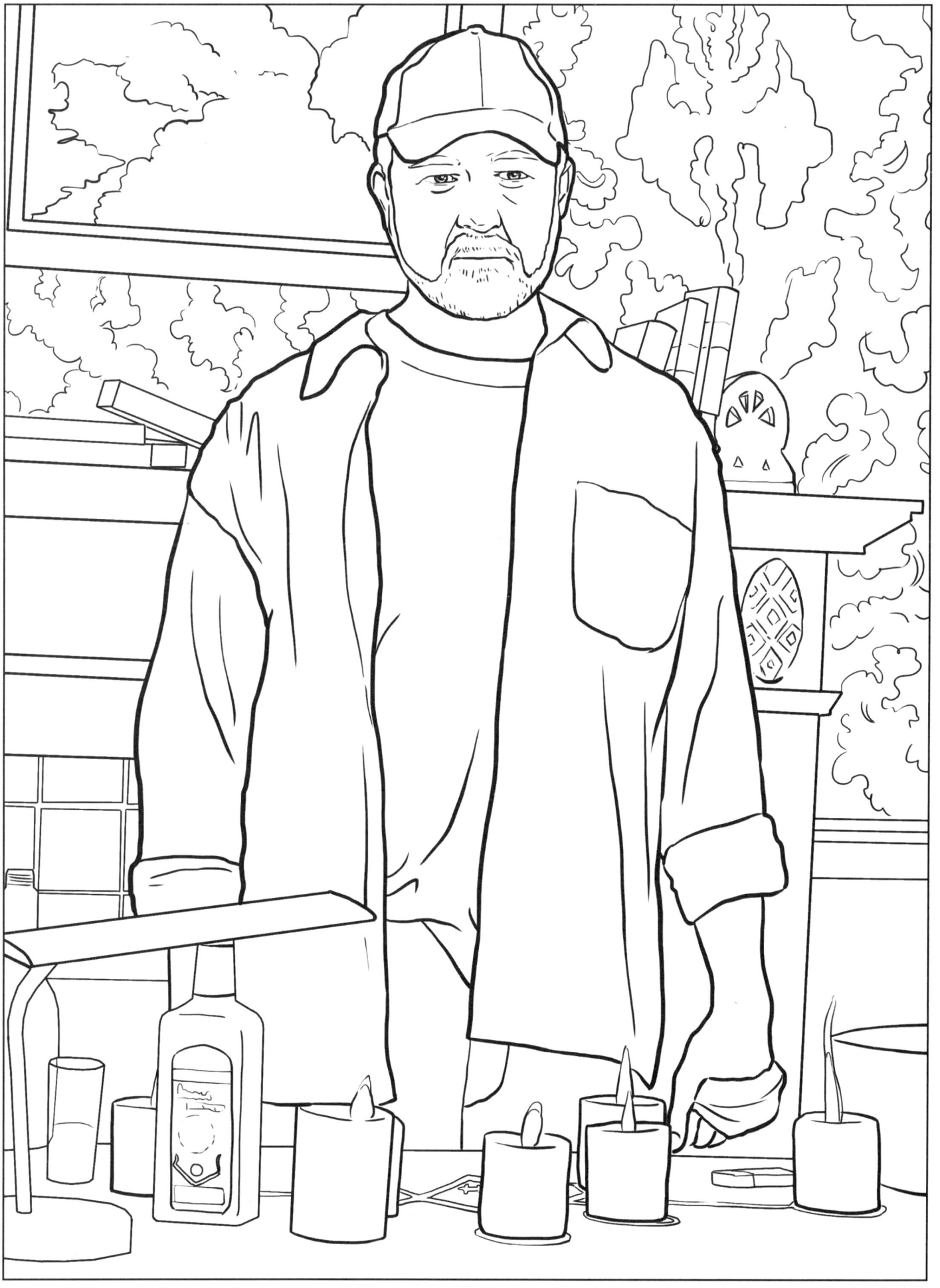

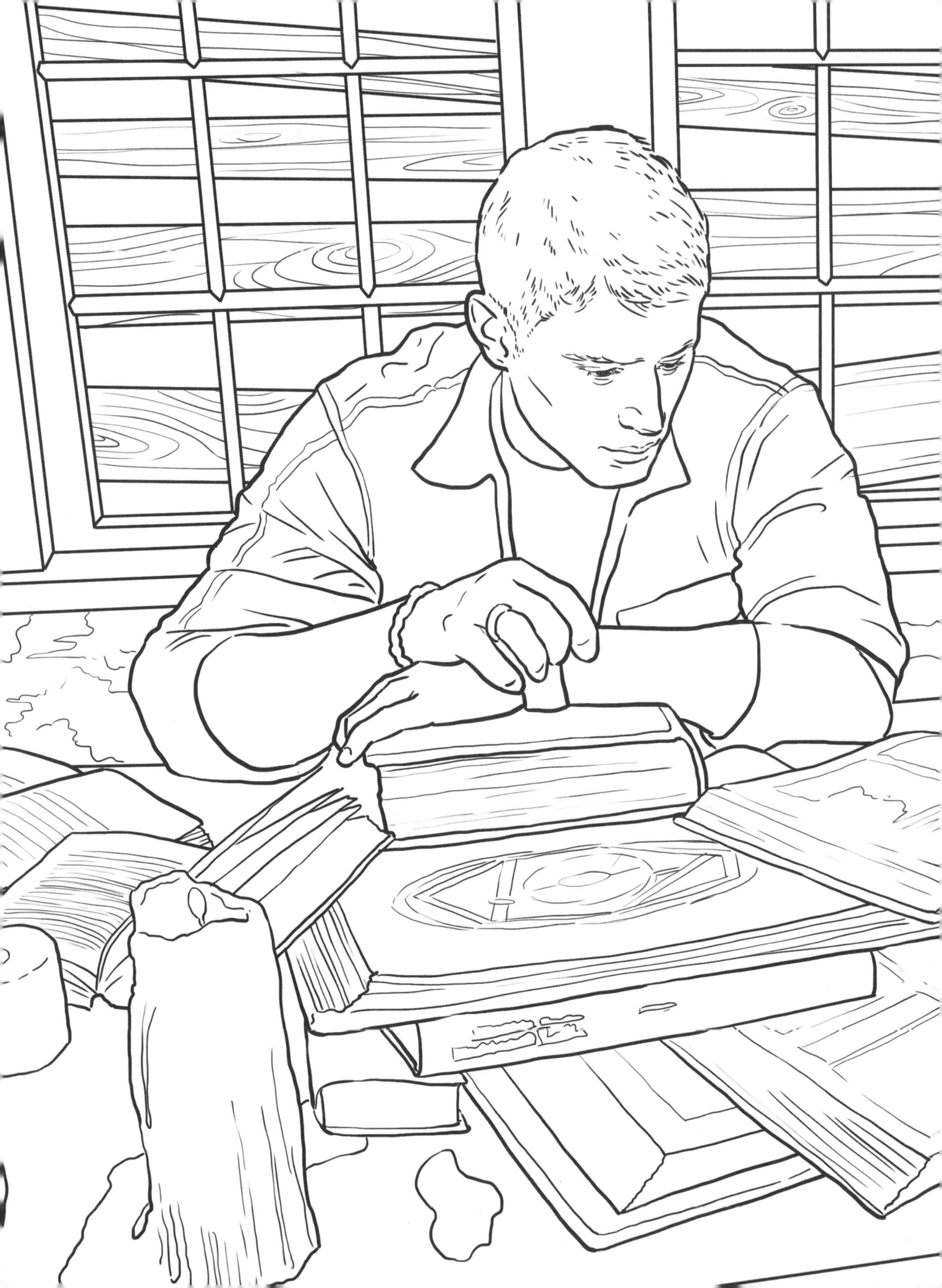

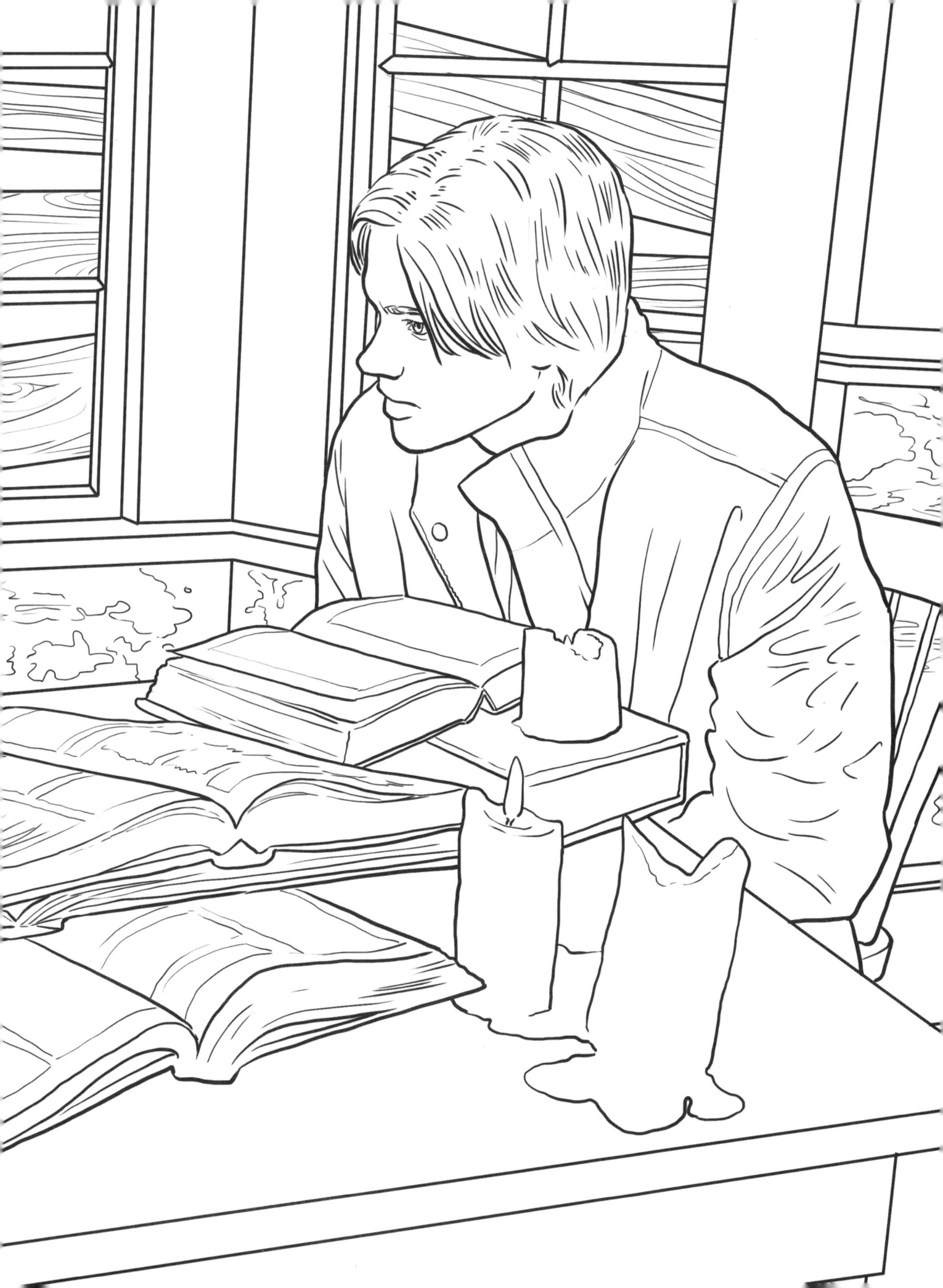

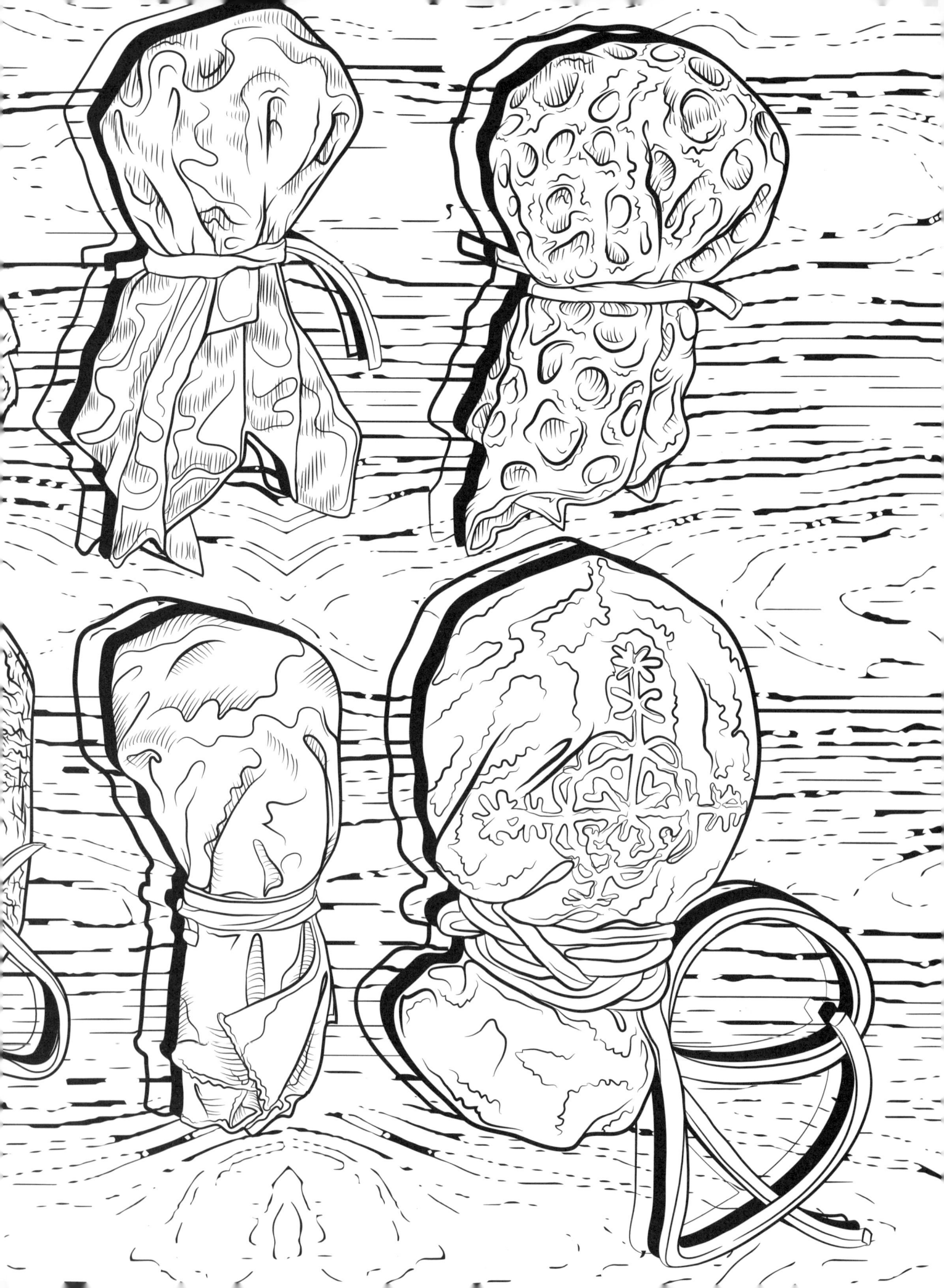

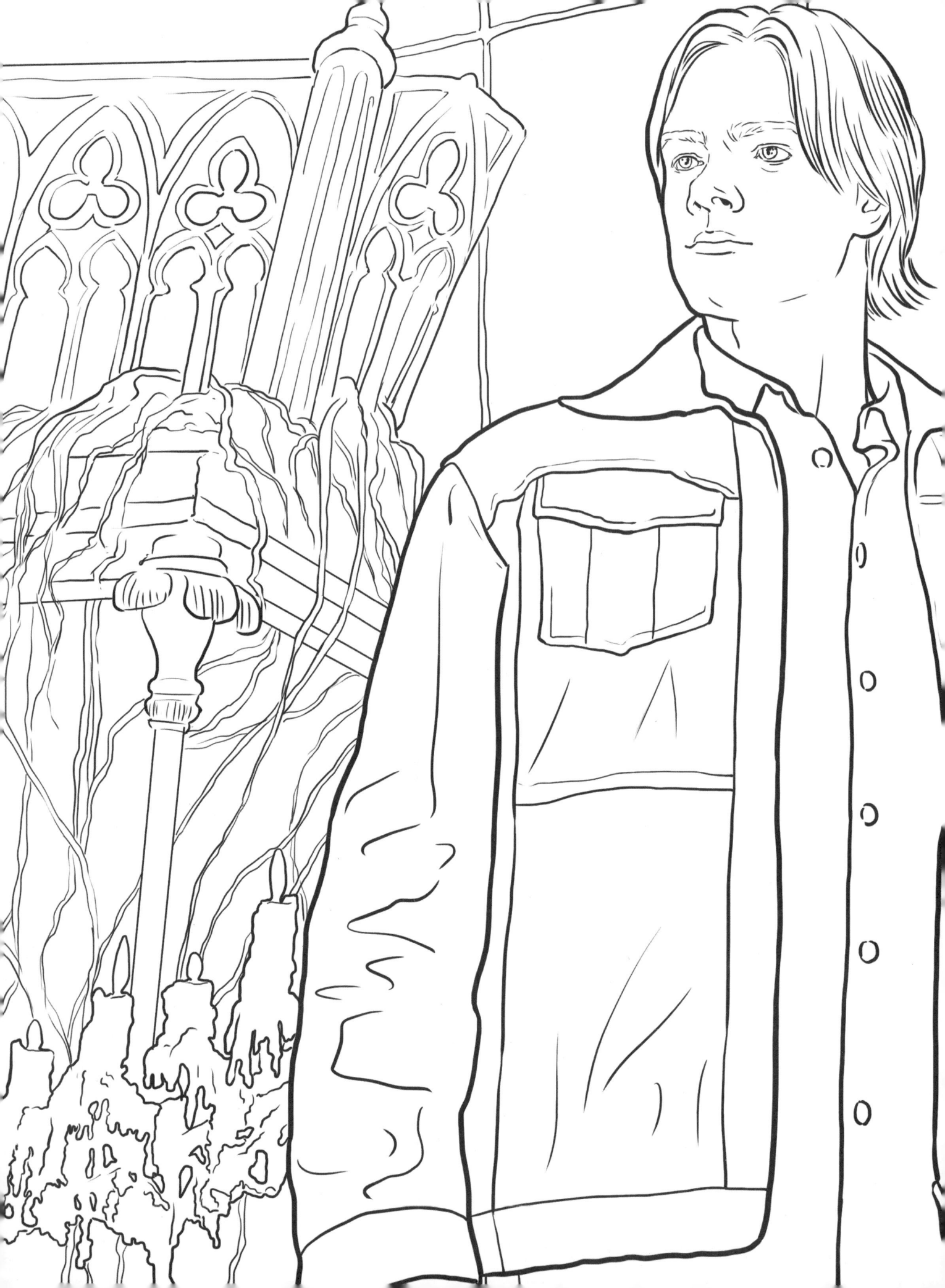

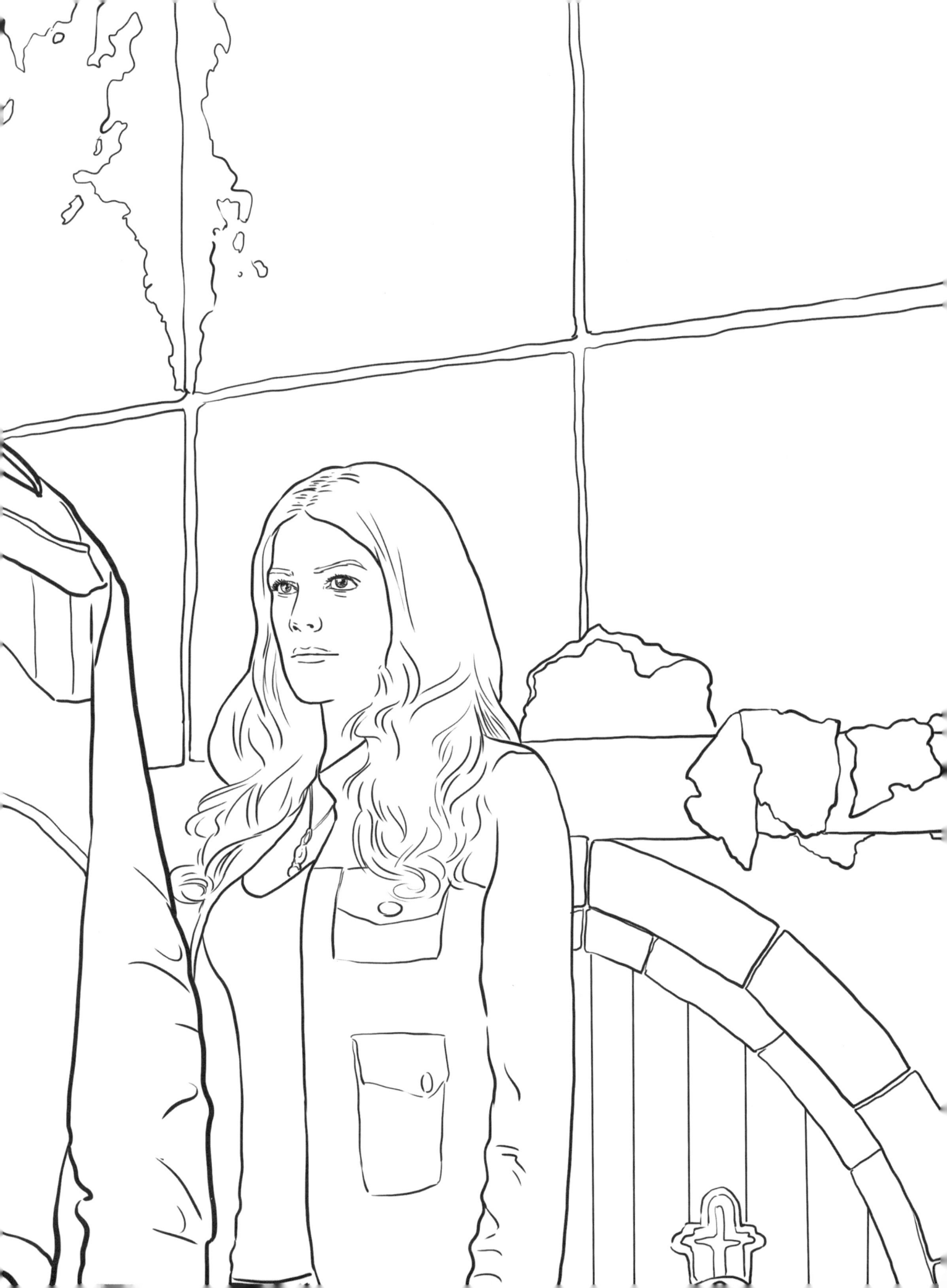

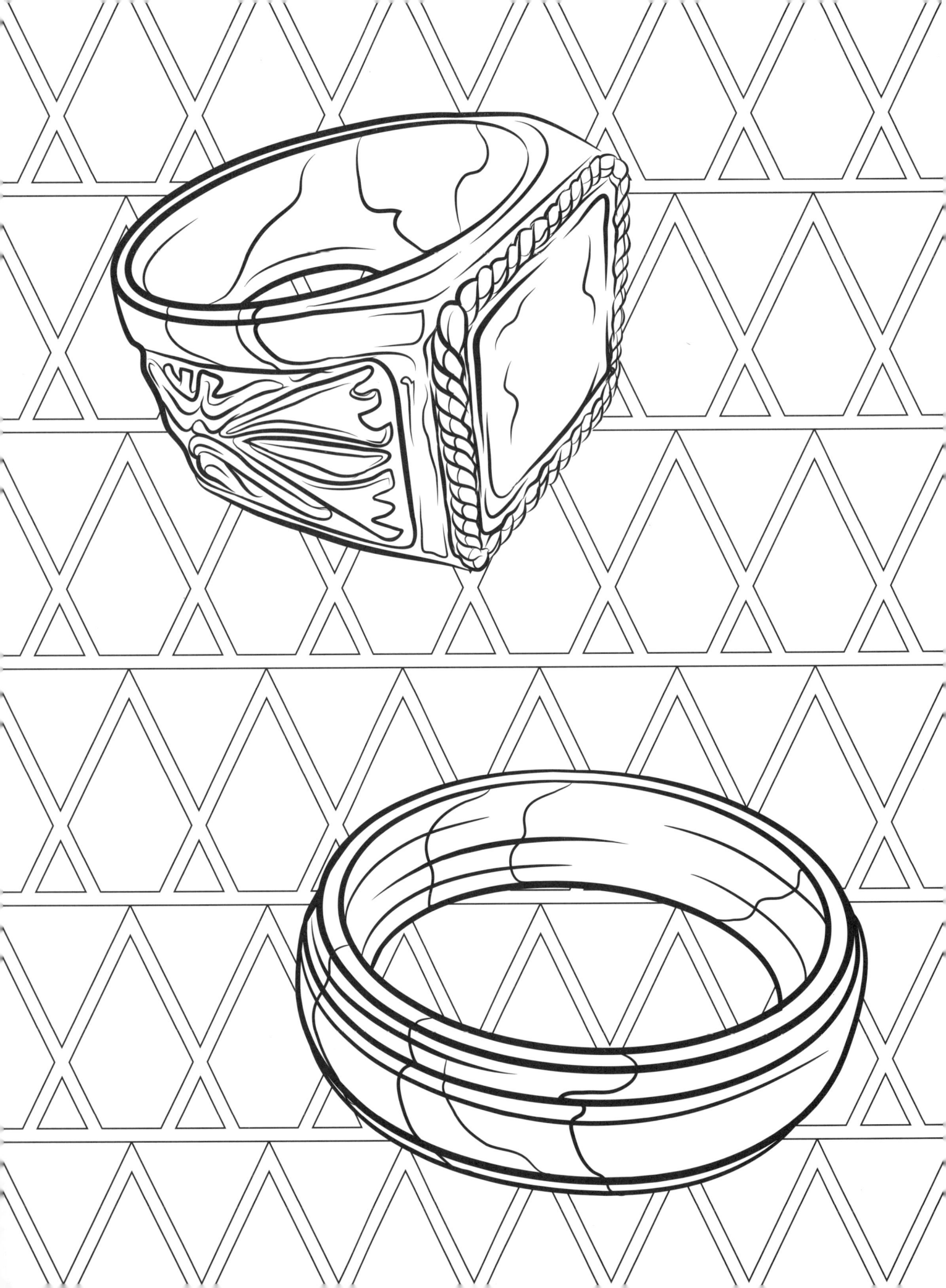

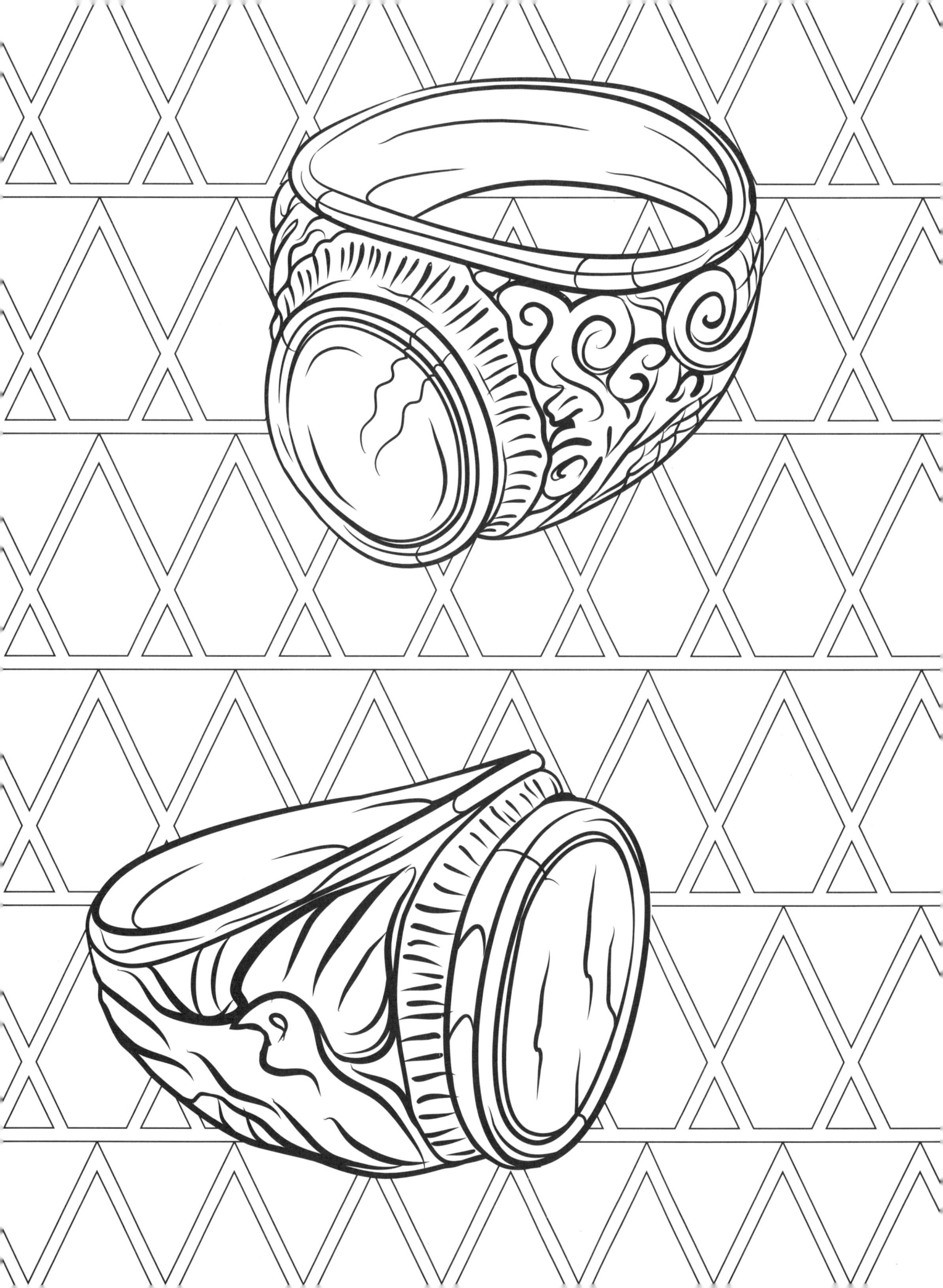

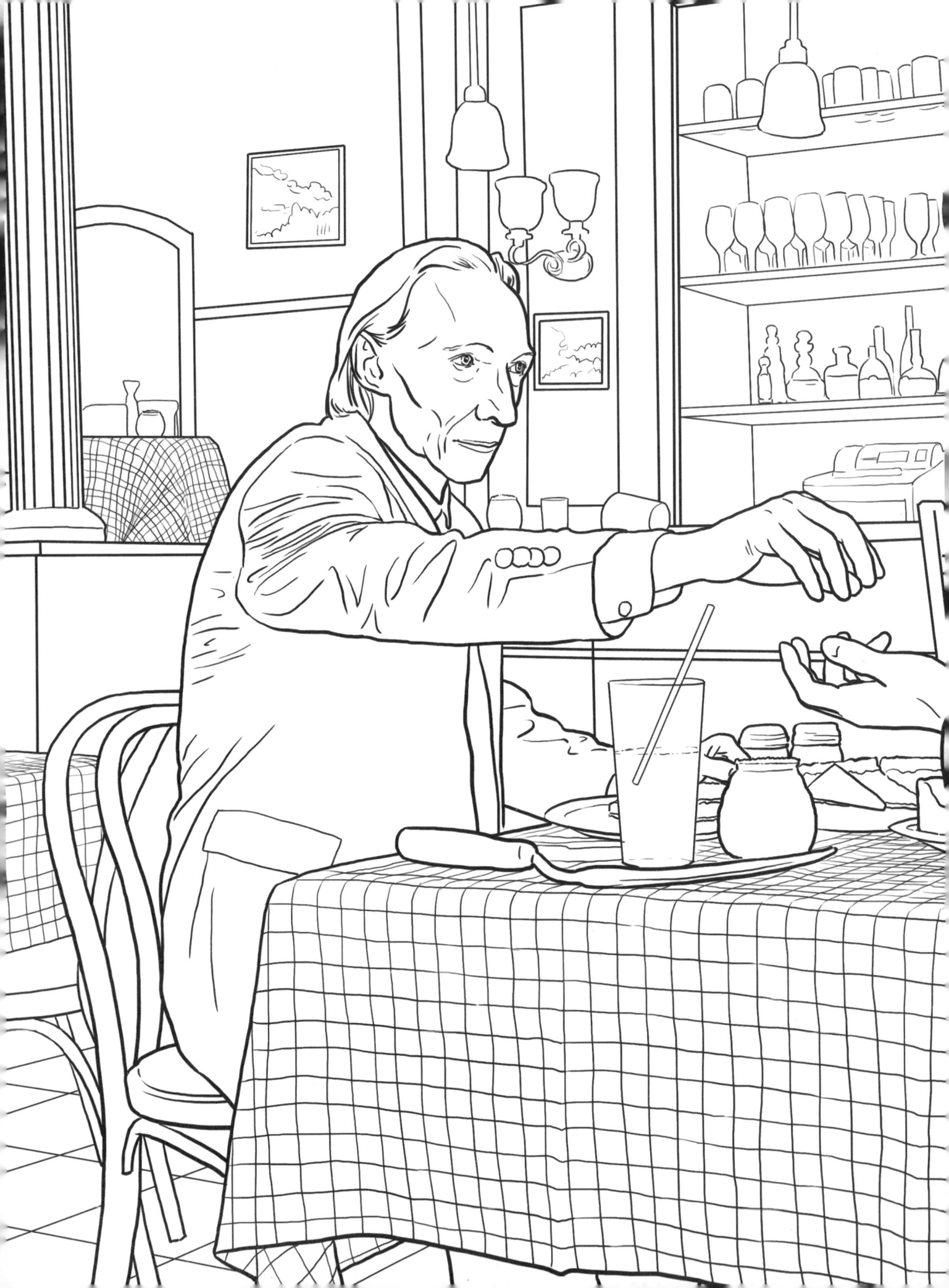

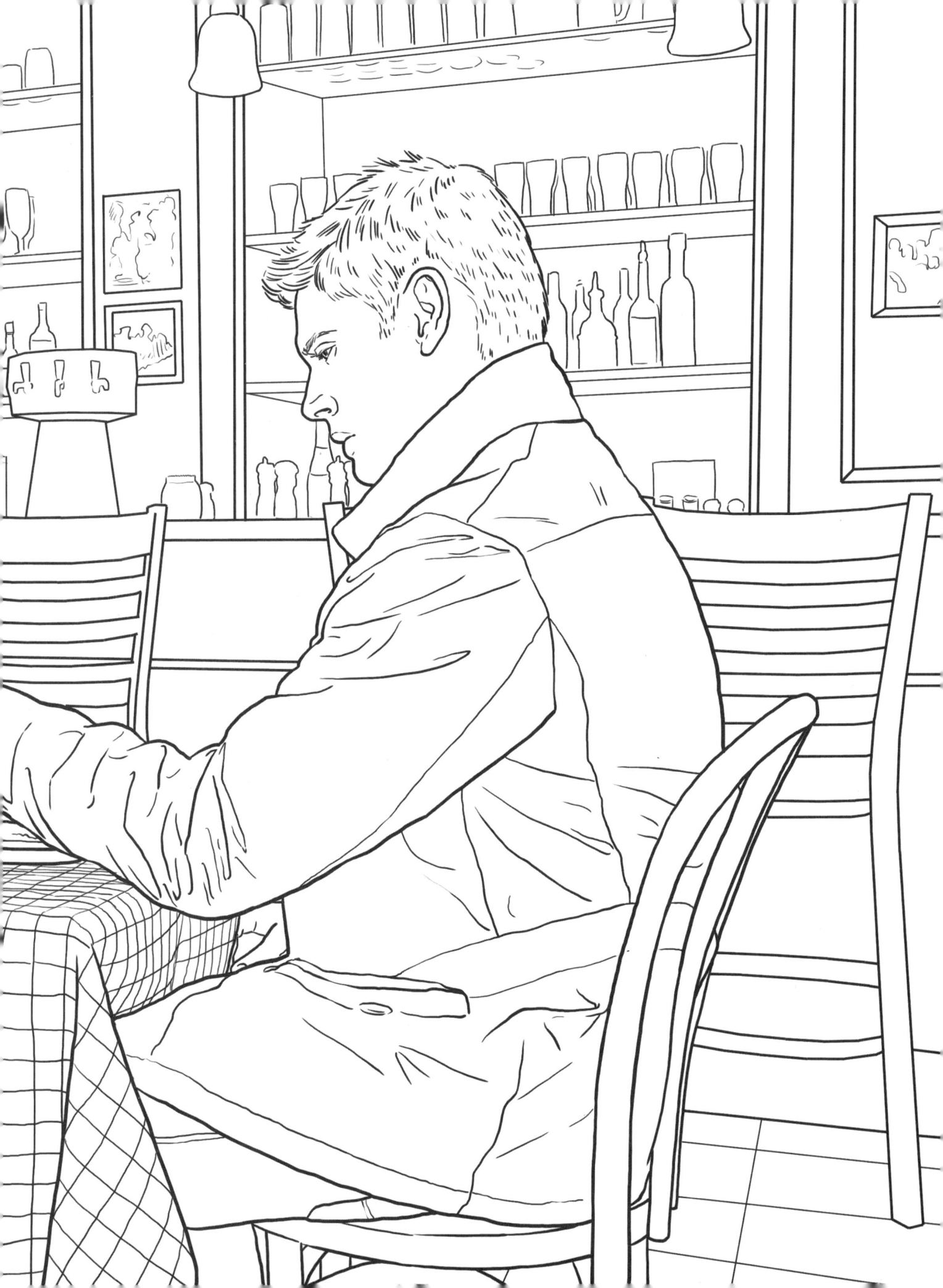

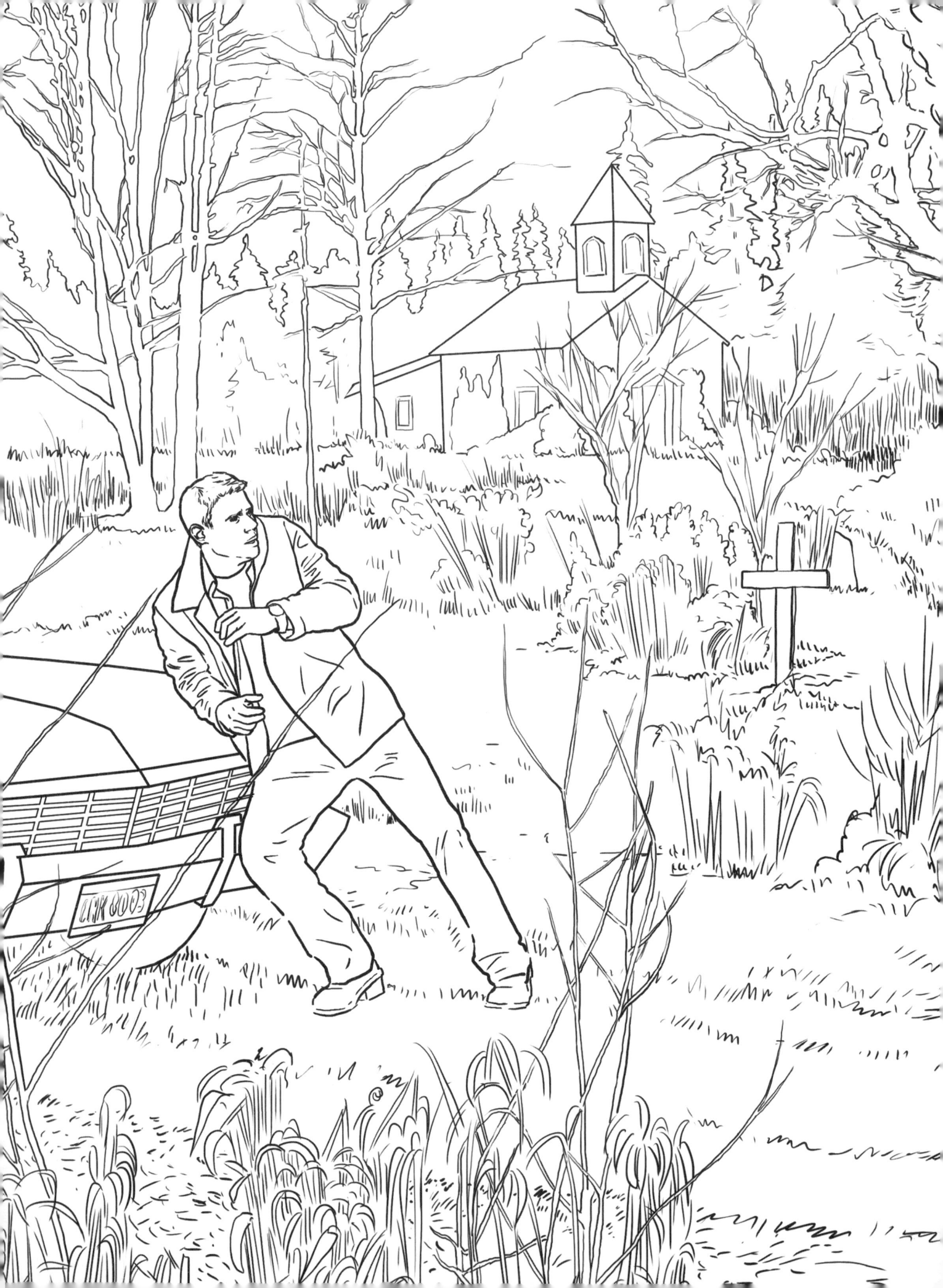

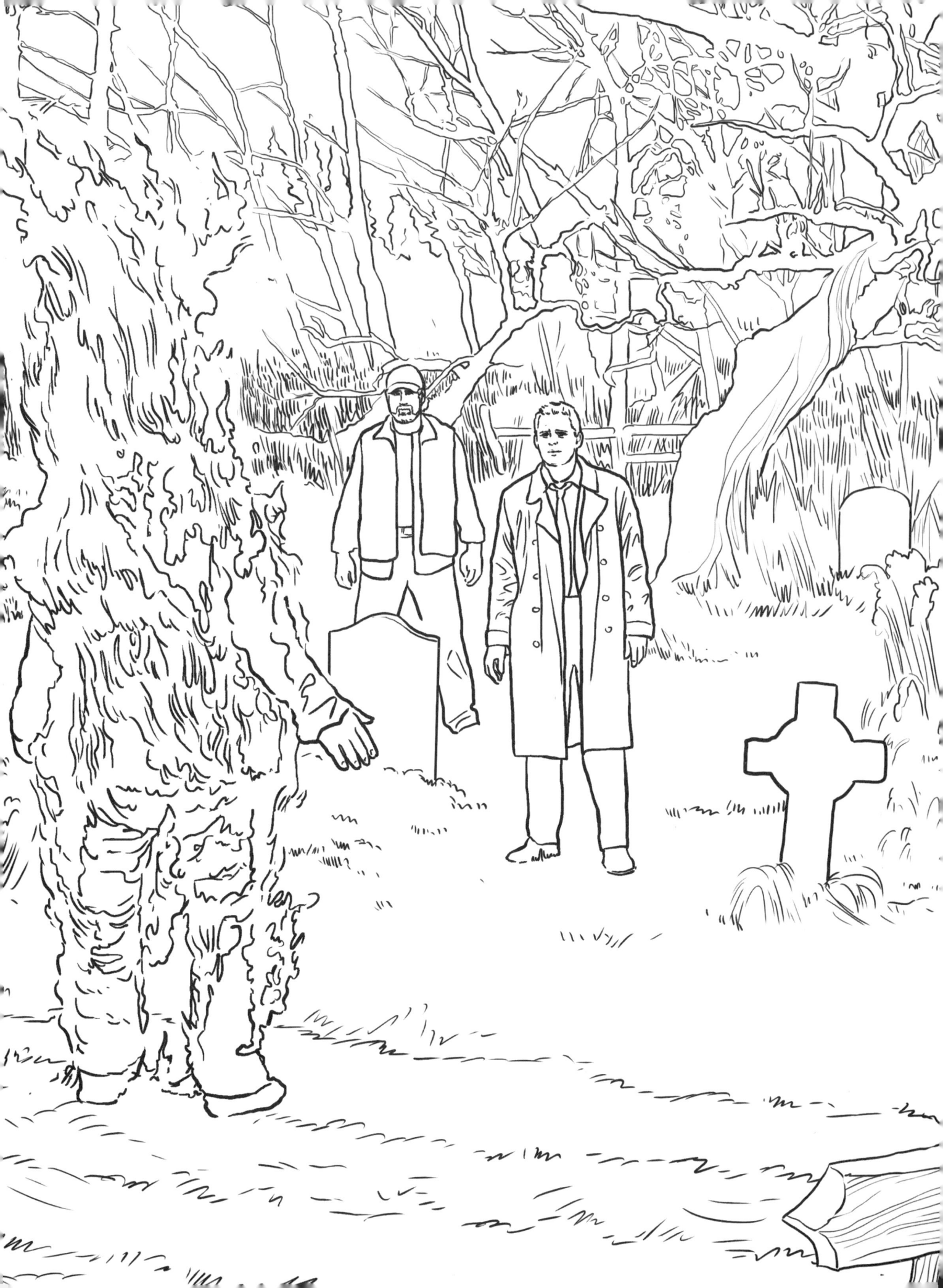

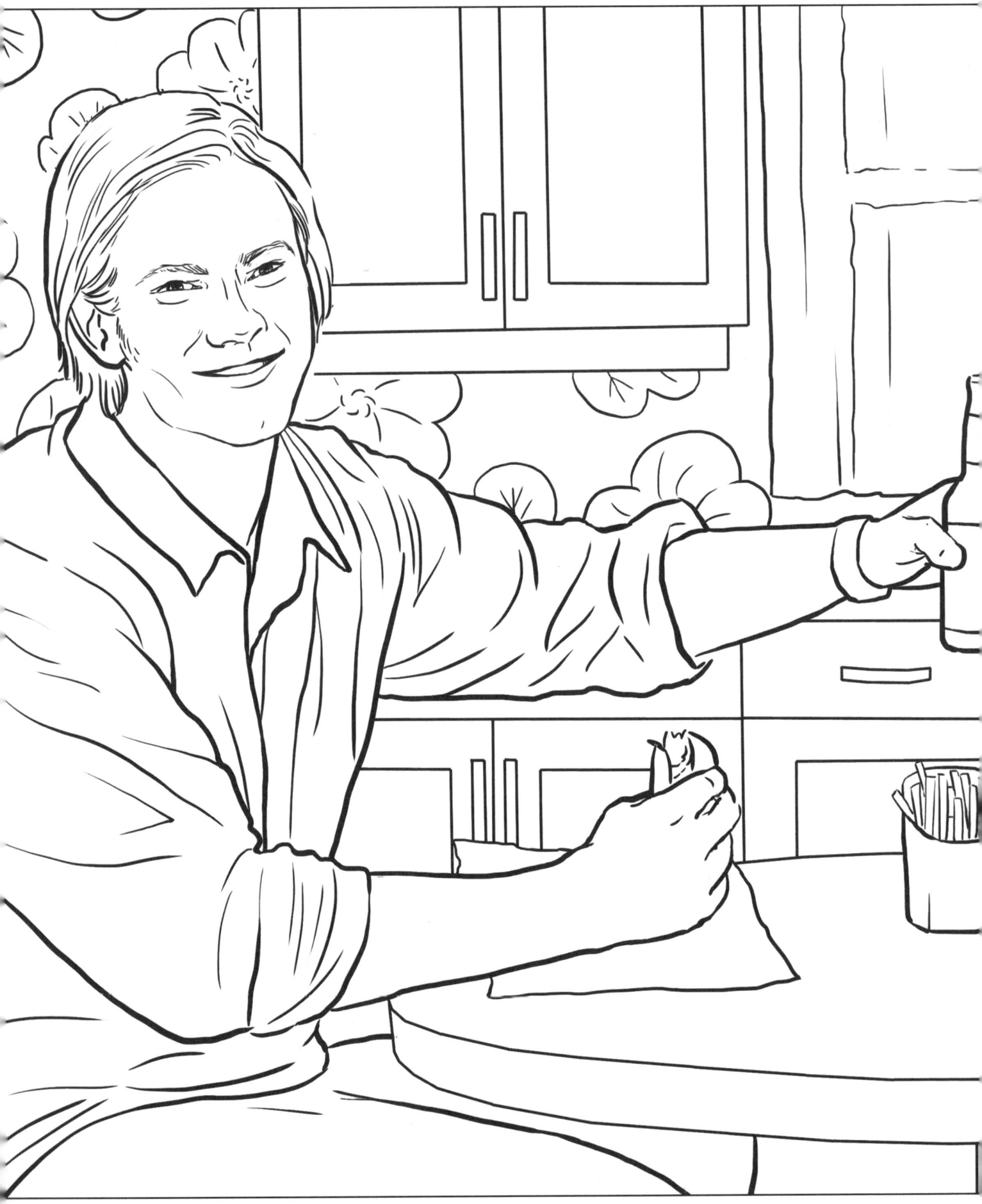

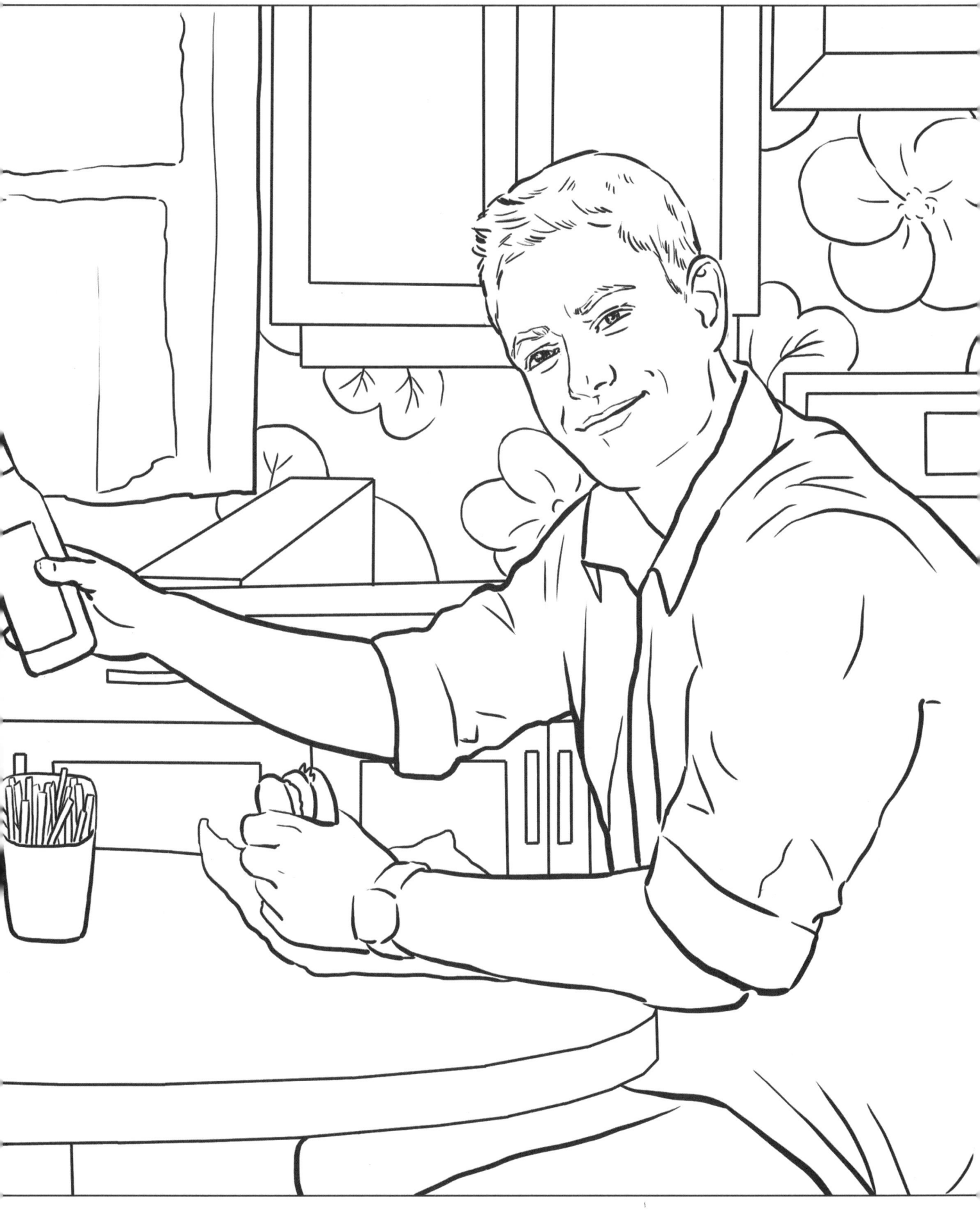

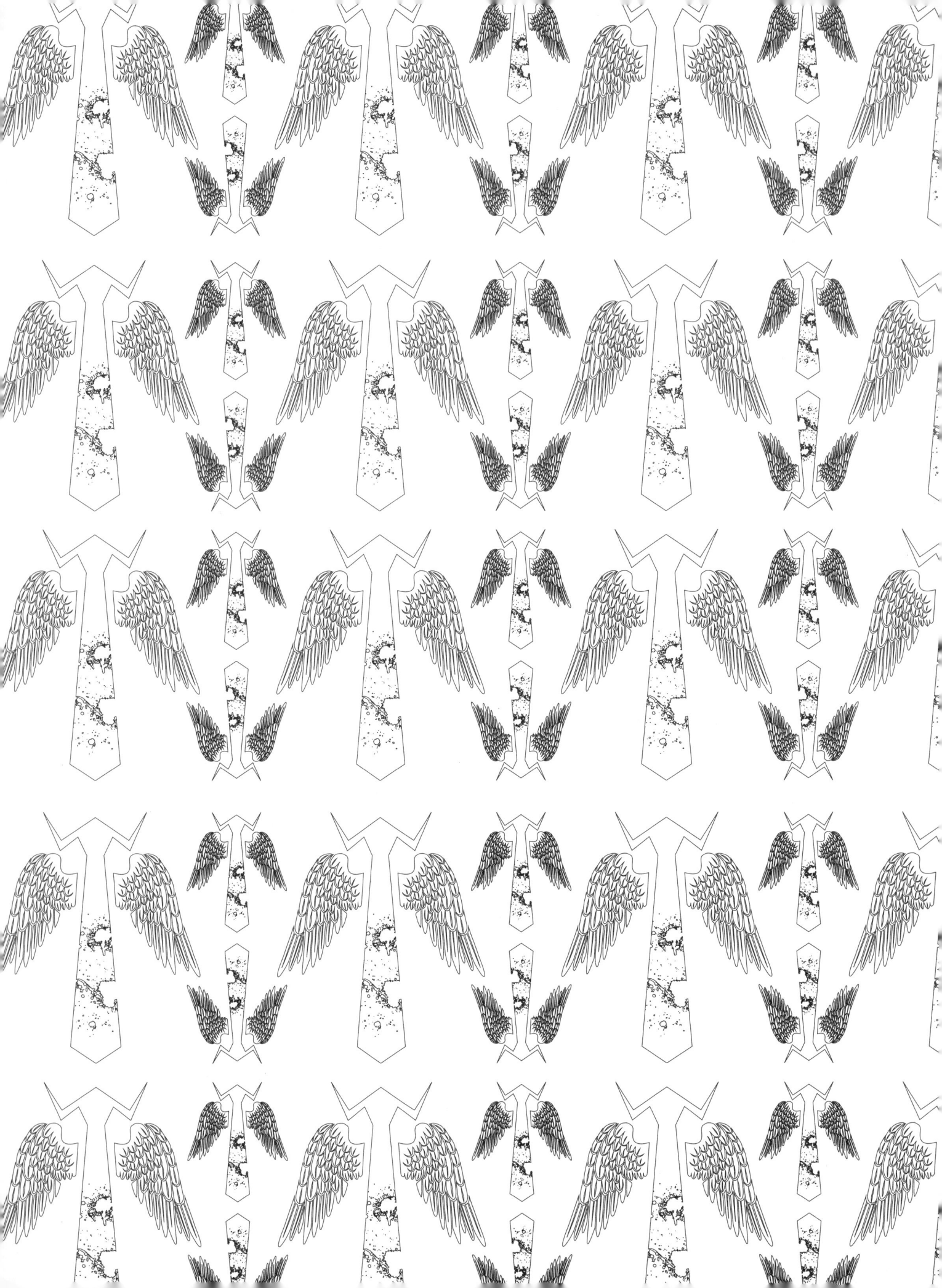

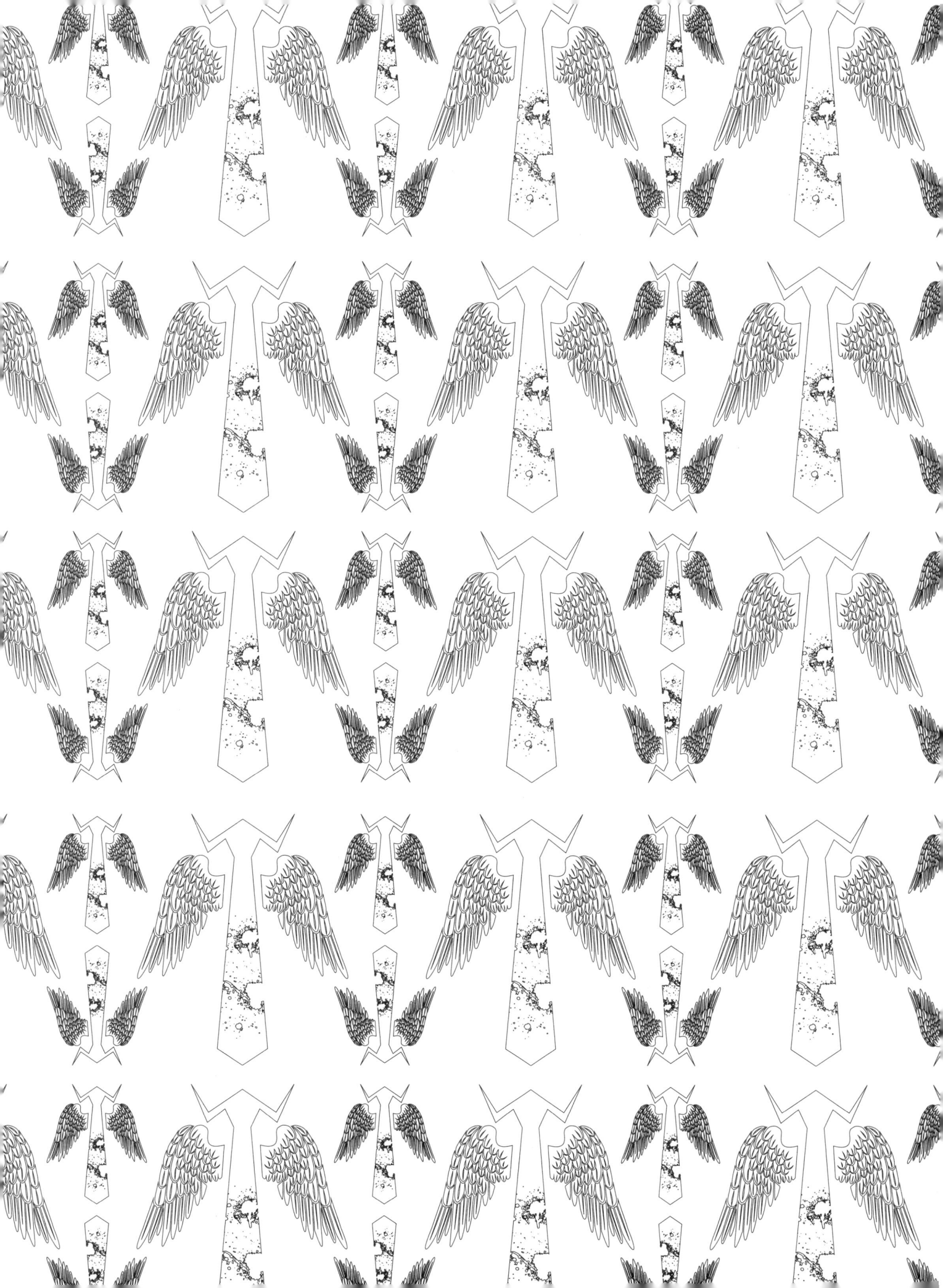

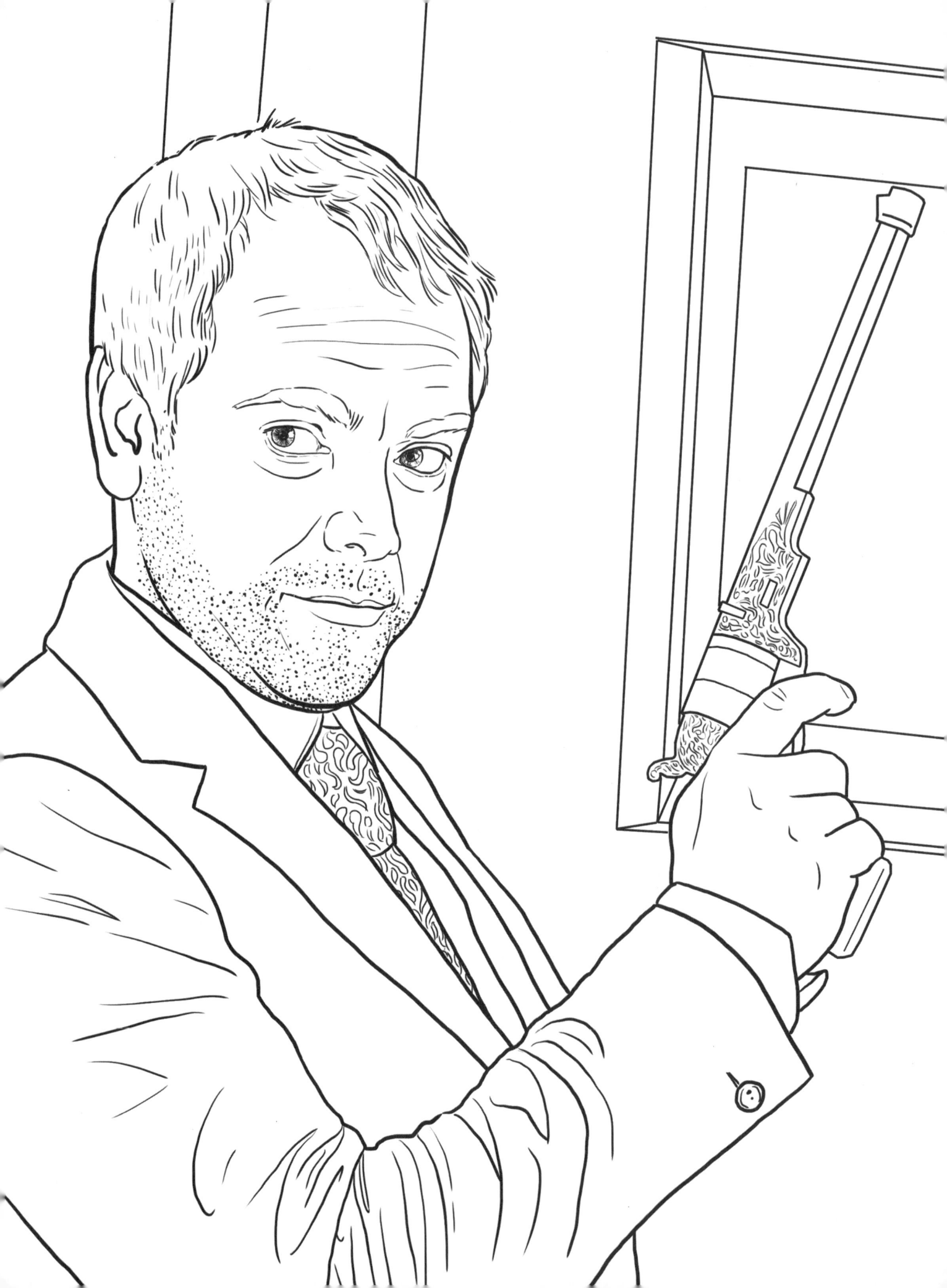

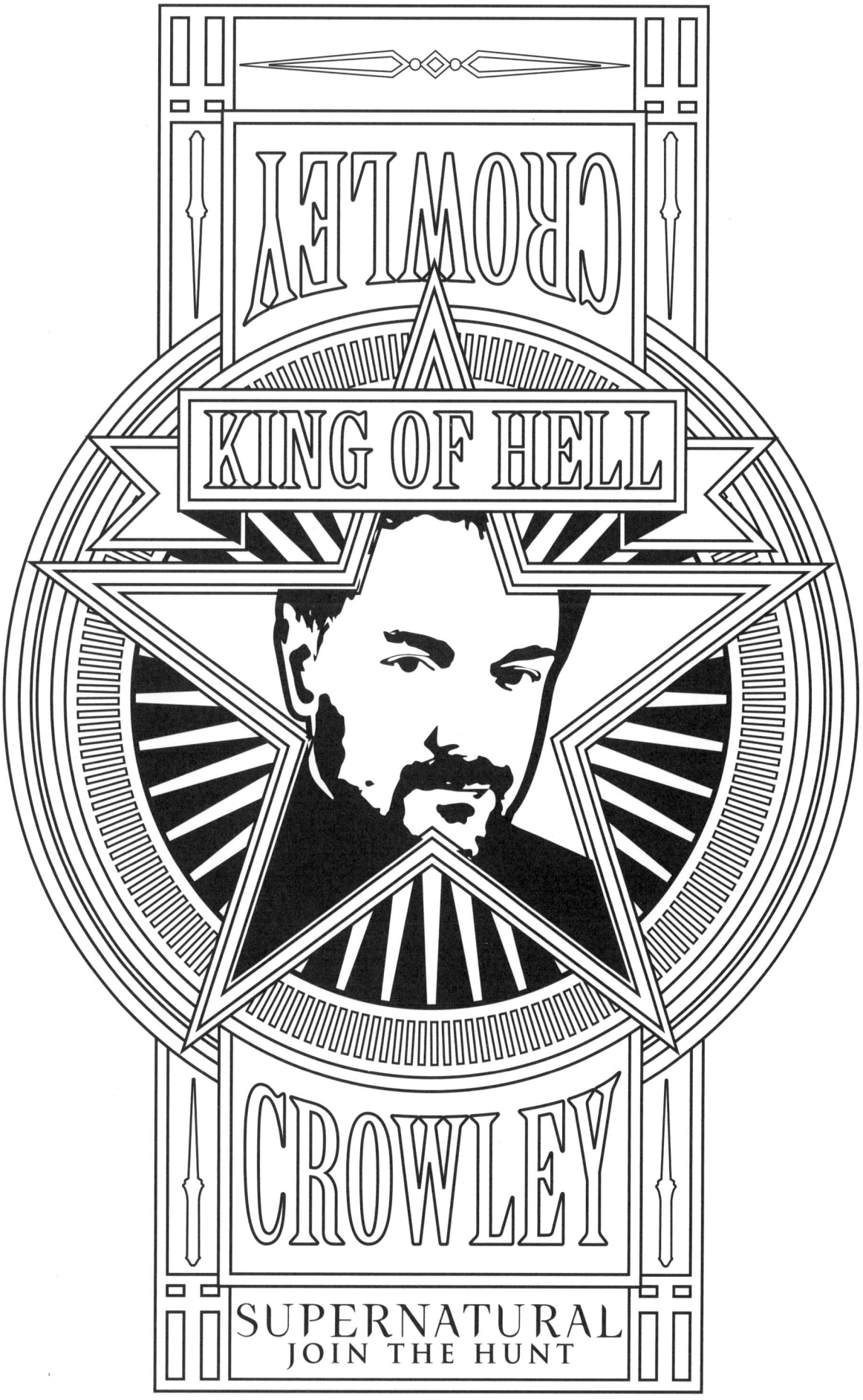
CROWLEY
KING OF HELL
CROWLEY
SUPERNATURAL
JOIN THE HUNT

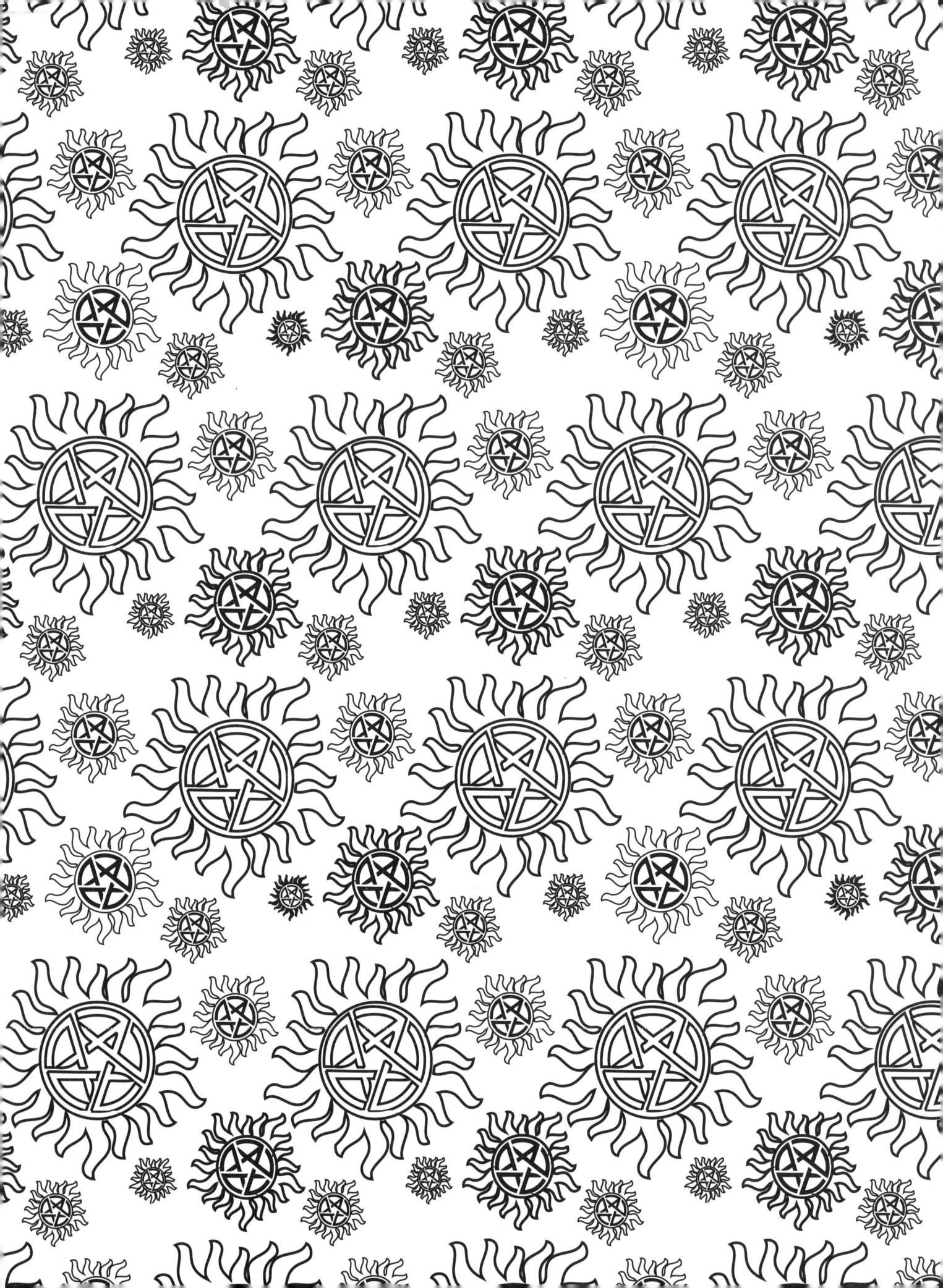

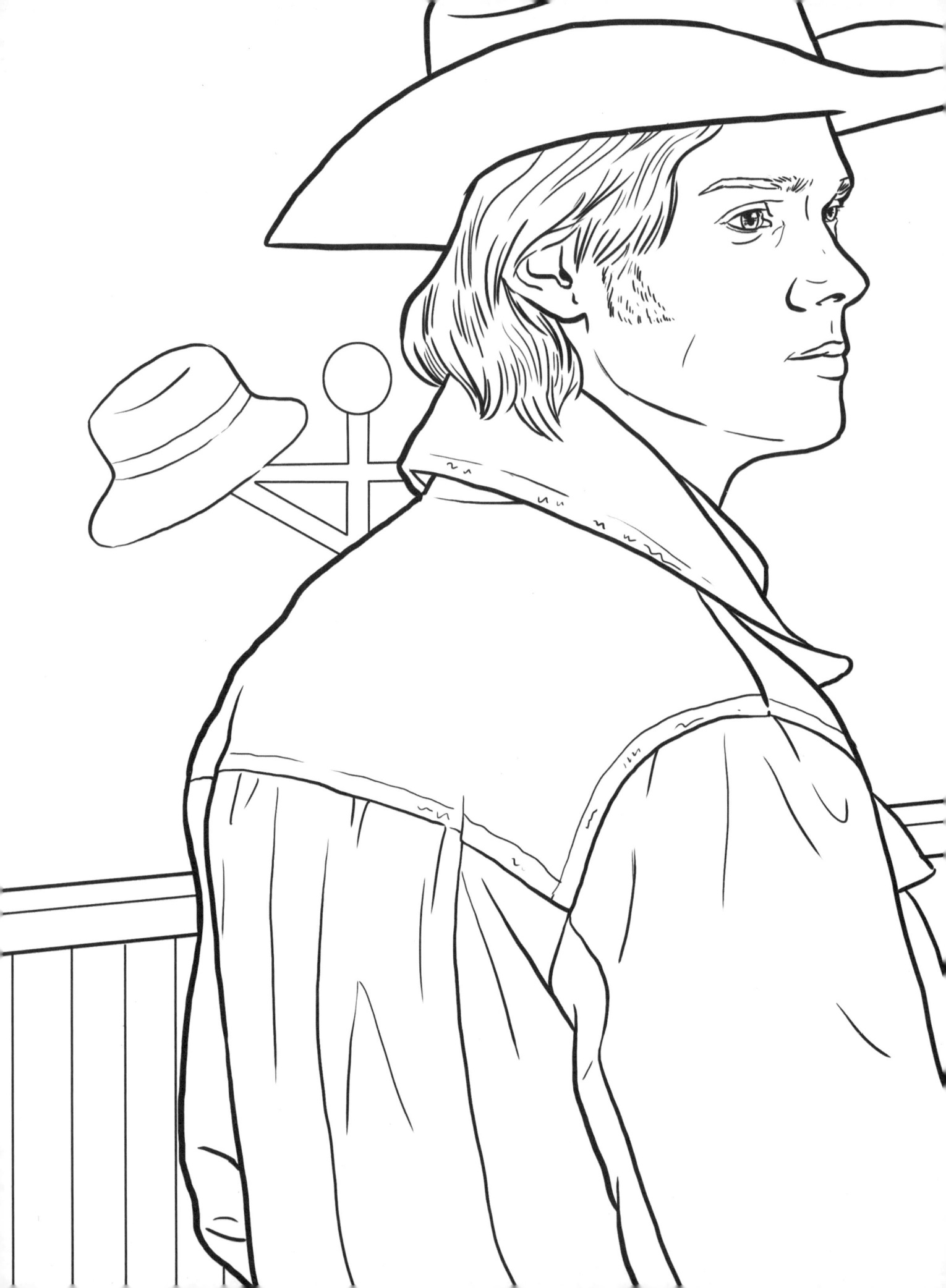

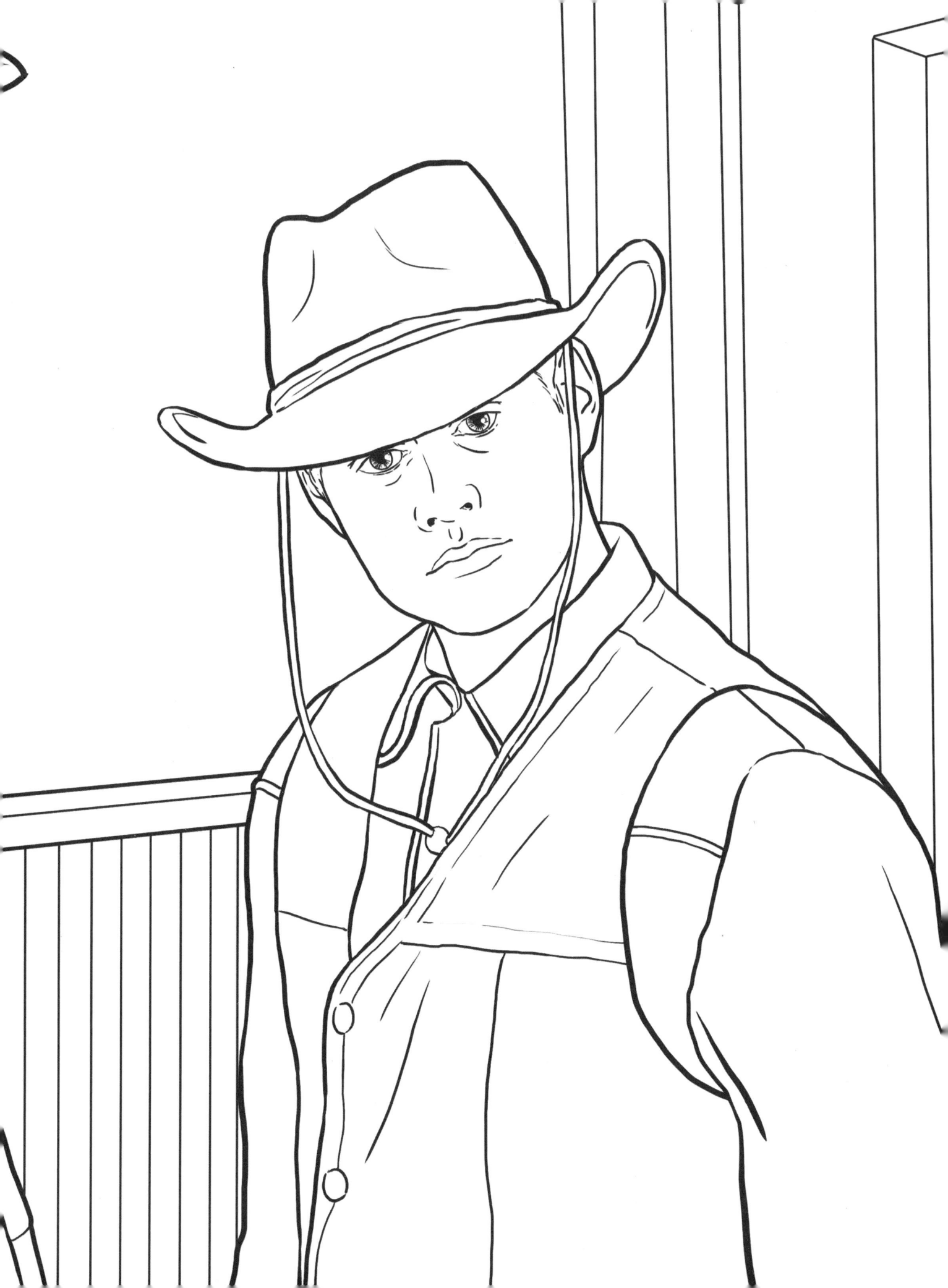

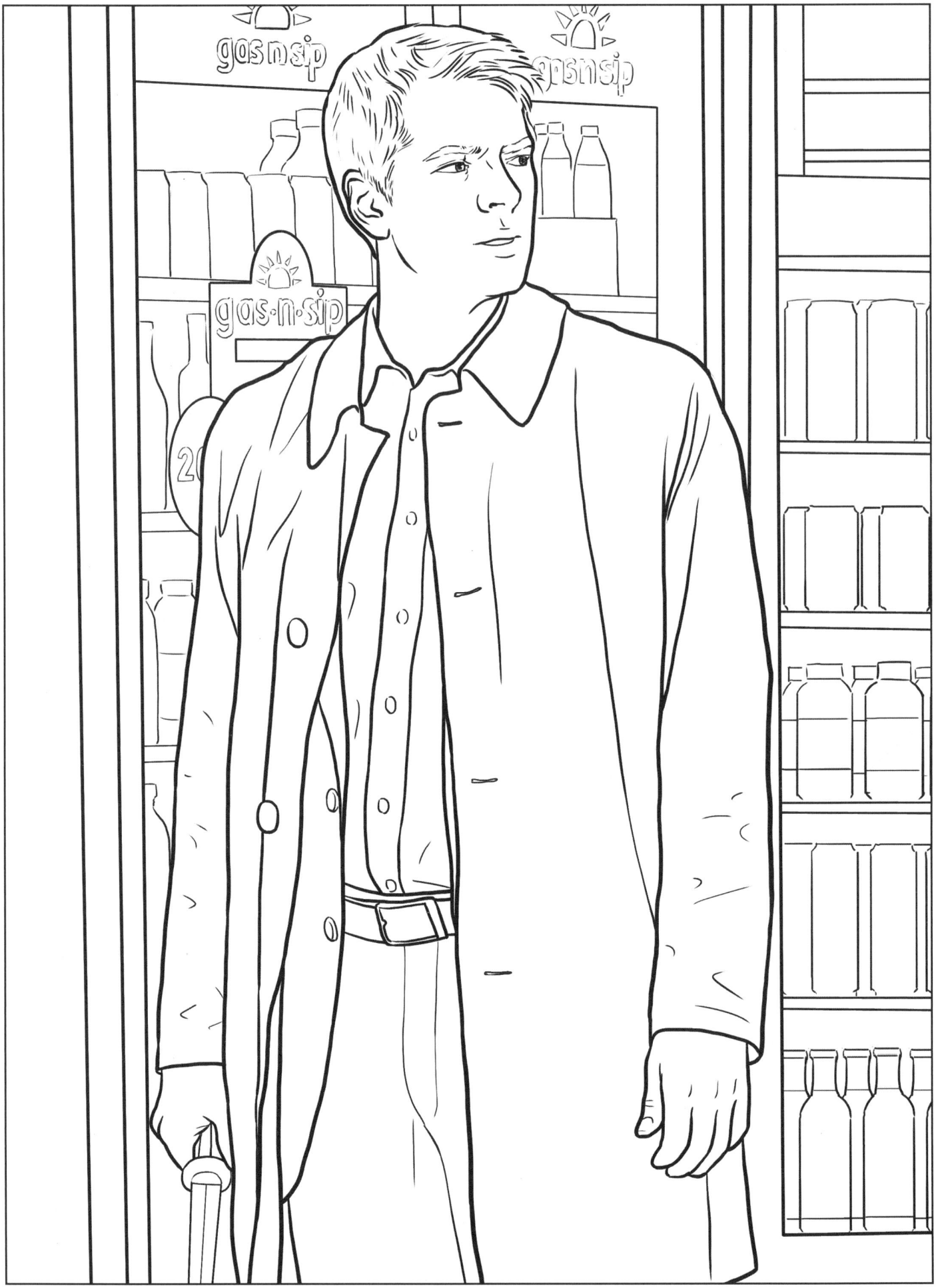
gasnsip
gasnsip
gas·n·sip

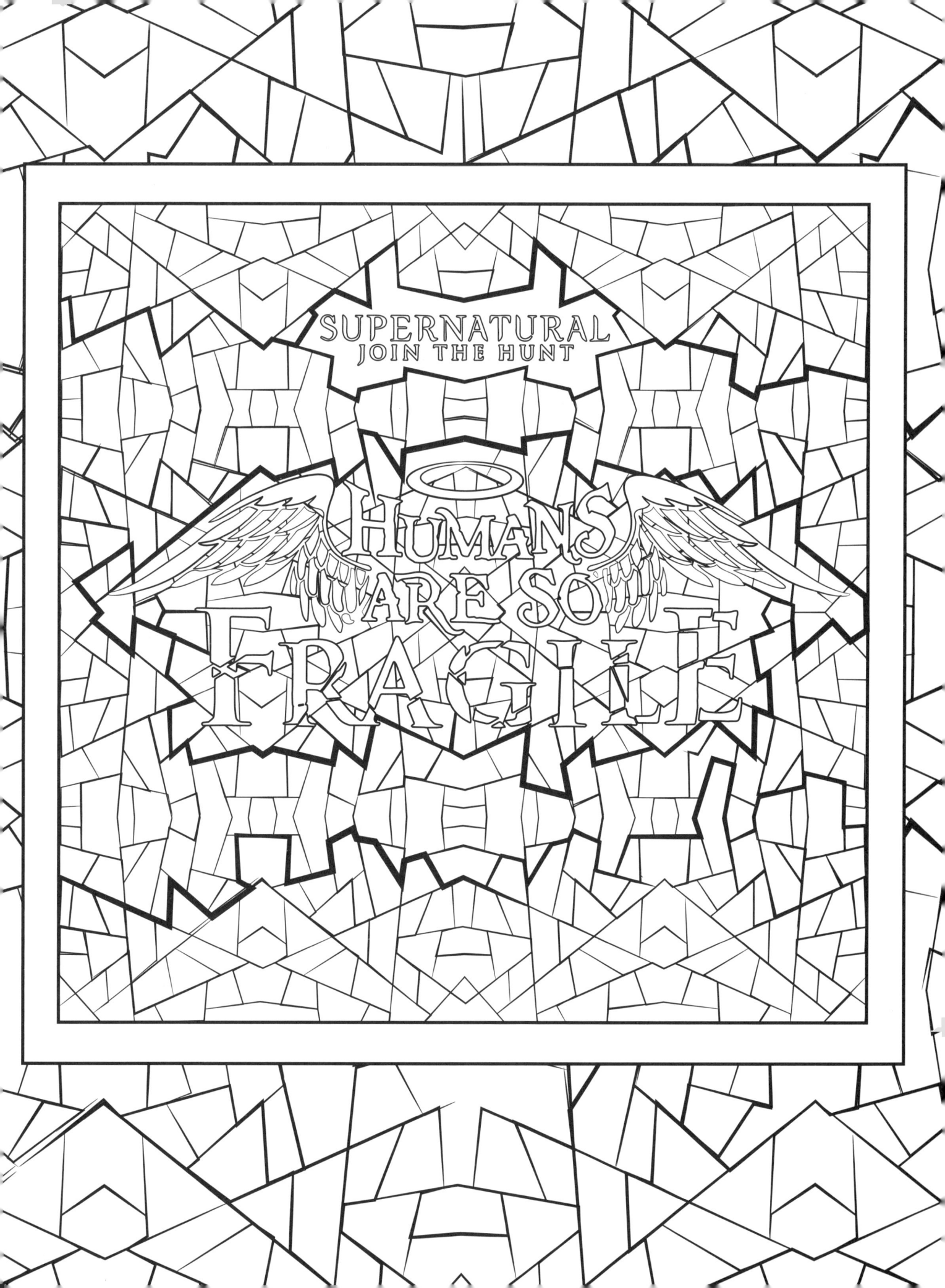
SUPERNATURAL
JOIN THE HUNT
HUMANS
ARE SO
FRAGILE

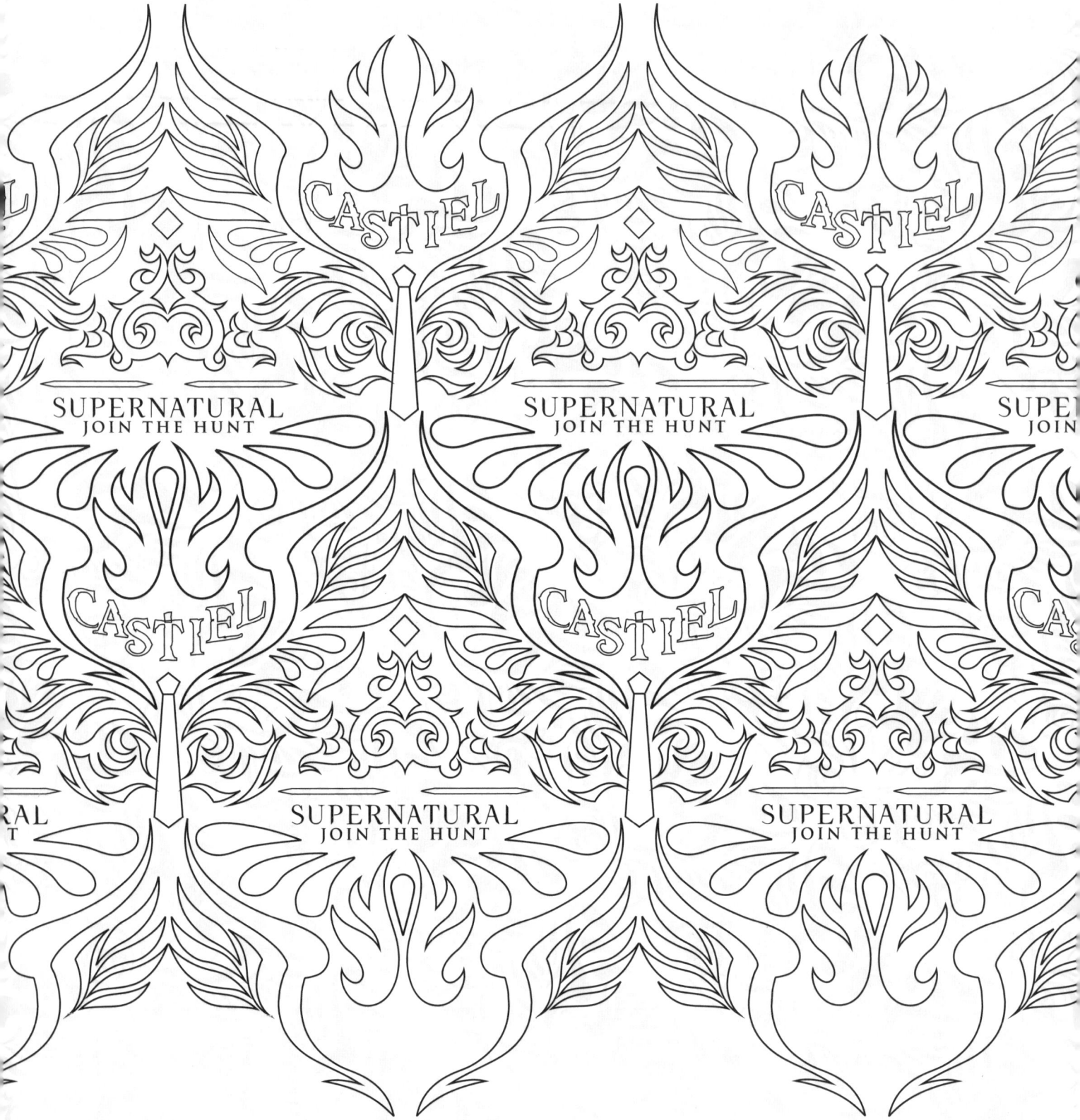
CASTIEL
SUPERNATURAL
JOIN THE HUNT
CASTIEL
SUPERNATURAL
JOIN THE HUNT
CASTIEL
SUPERNATURAL
JOIN THE HUNT
CASTIEL
SUPERNATURAL
JOIN THE HUNT

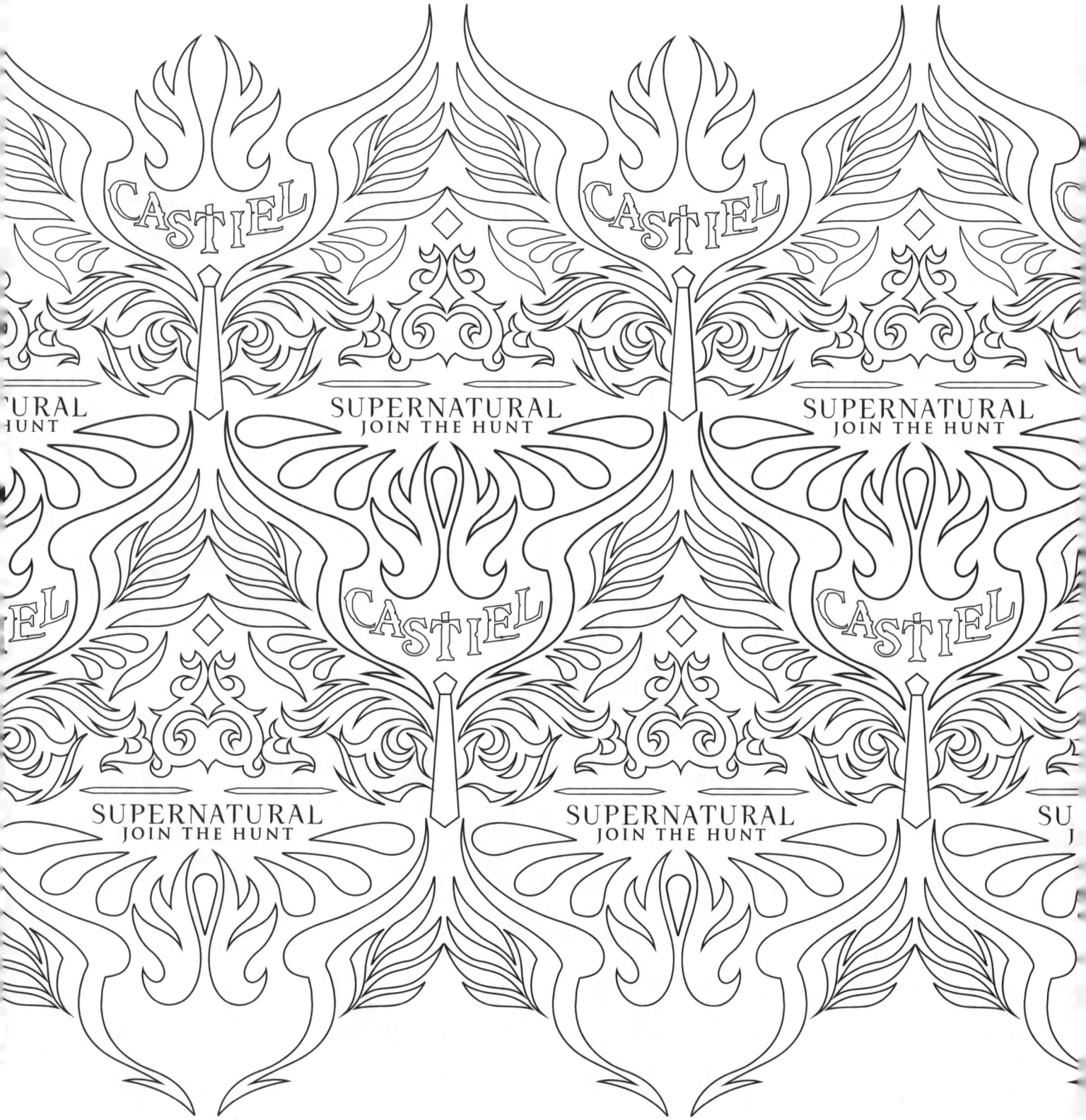
CASTIEL
CASTIEL
SUPERNATURAL
JOIN THE HUNT
SUPERNATURAL
JOIN THE HUNT
CASTIEL
CASTIEL
SUPERNATURAL
JOIN THE HUNT
SUPERNATURAL
JOIN THE HUNT

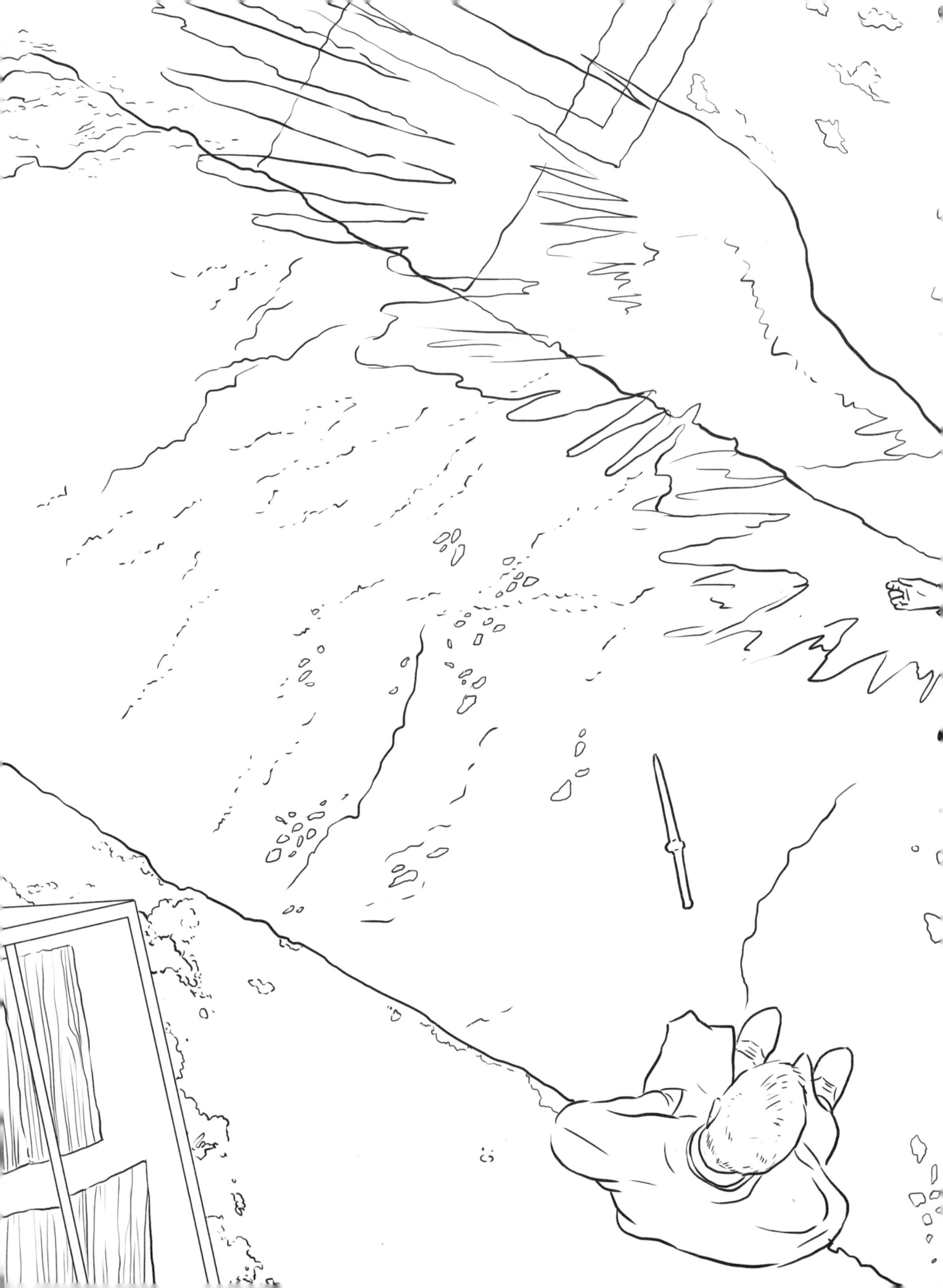

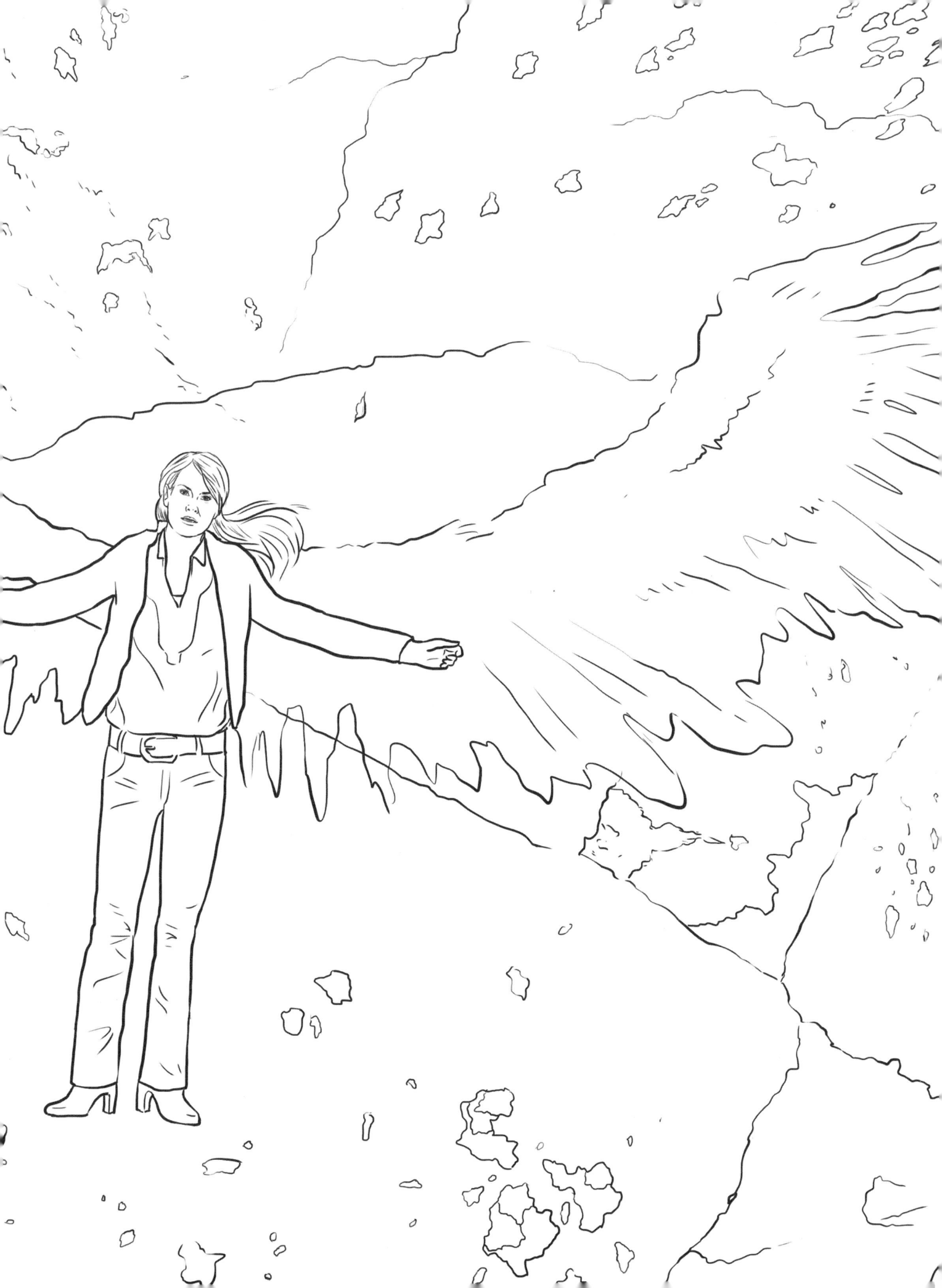

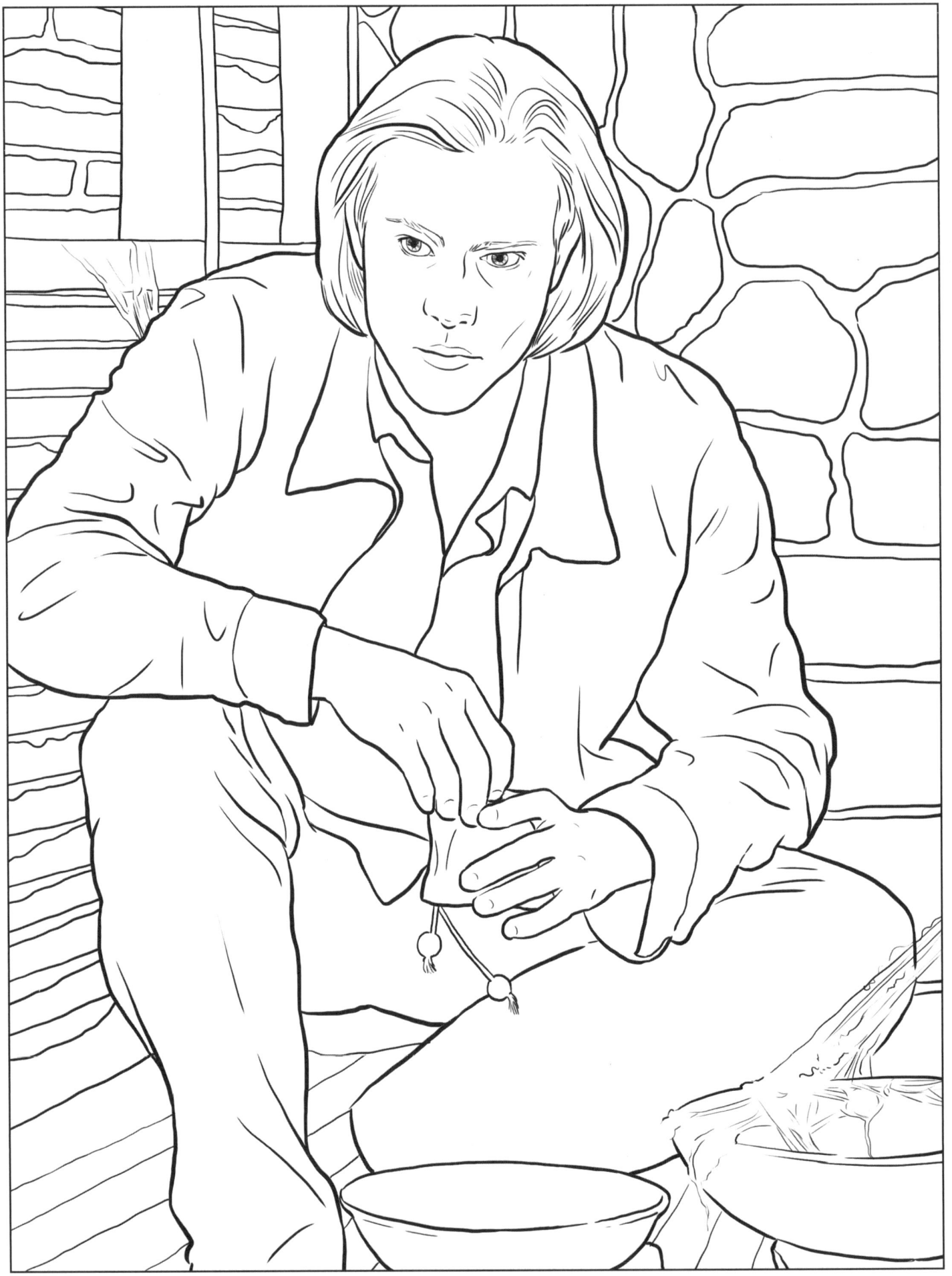

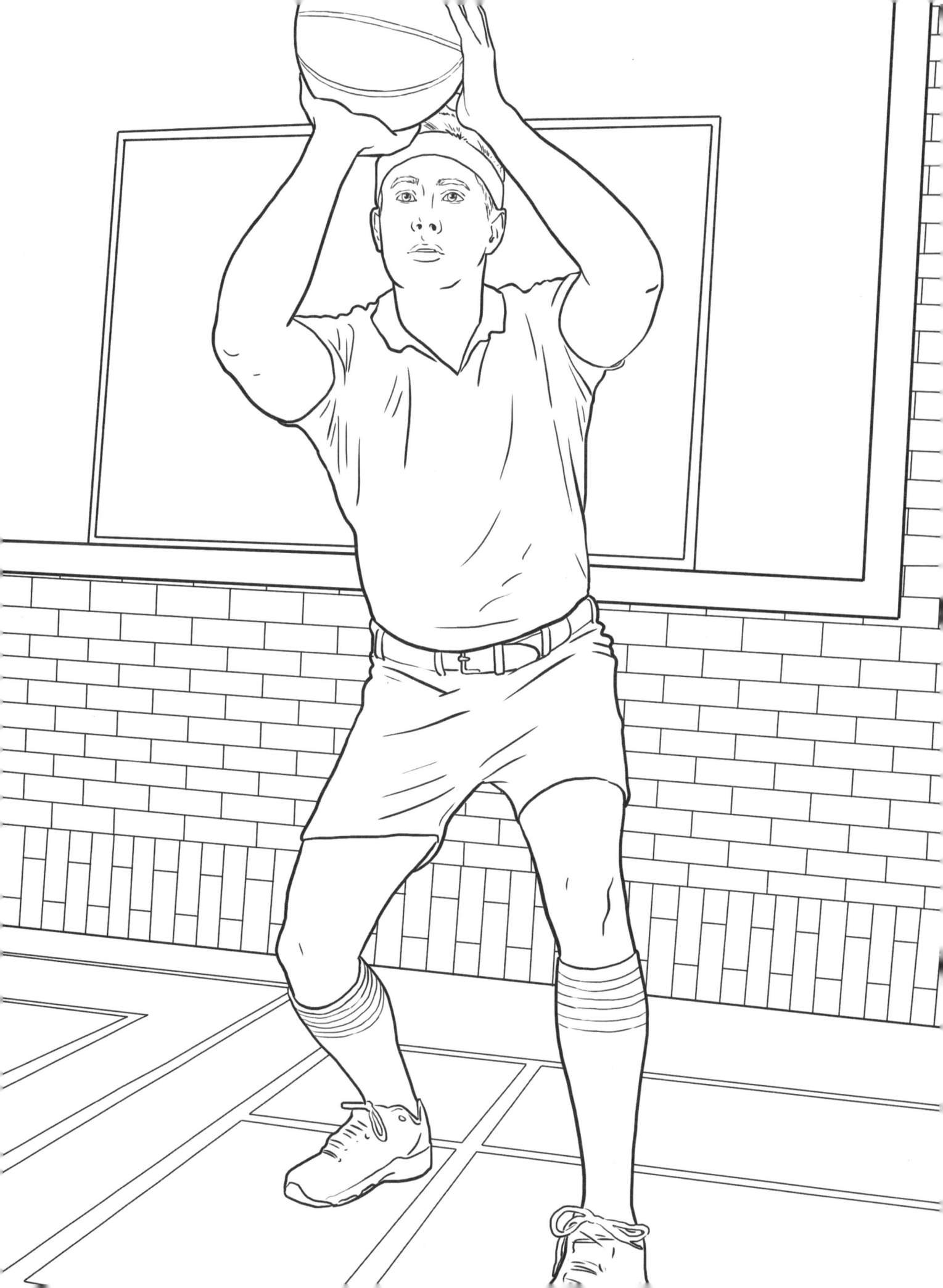

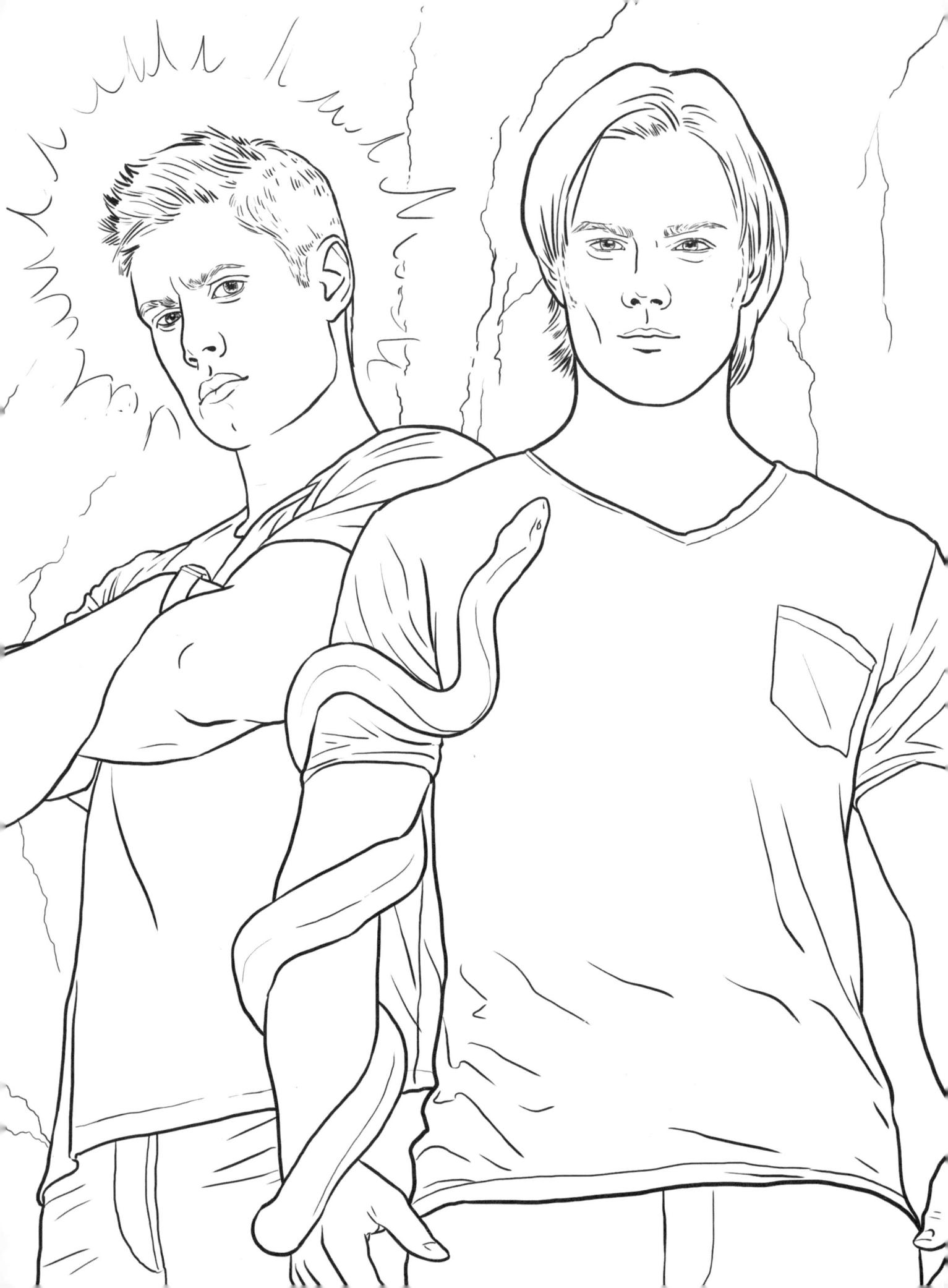

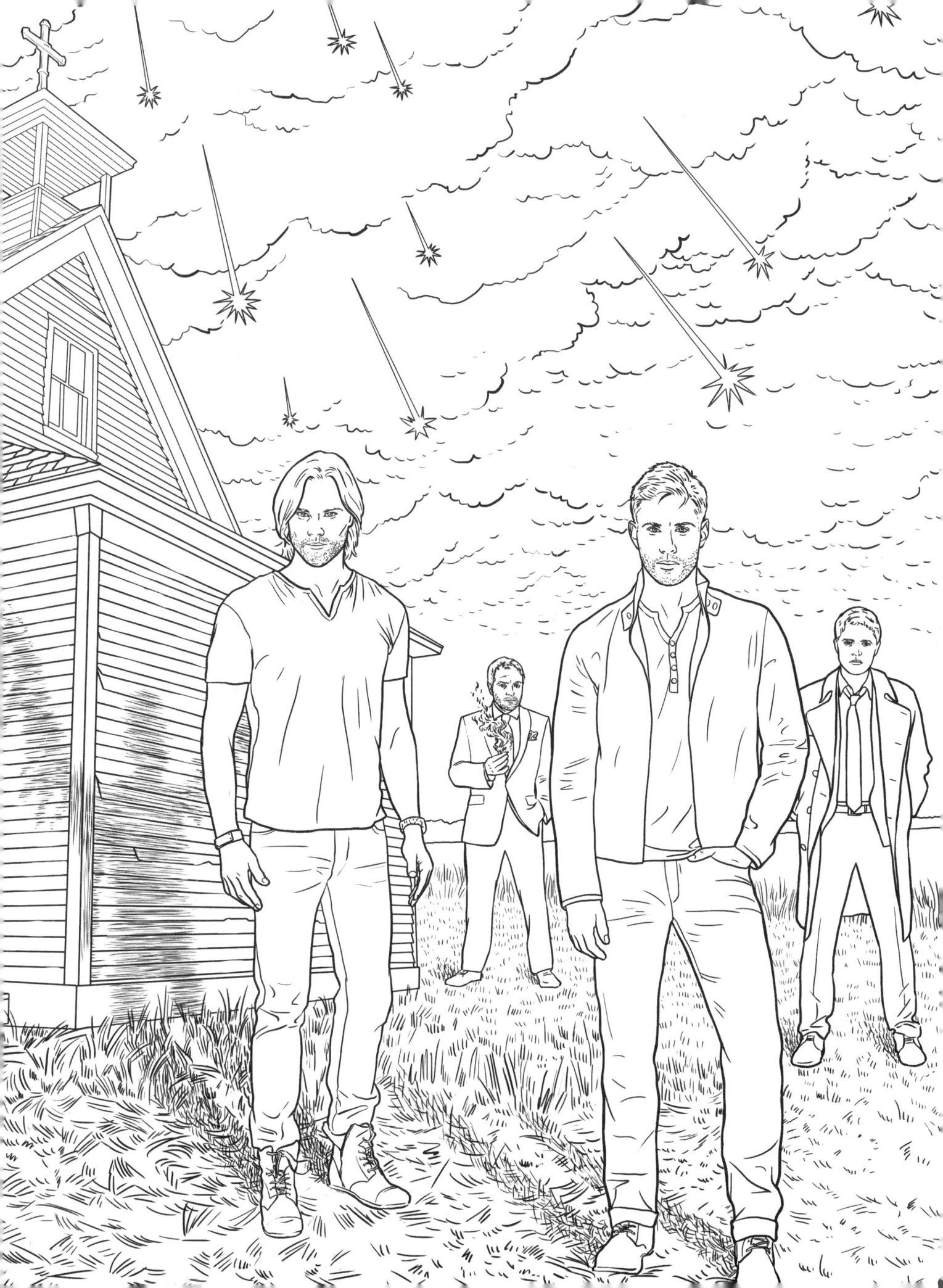

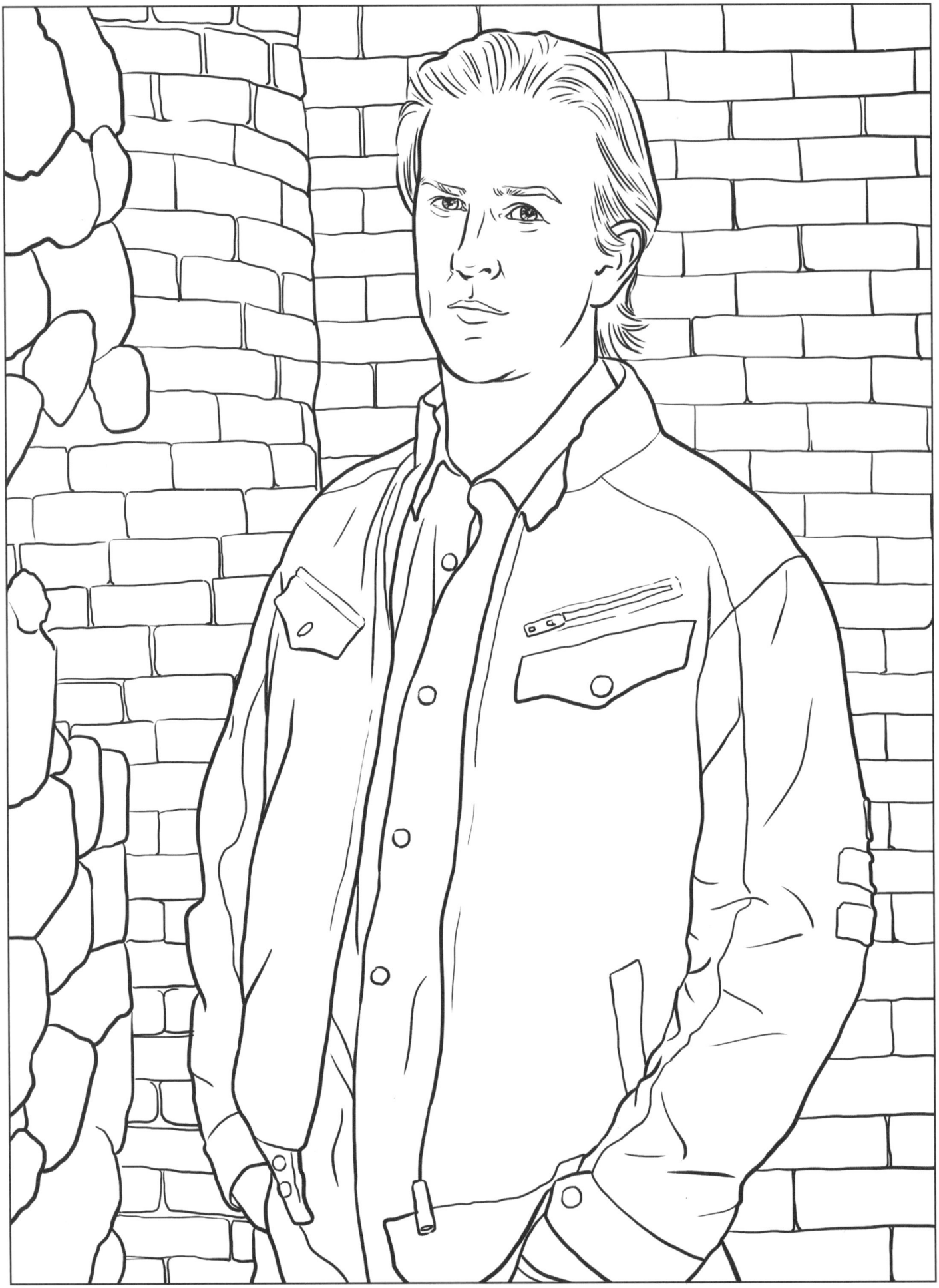

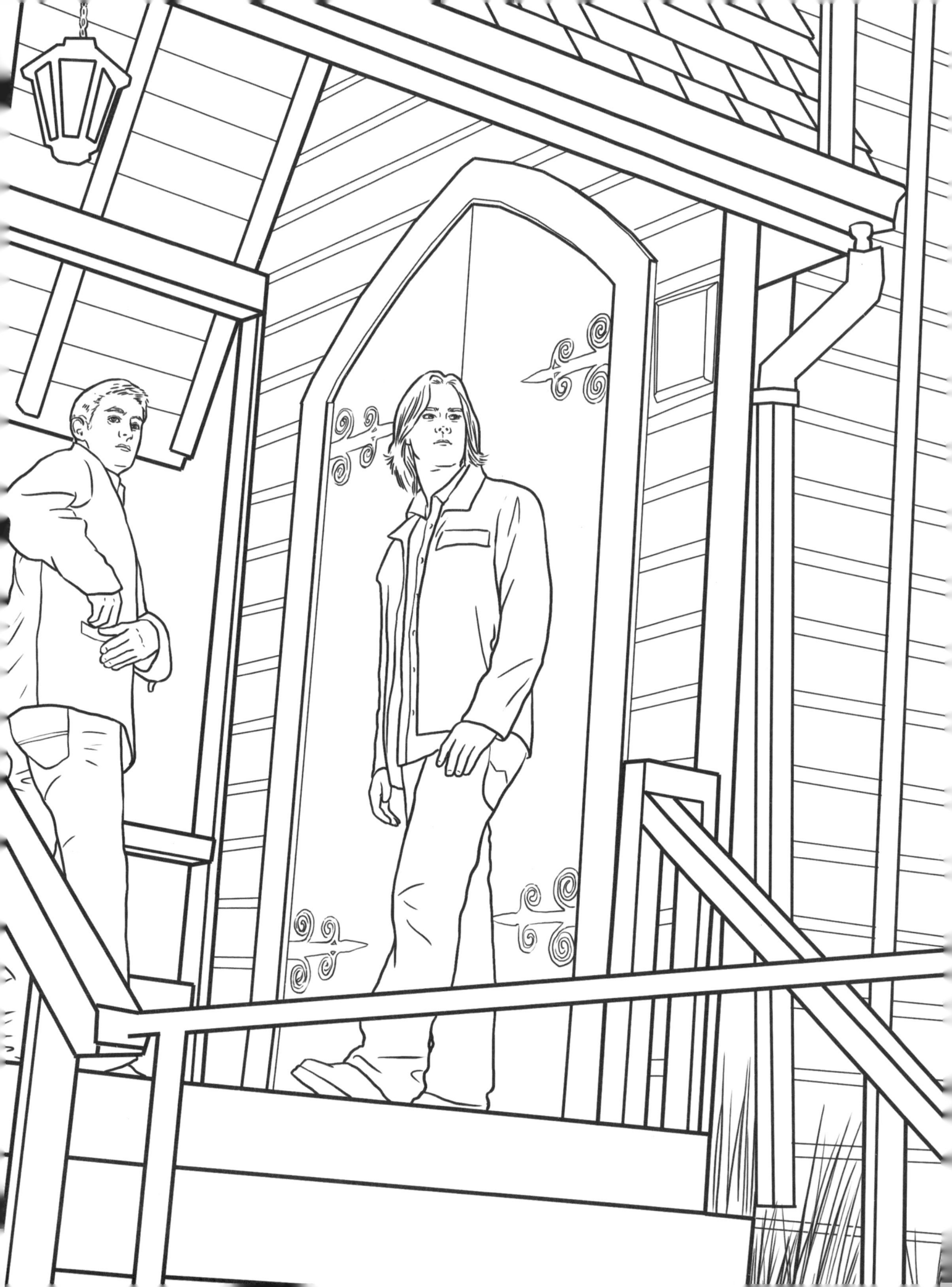

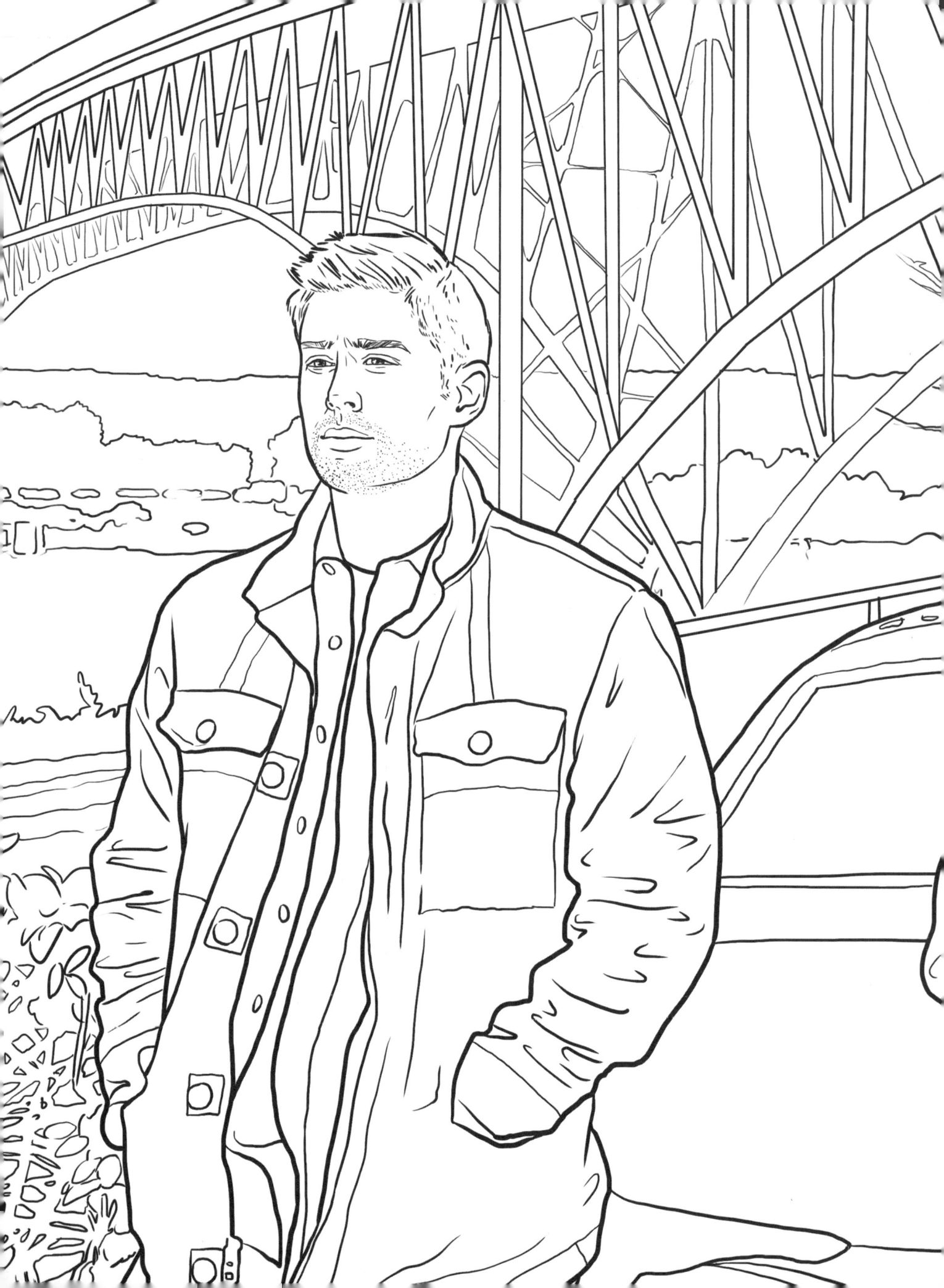

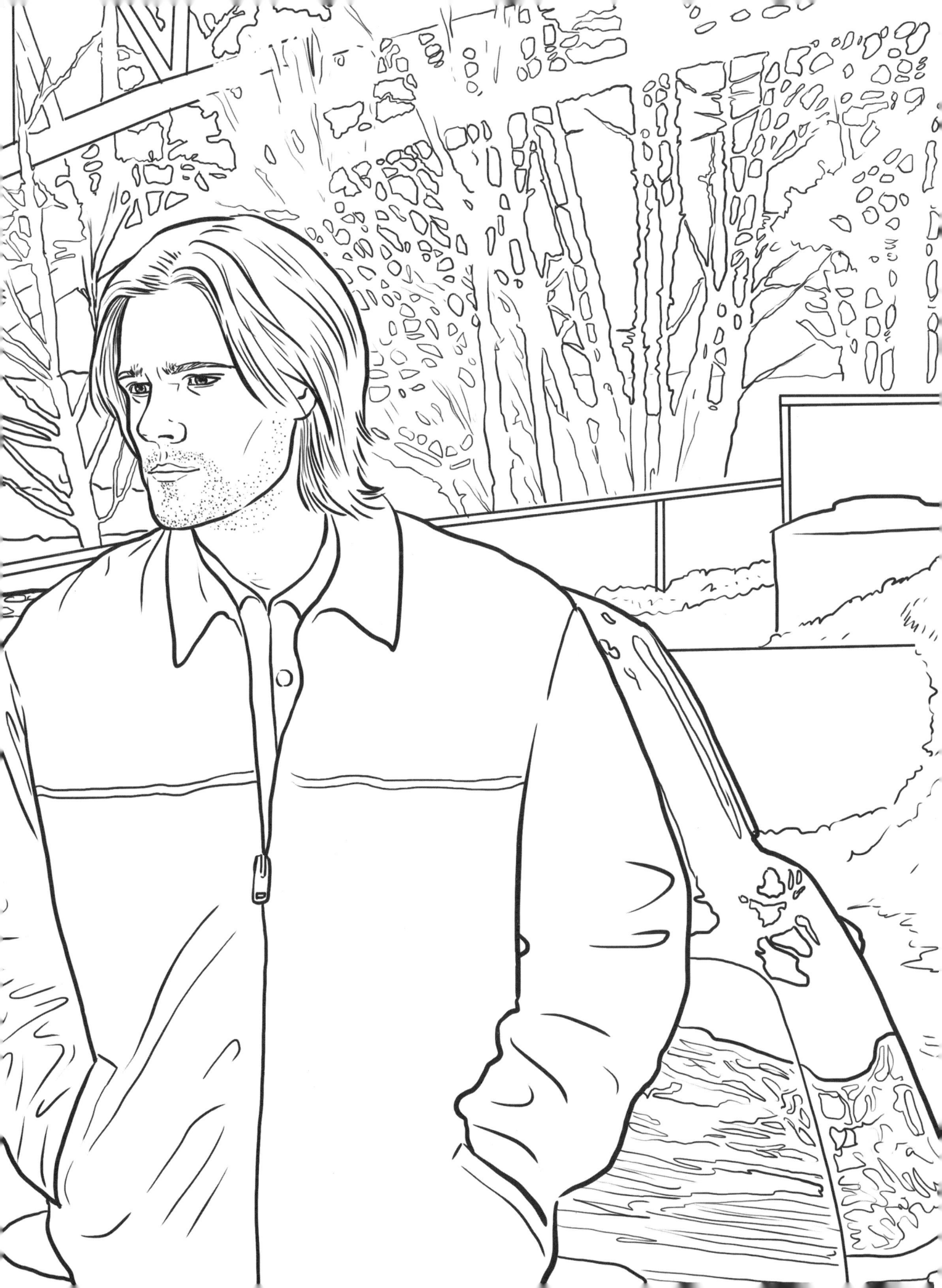

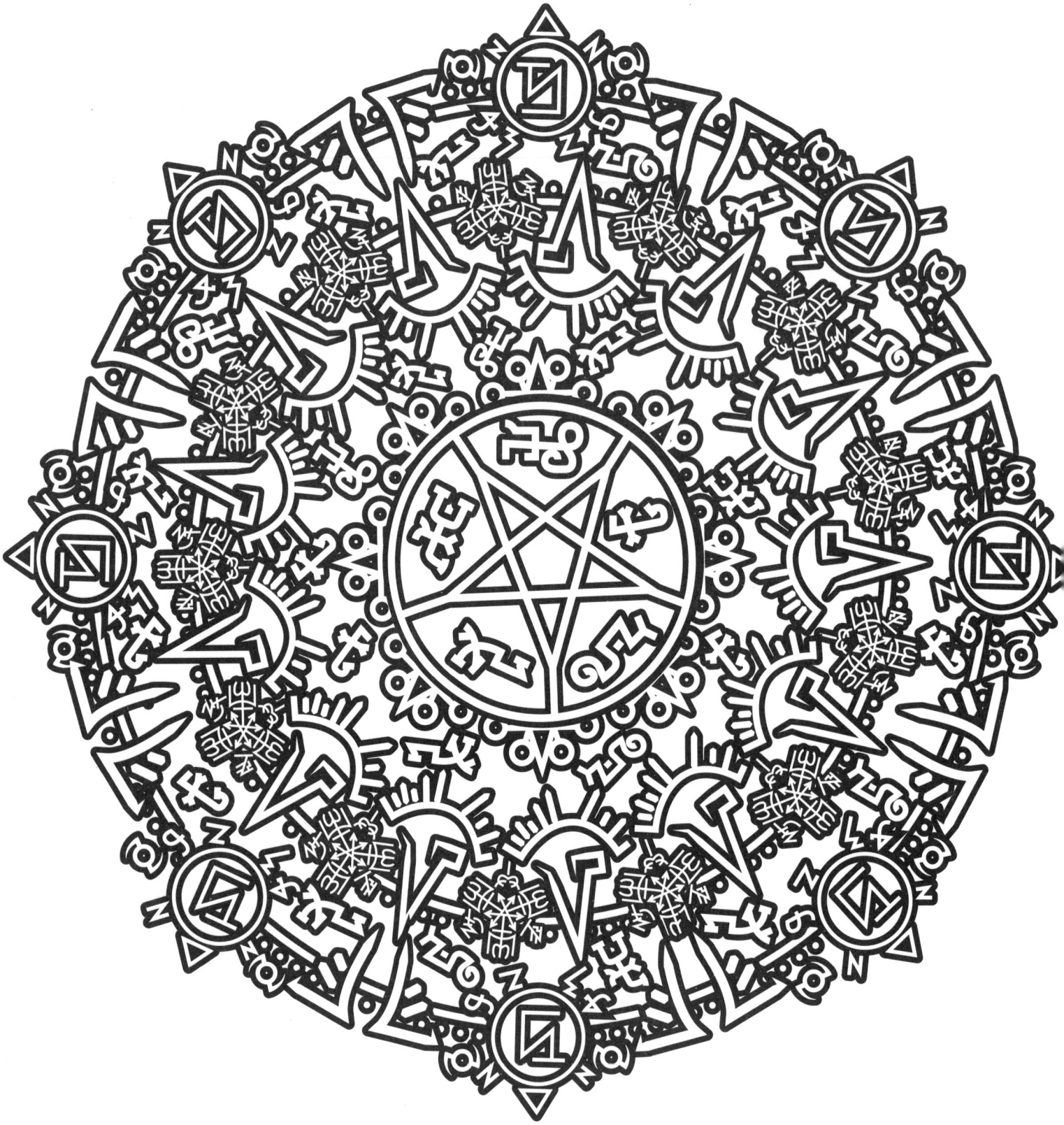

SUPERNATURAL

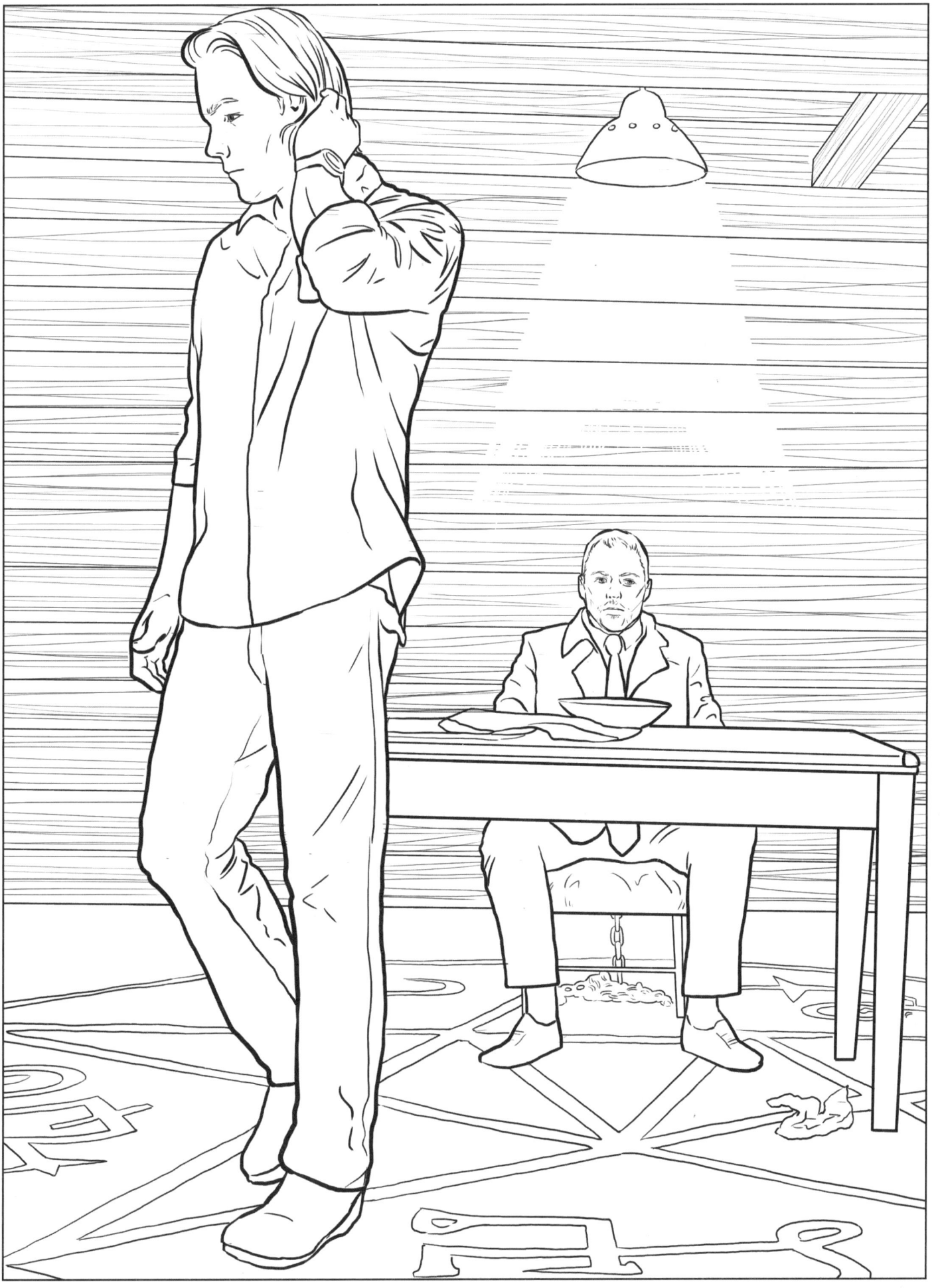

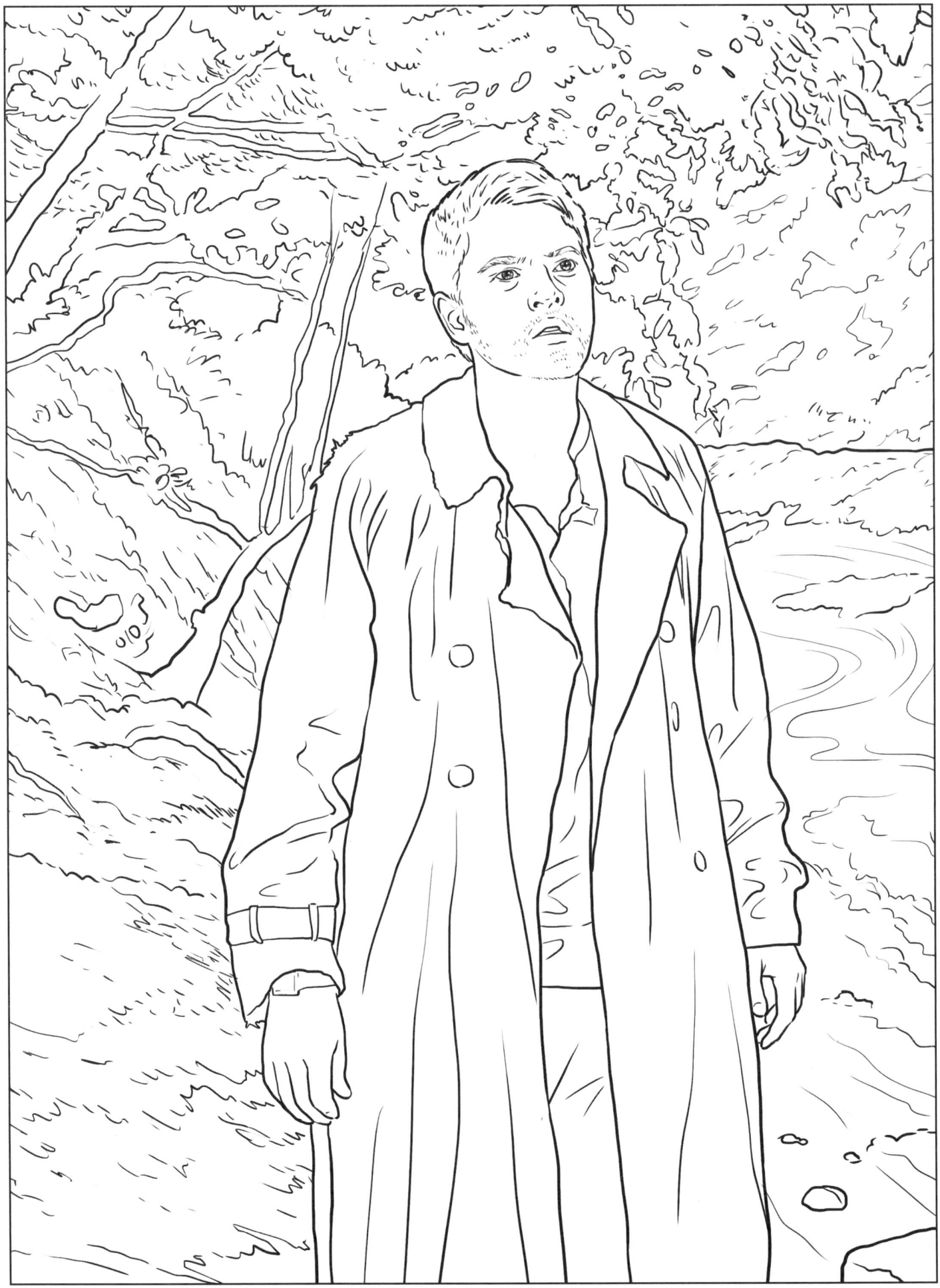

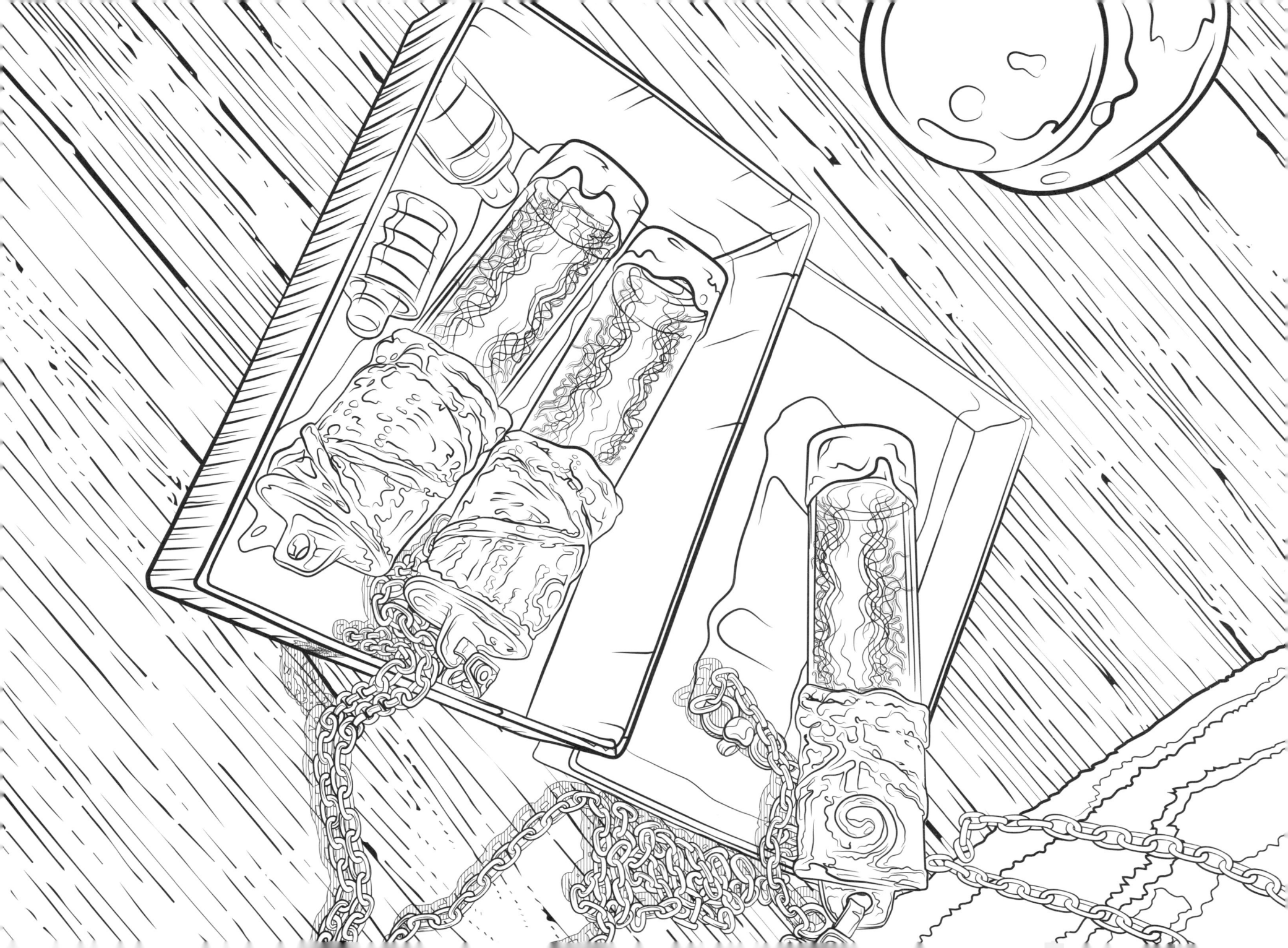

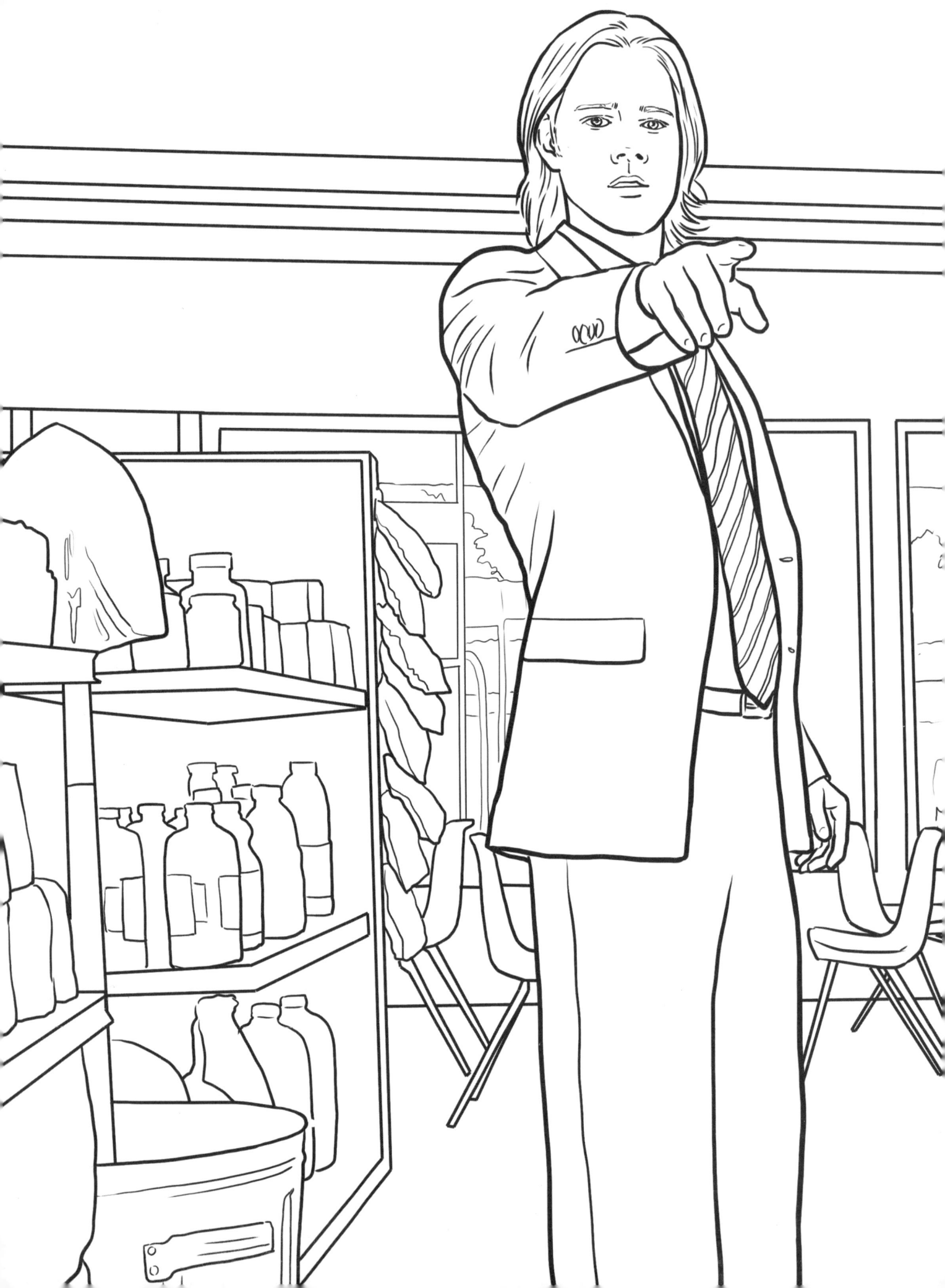

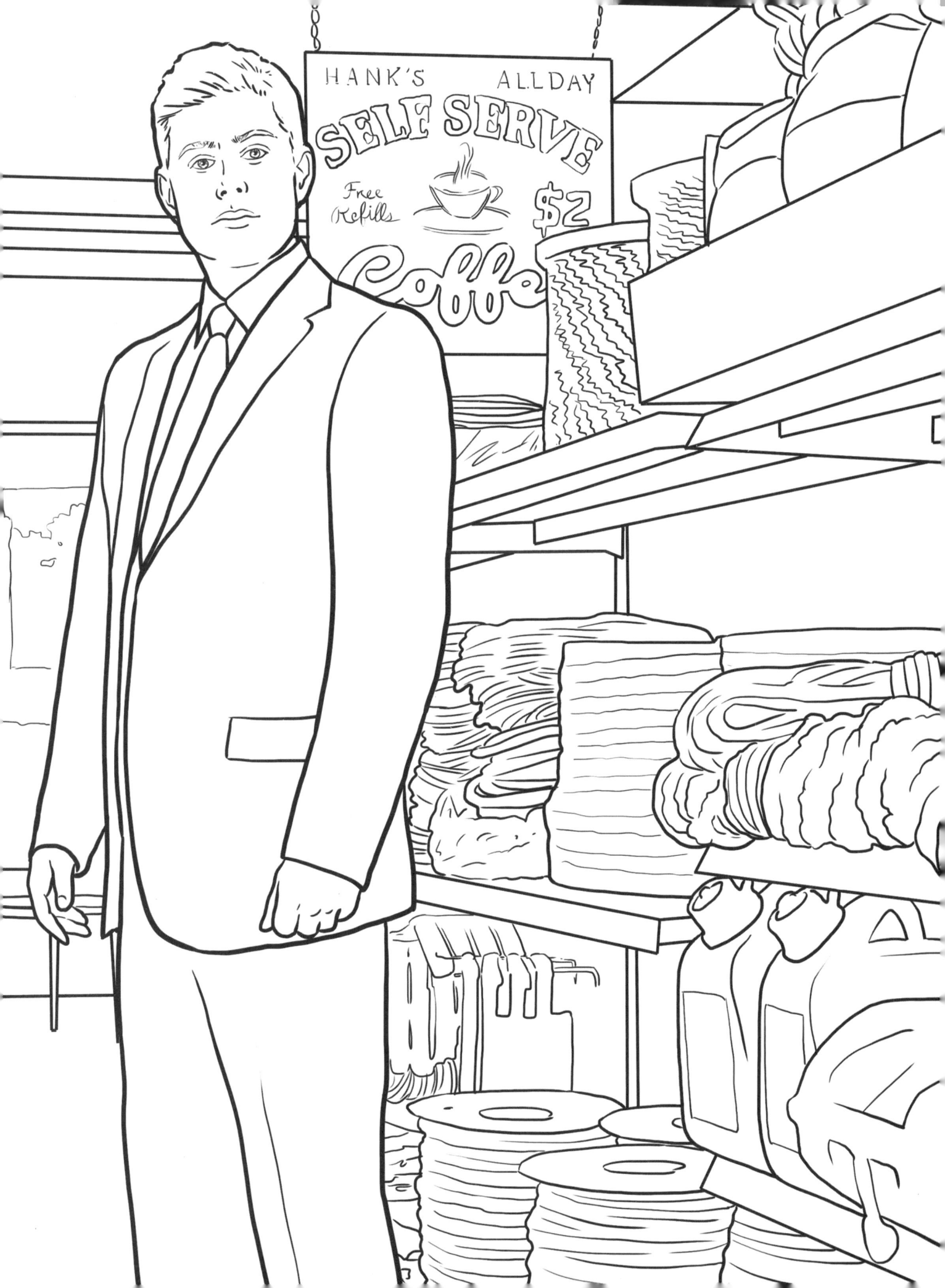
HANK'S
ALL DAY
SELF SERVE
Free Refills
$2
Coffee

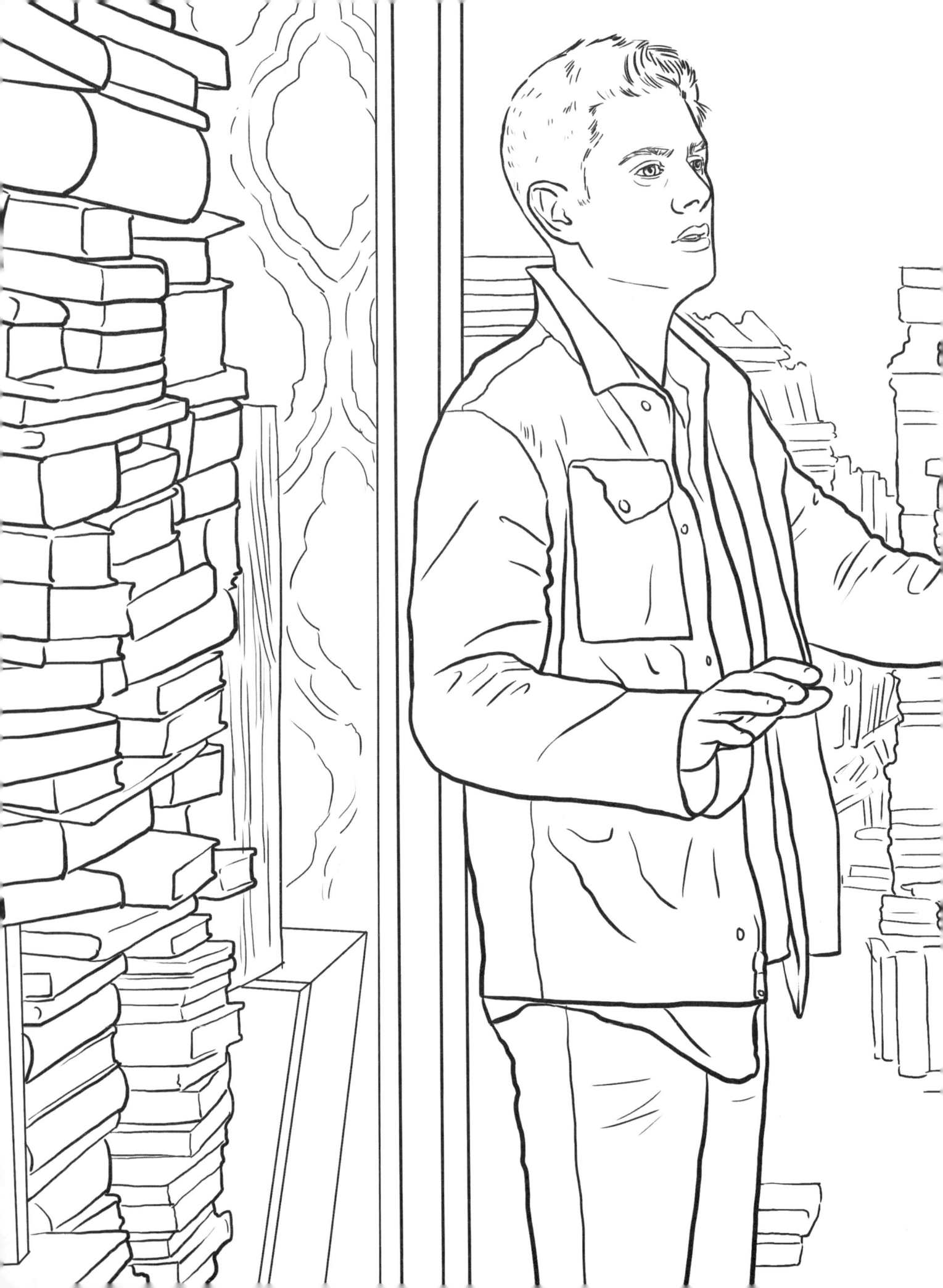

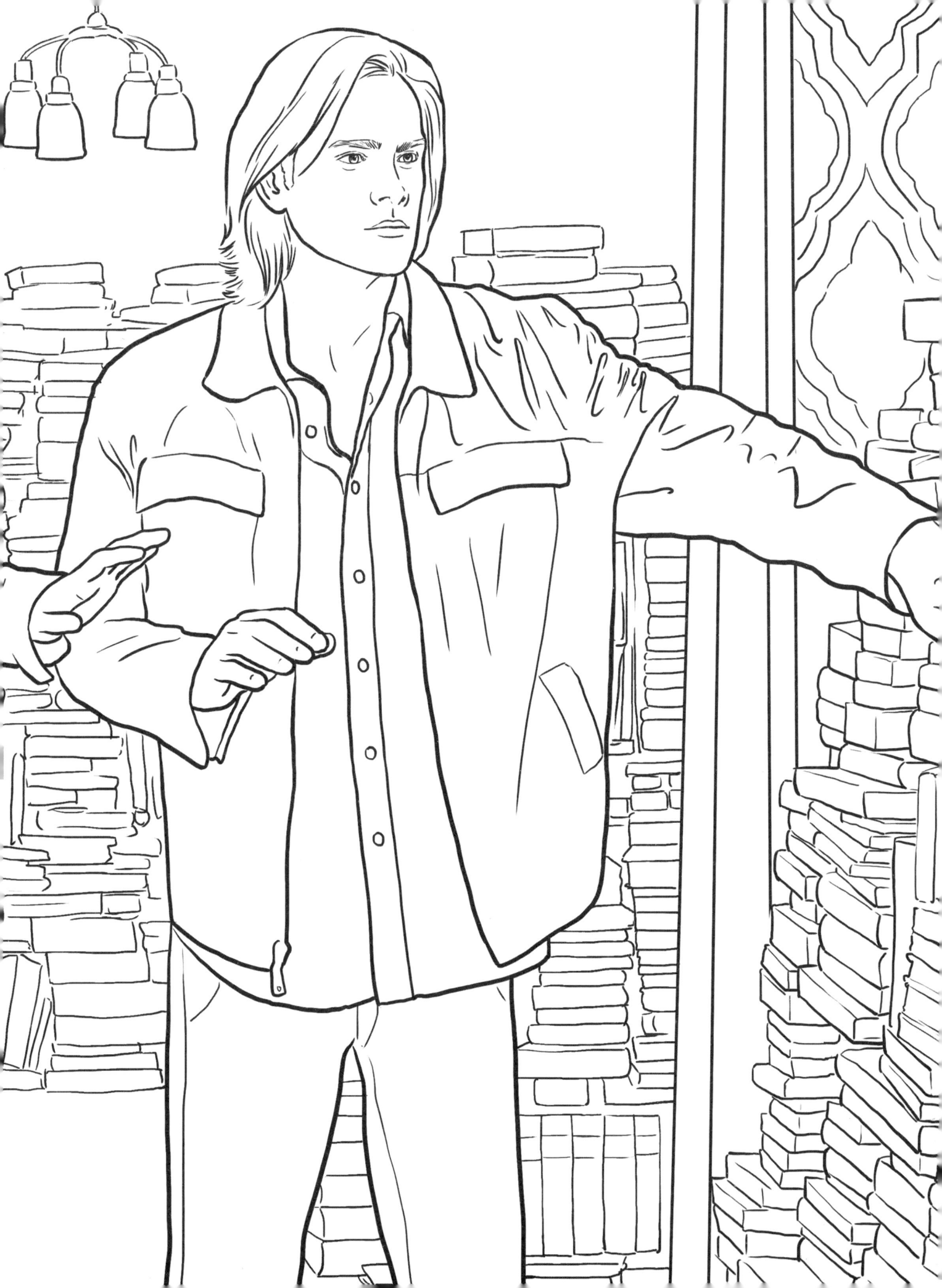

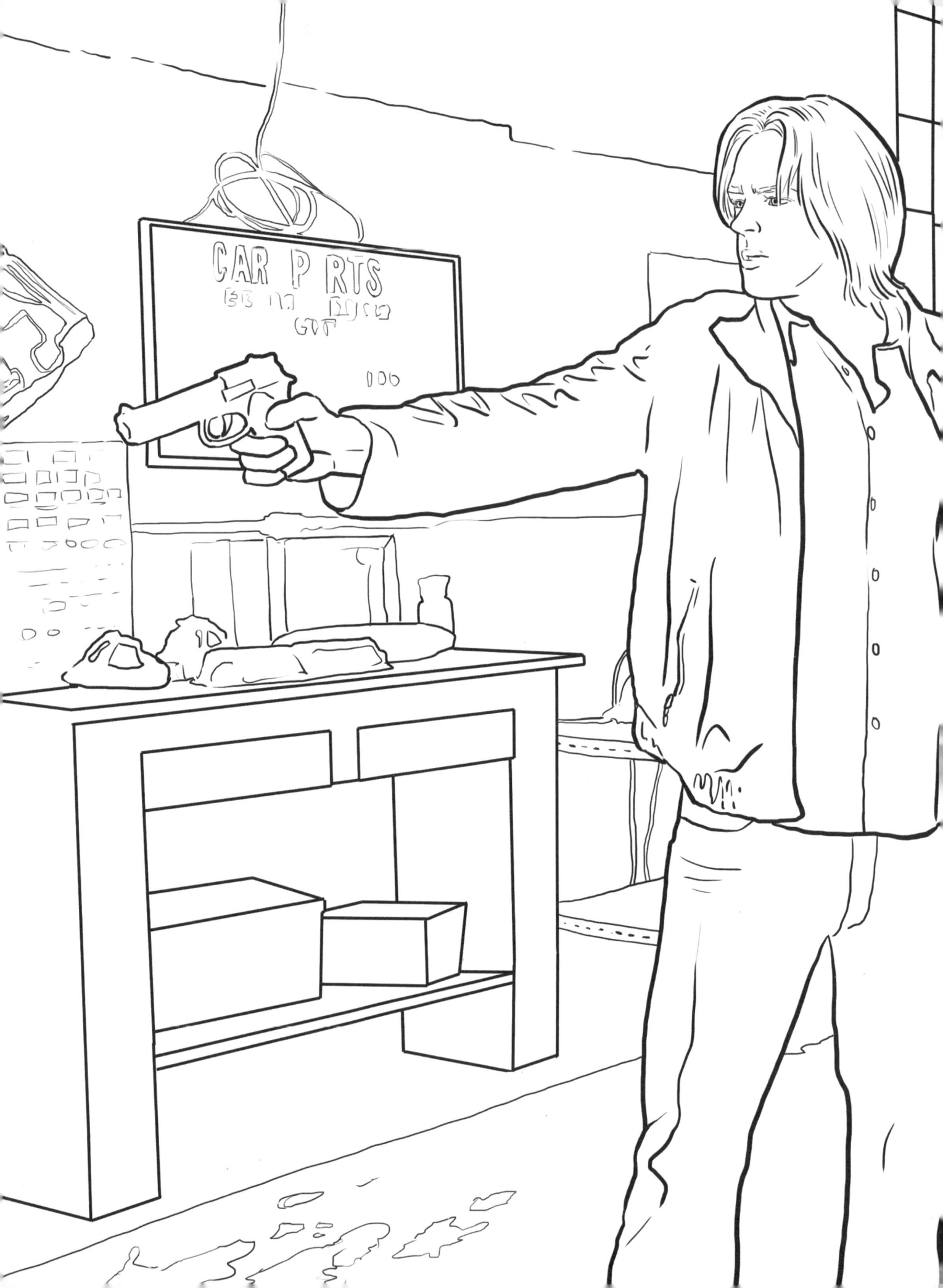
CAR P RTS

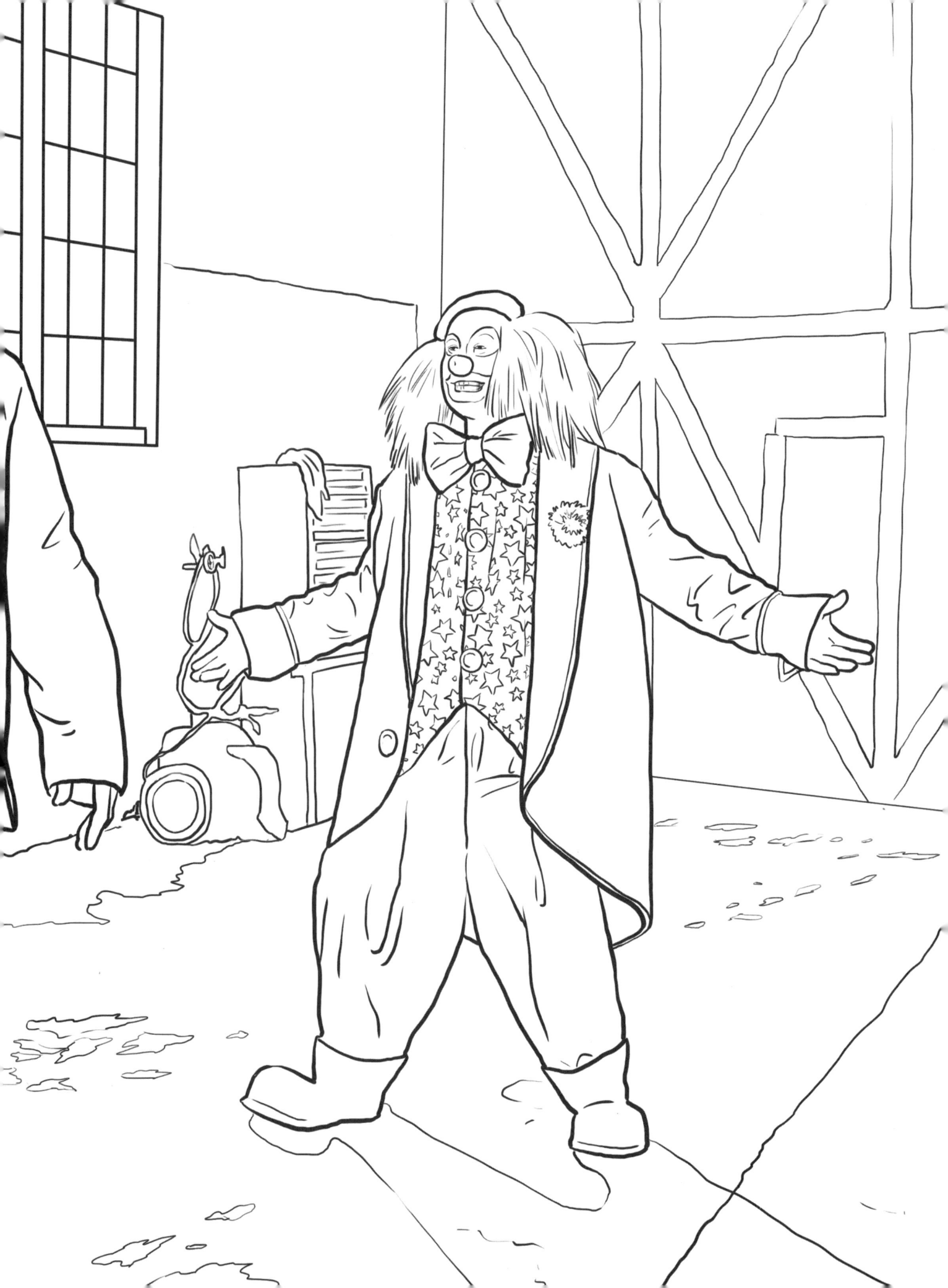

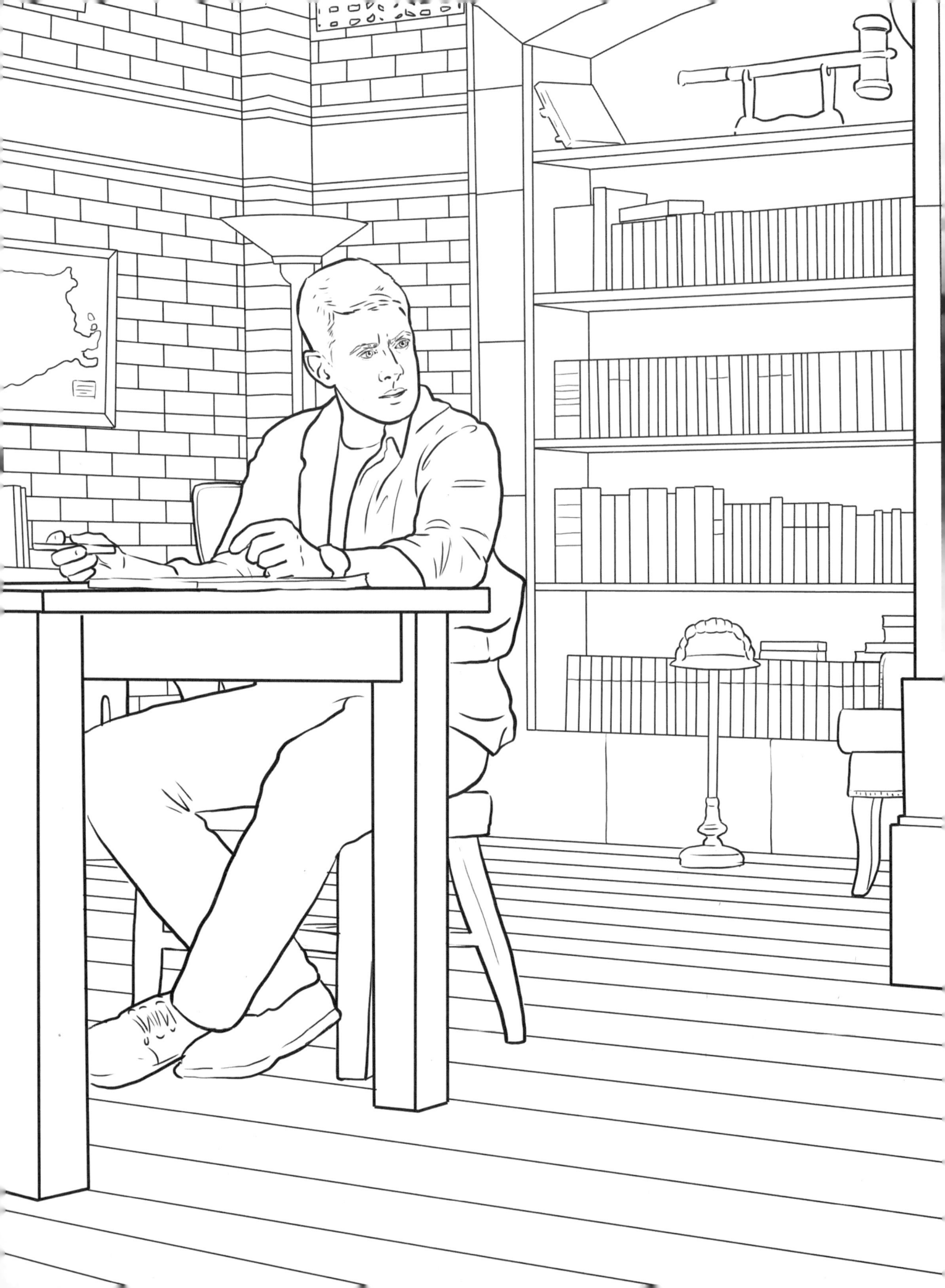

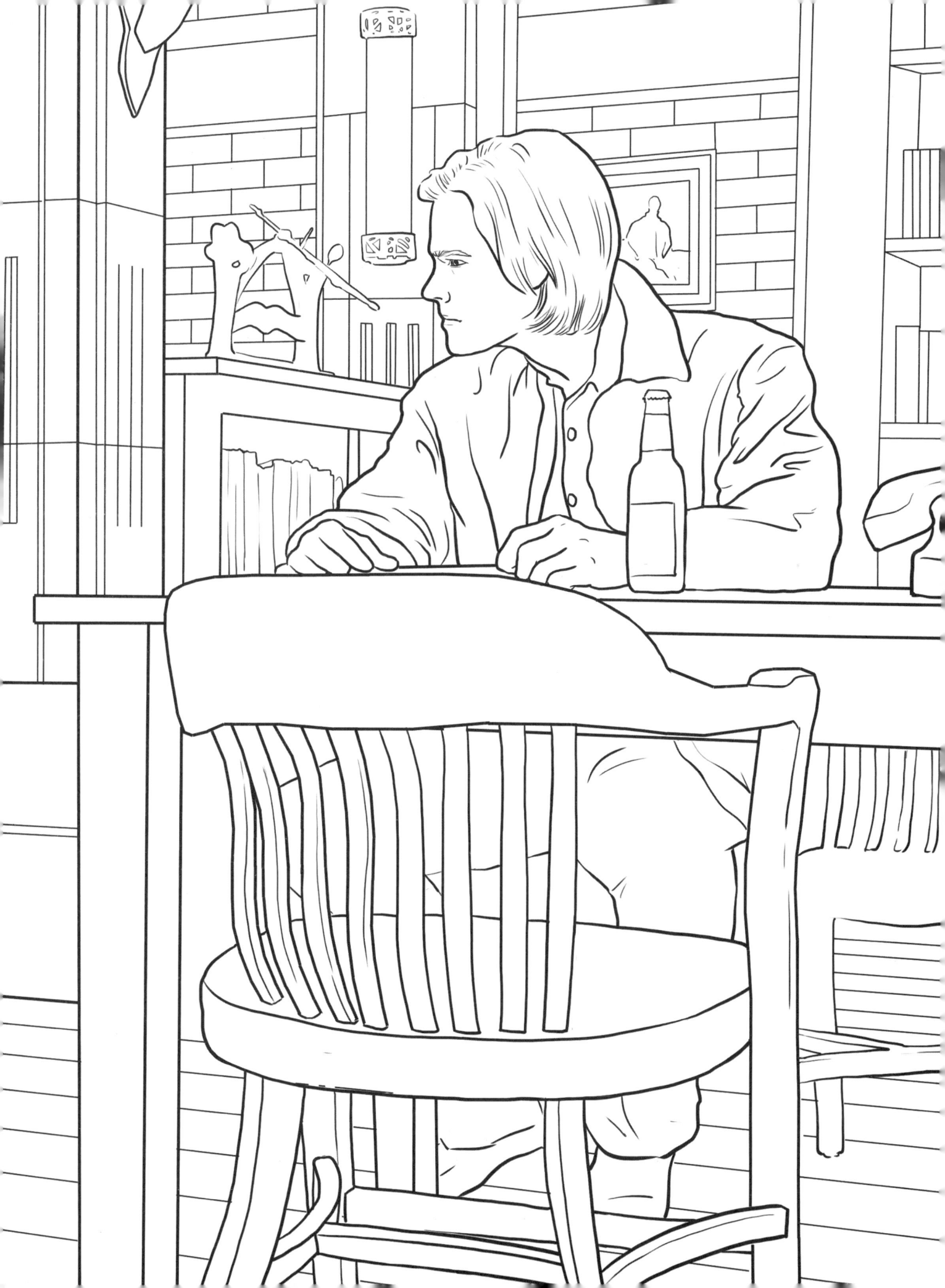

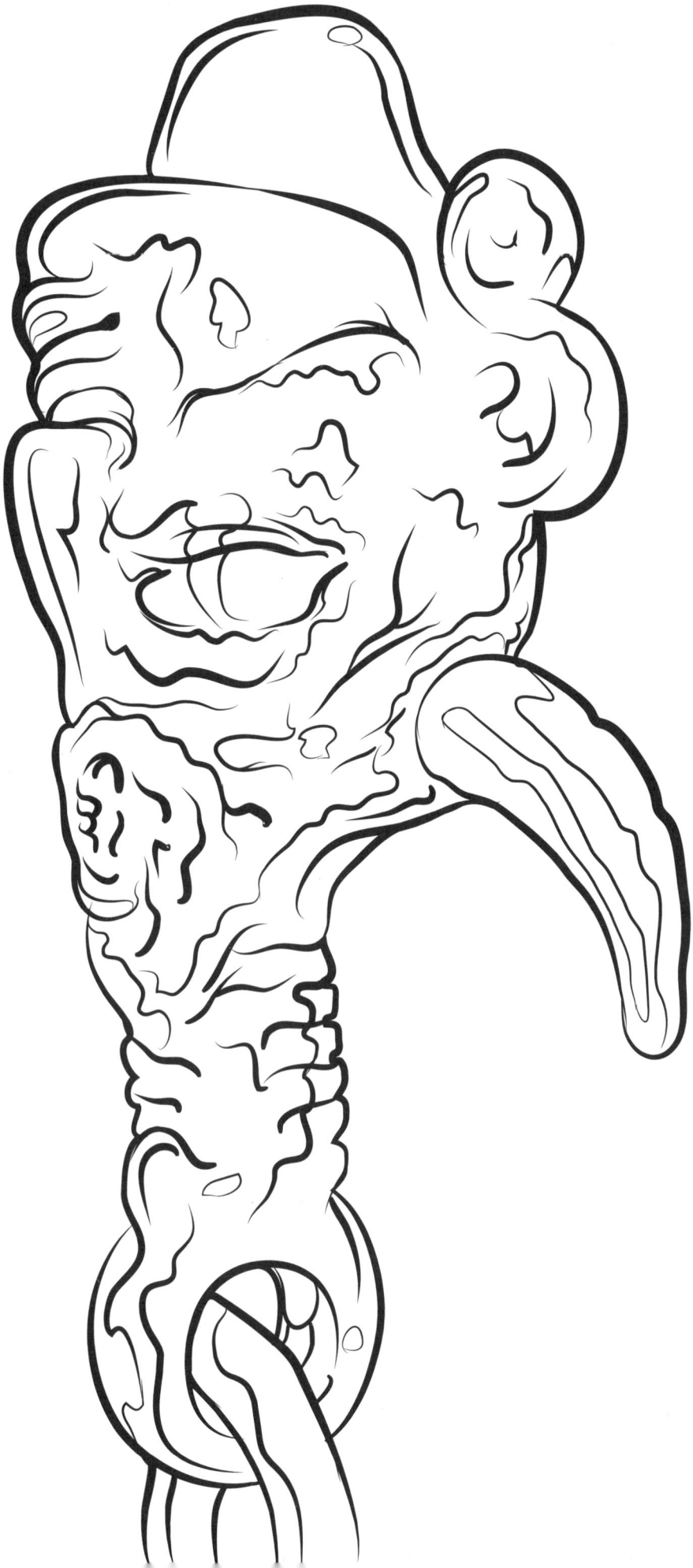

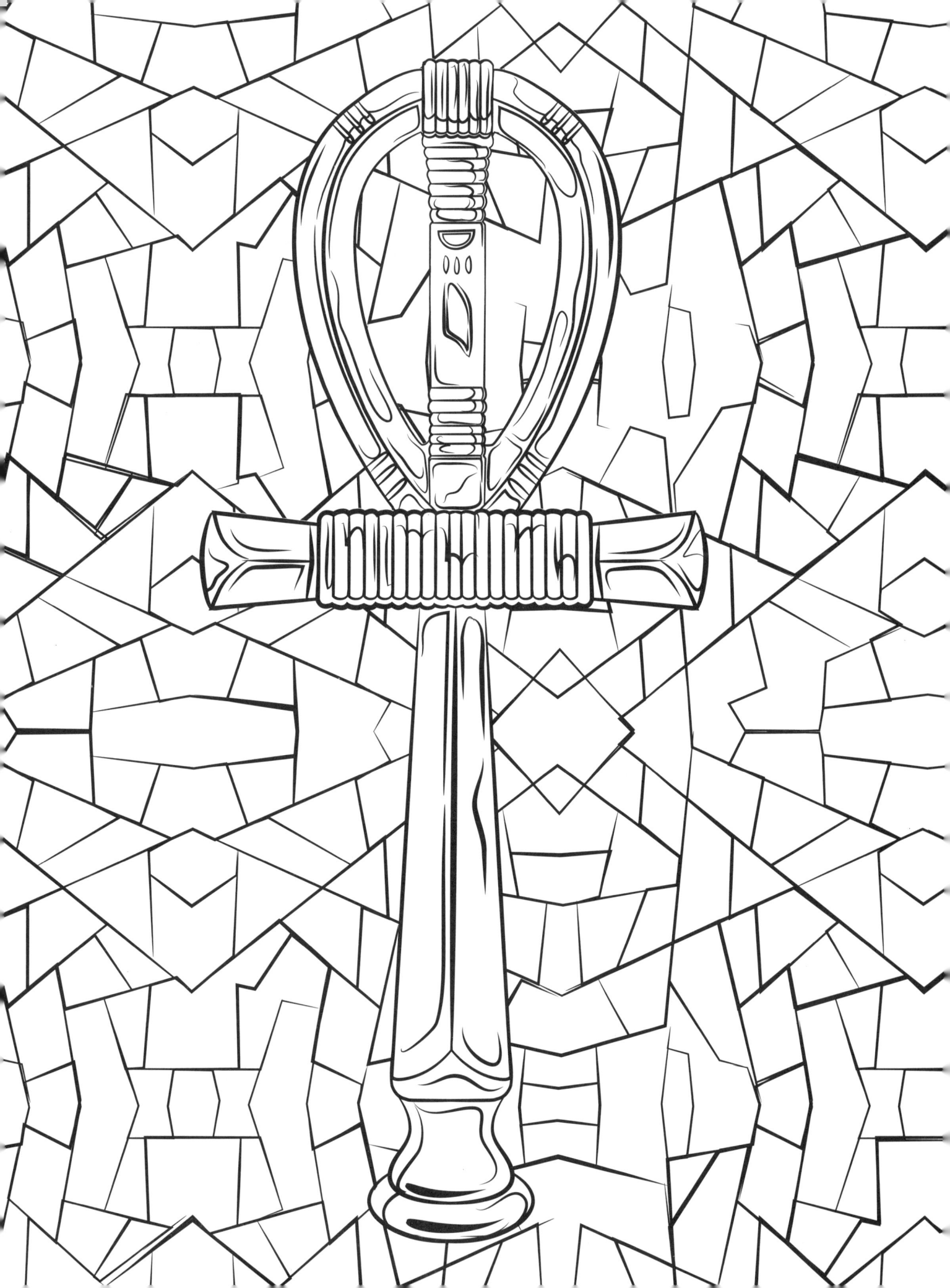

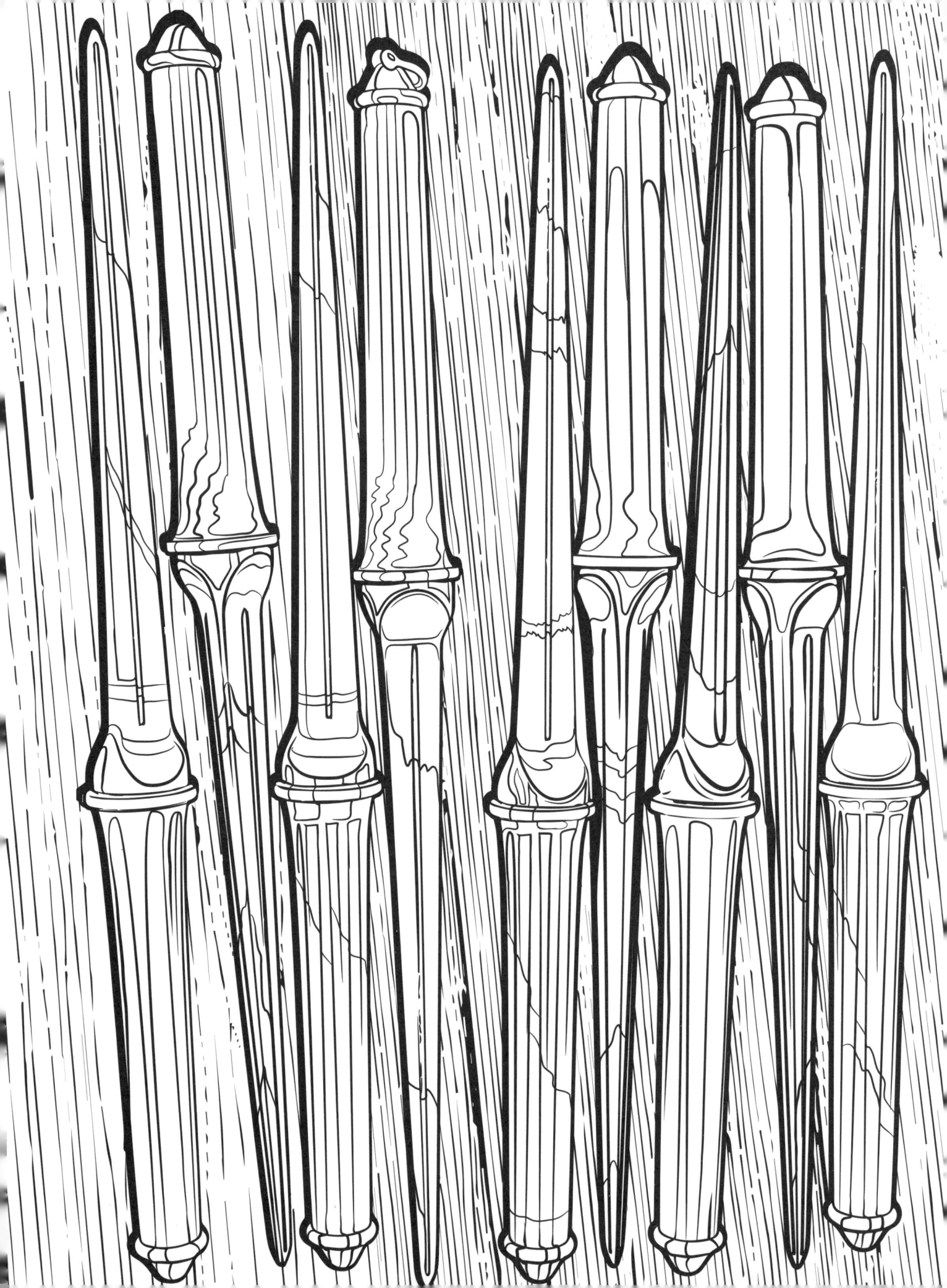

DRAW YOUR WORST FEAR

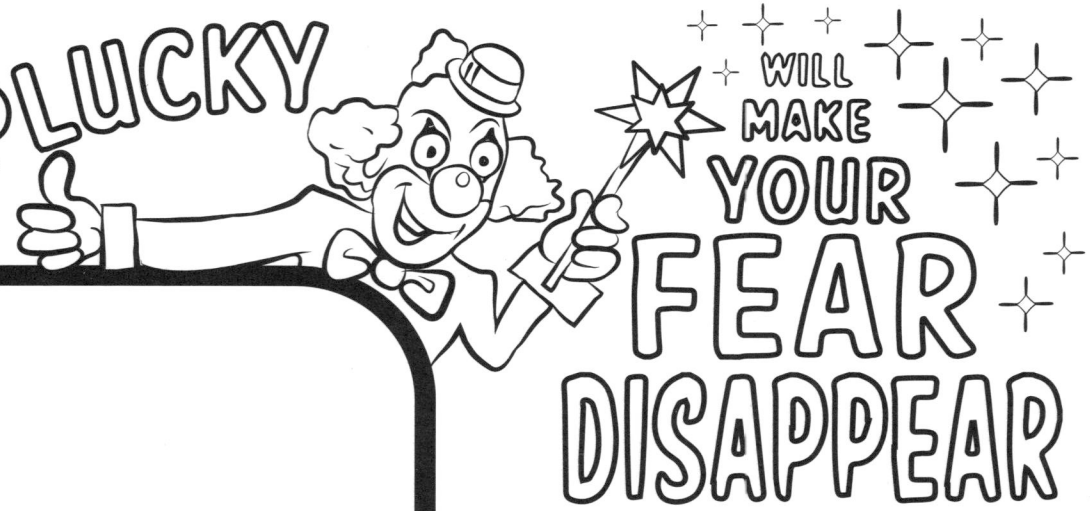

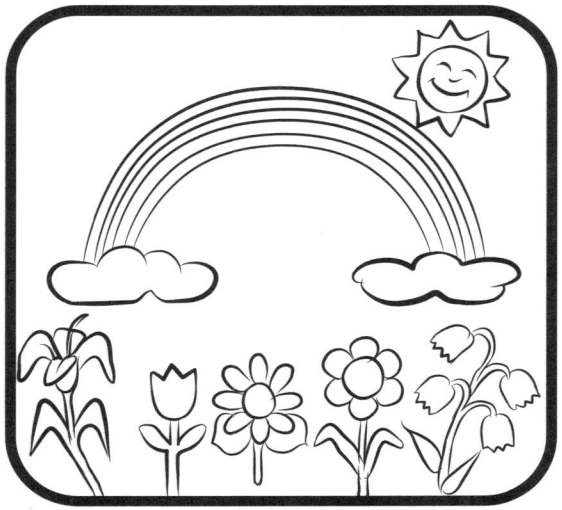

PLUCKY PENNYWHISTLE'S MAGICAL MENAGERIE!

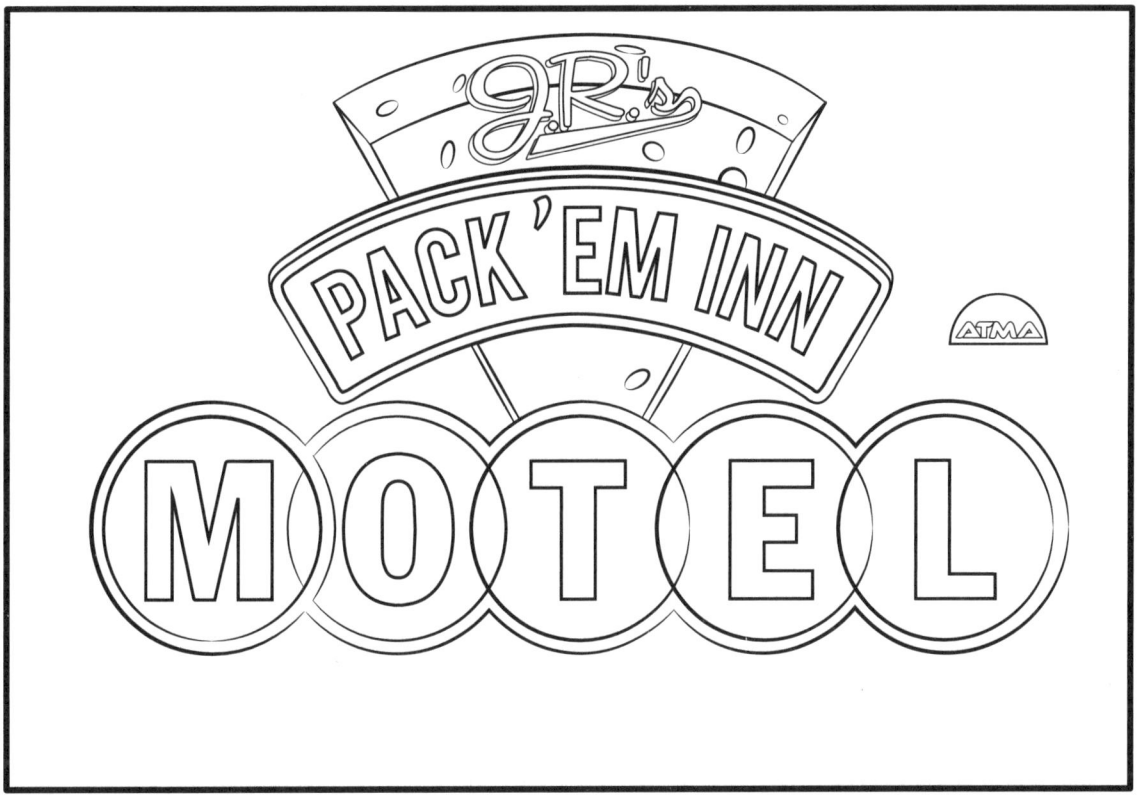
J.R.'s
PACK 'EM INN
MOTEL
ATMA

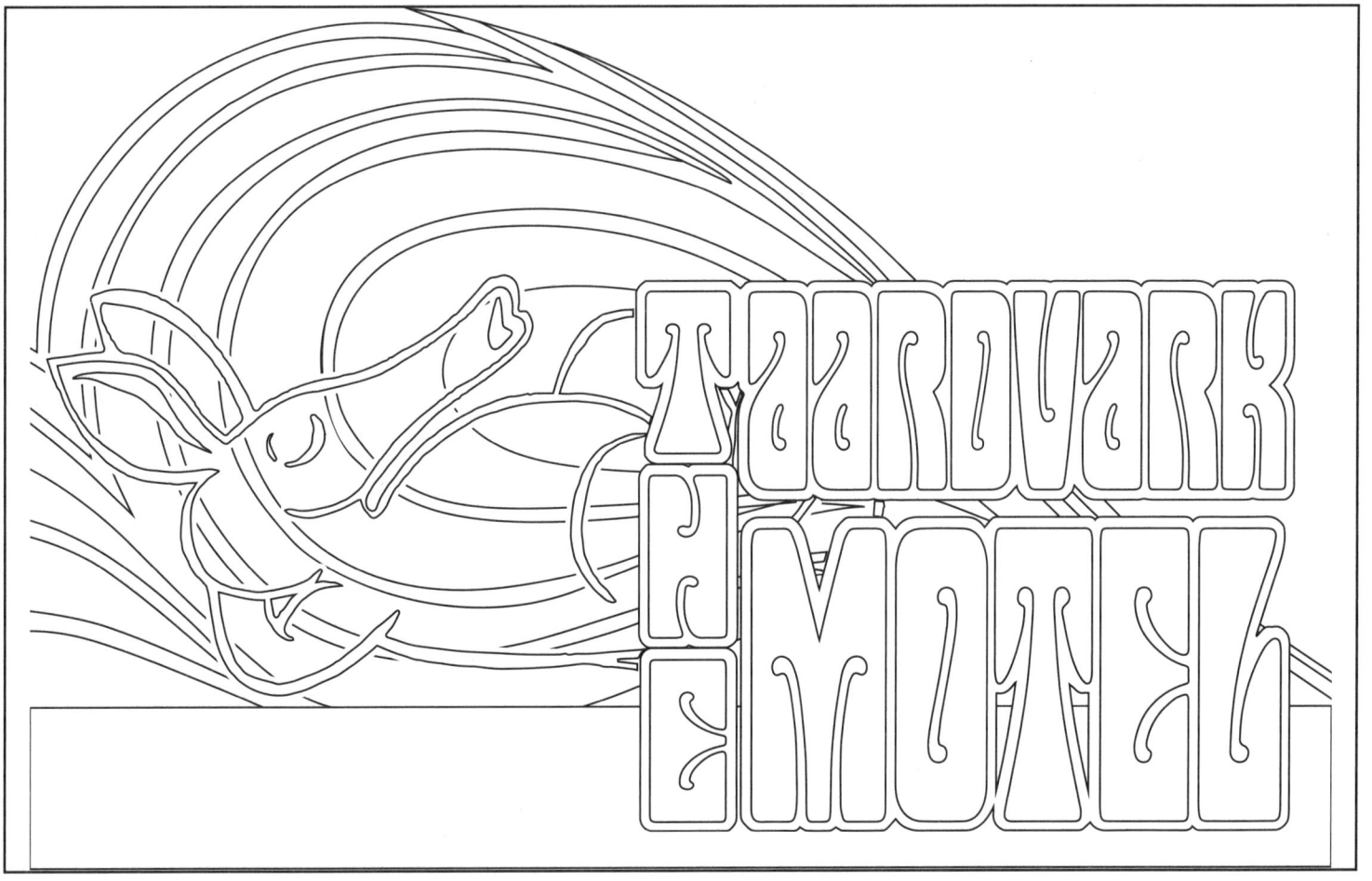
TASMAN
MOTEL

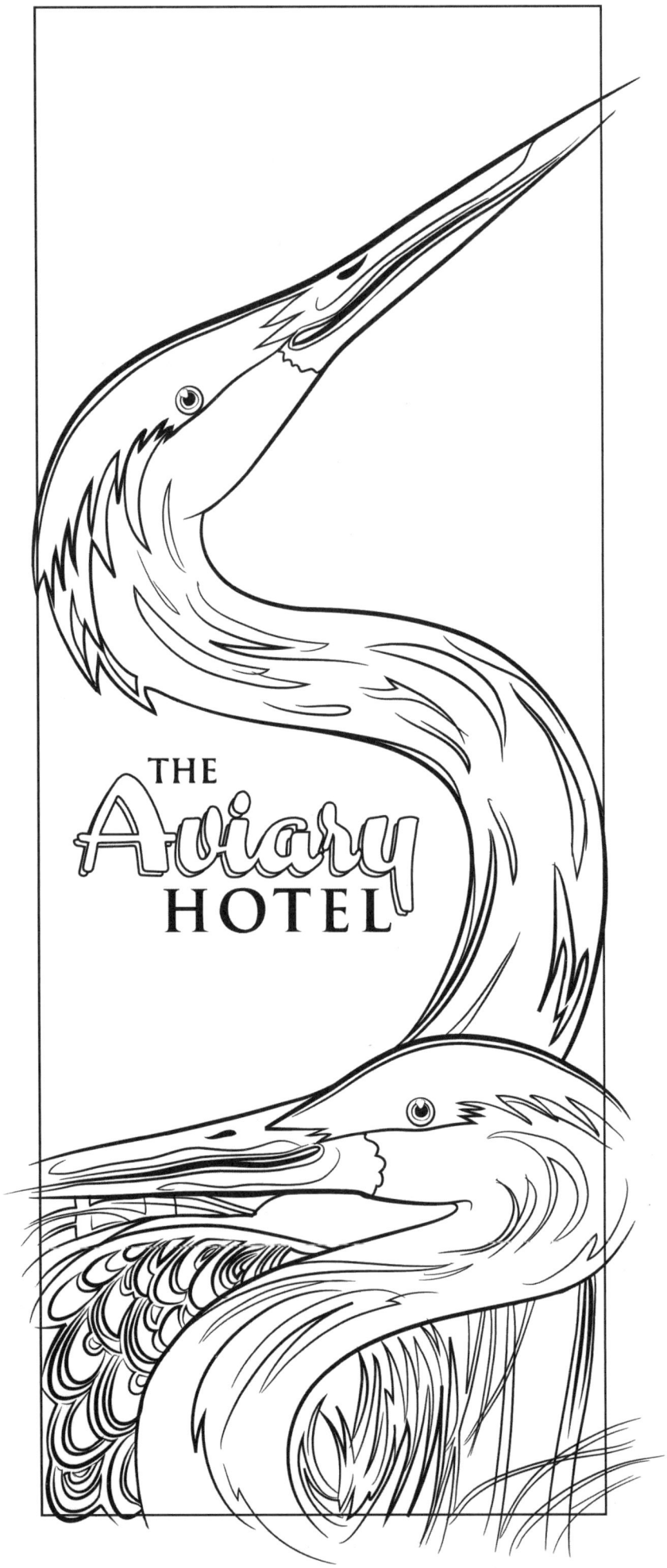
THE
Aviary
HOTEL

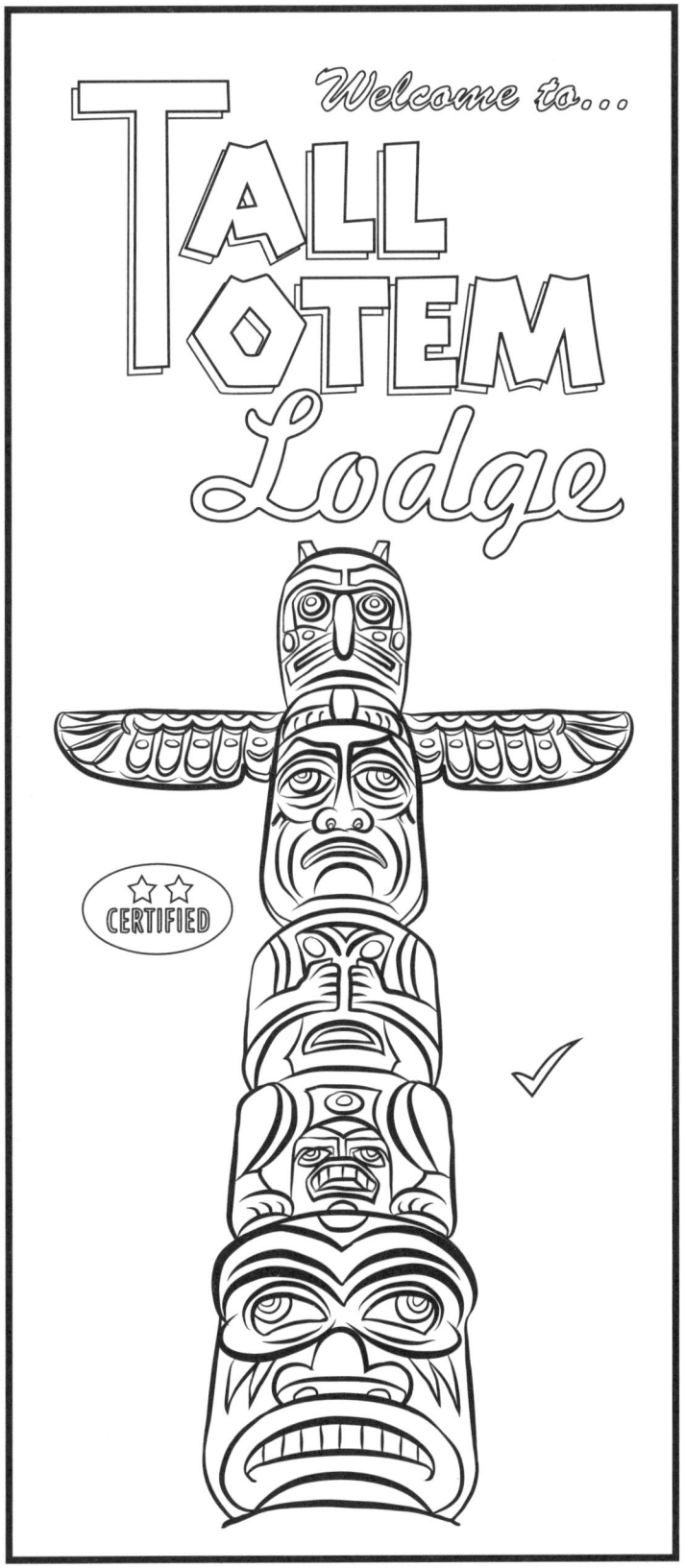
Welcome to...
TALL TOTEM Lodge
CERTIFIED

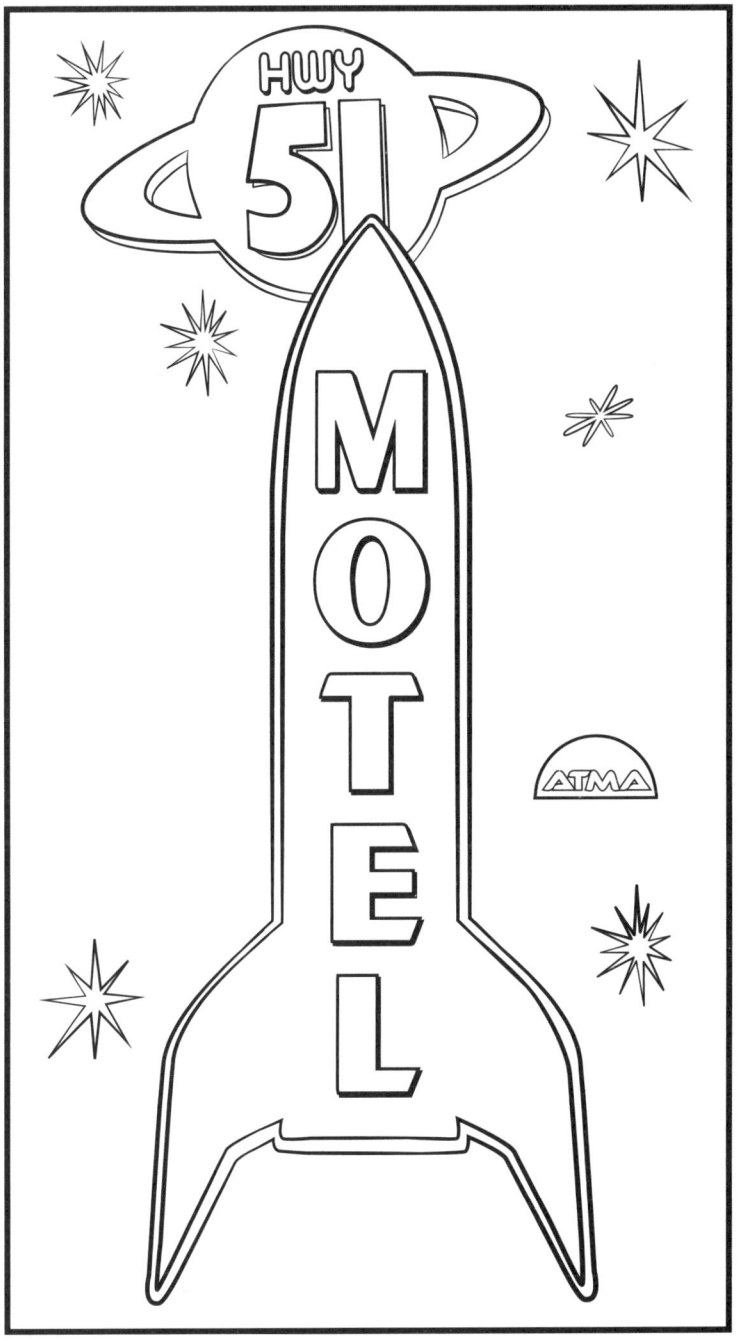
HWY
51
MOTEL
ATMA

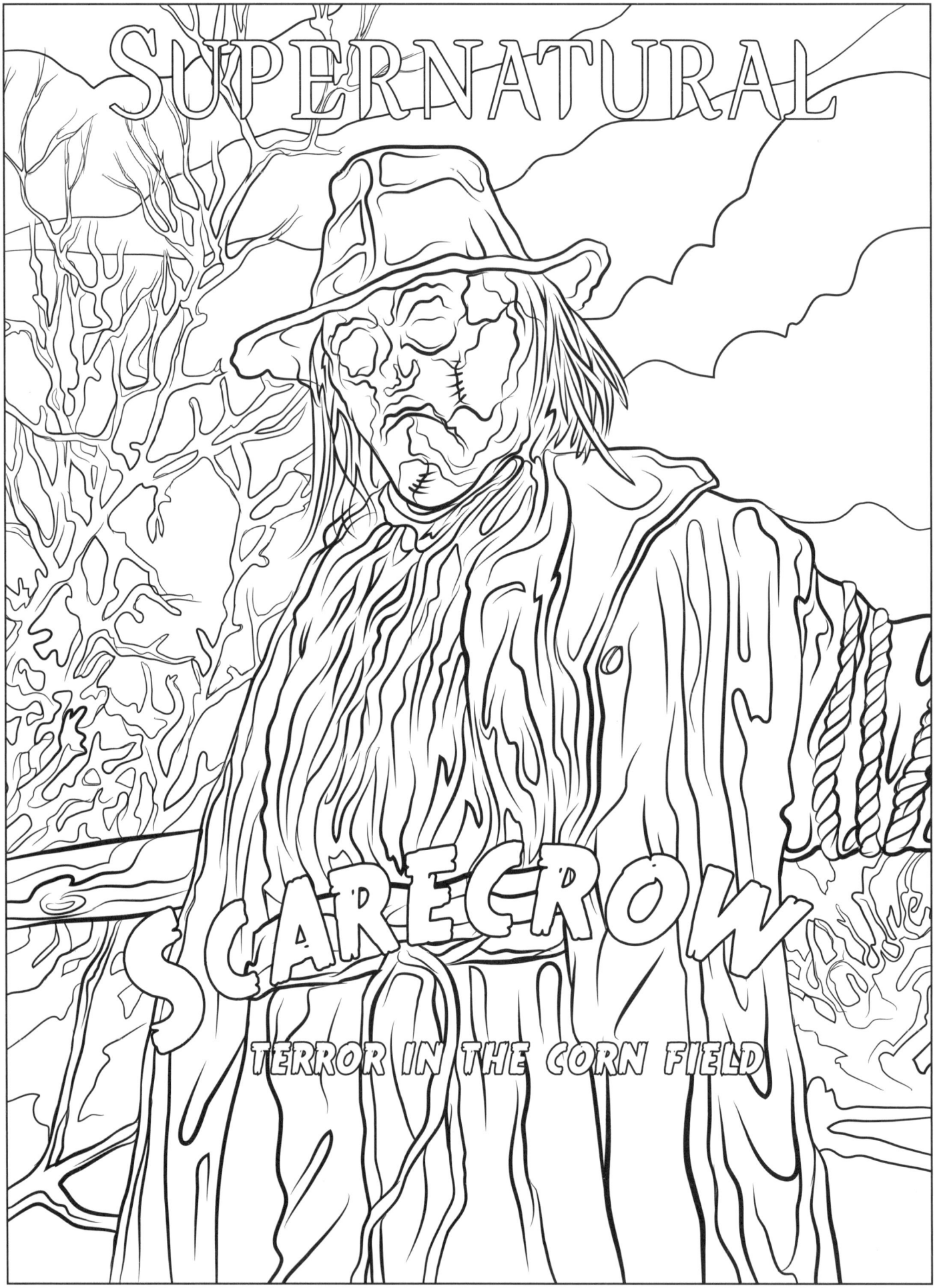
SUPERNATURAL
SCARECROW
TERROR IN THE CORN FIELD

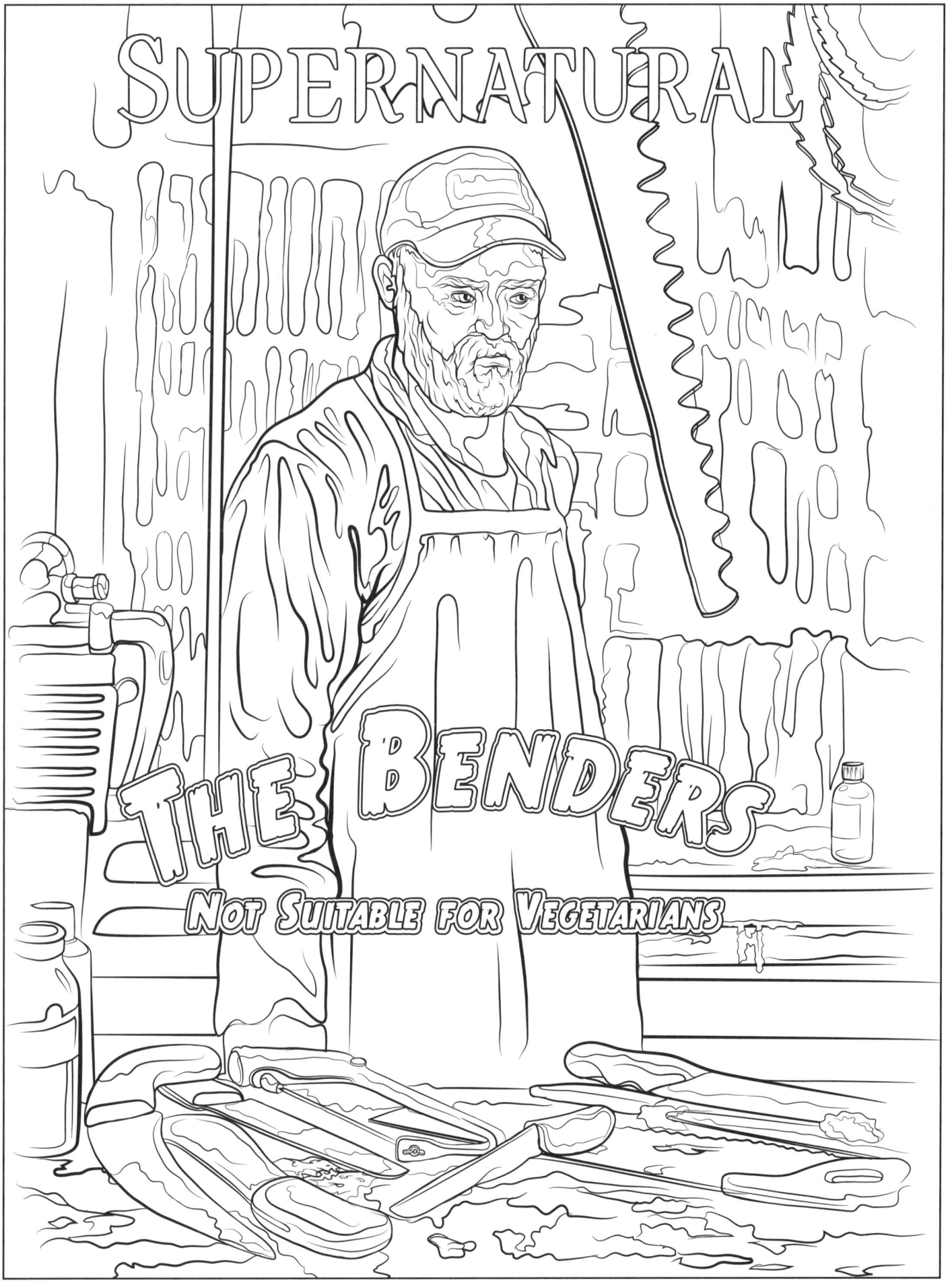
SUPERNATURAL
THE BENDERS
NOT SUITABLE FOR VEGETARIANS

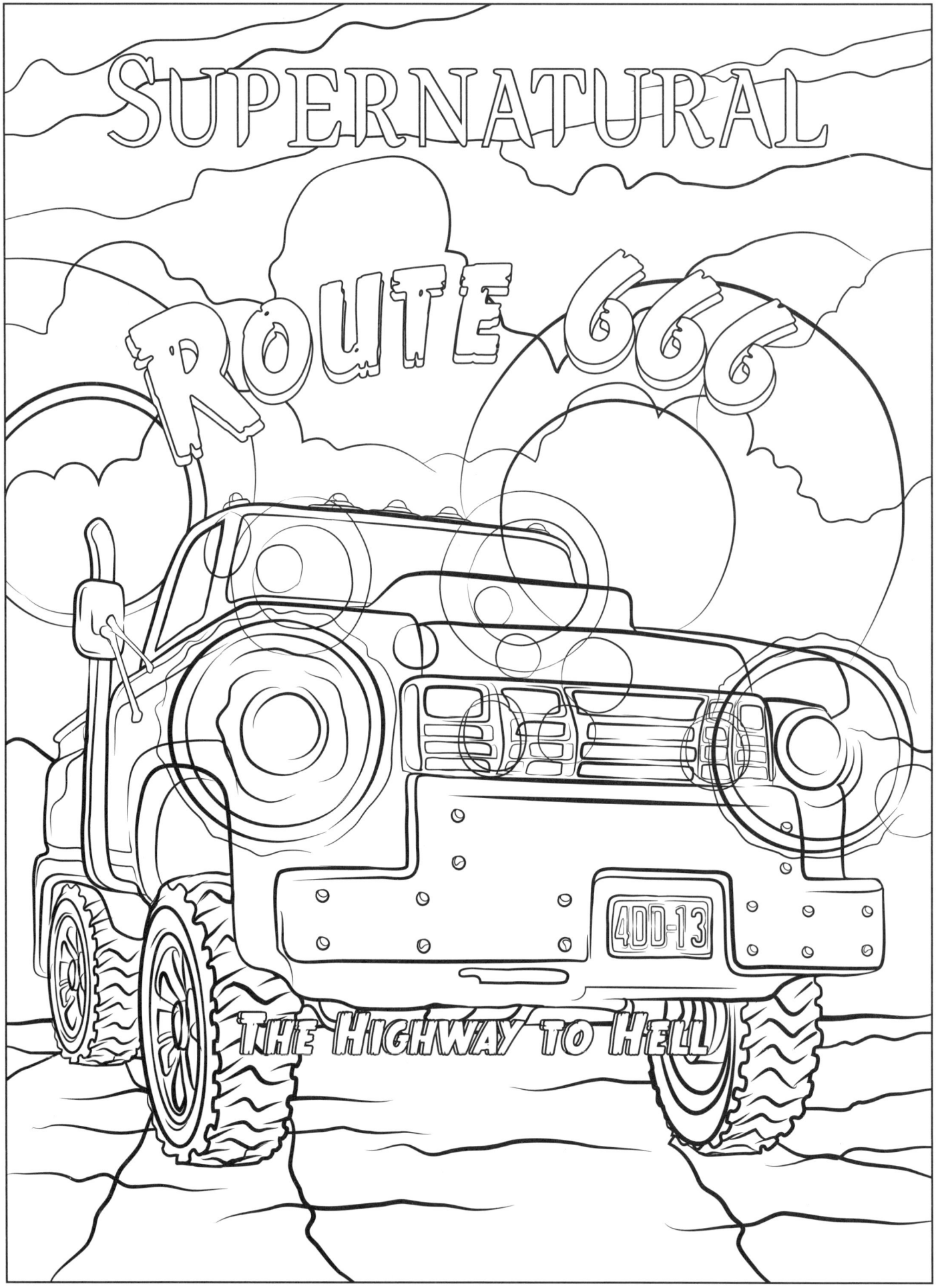
SUPERNATURAL
ROUTE 666
4DD-13
THE HIGHWAY TO HELL

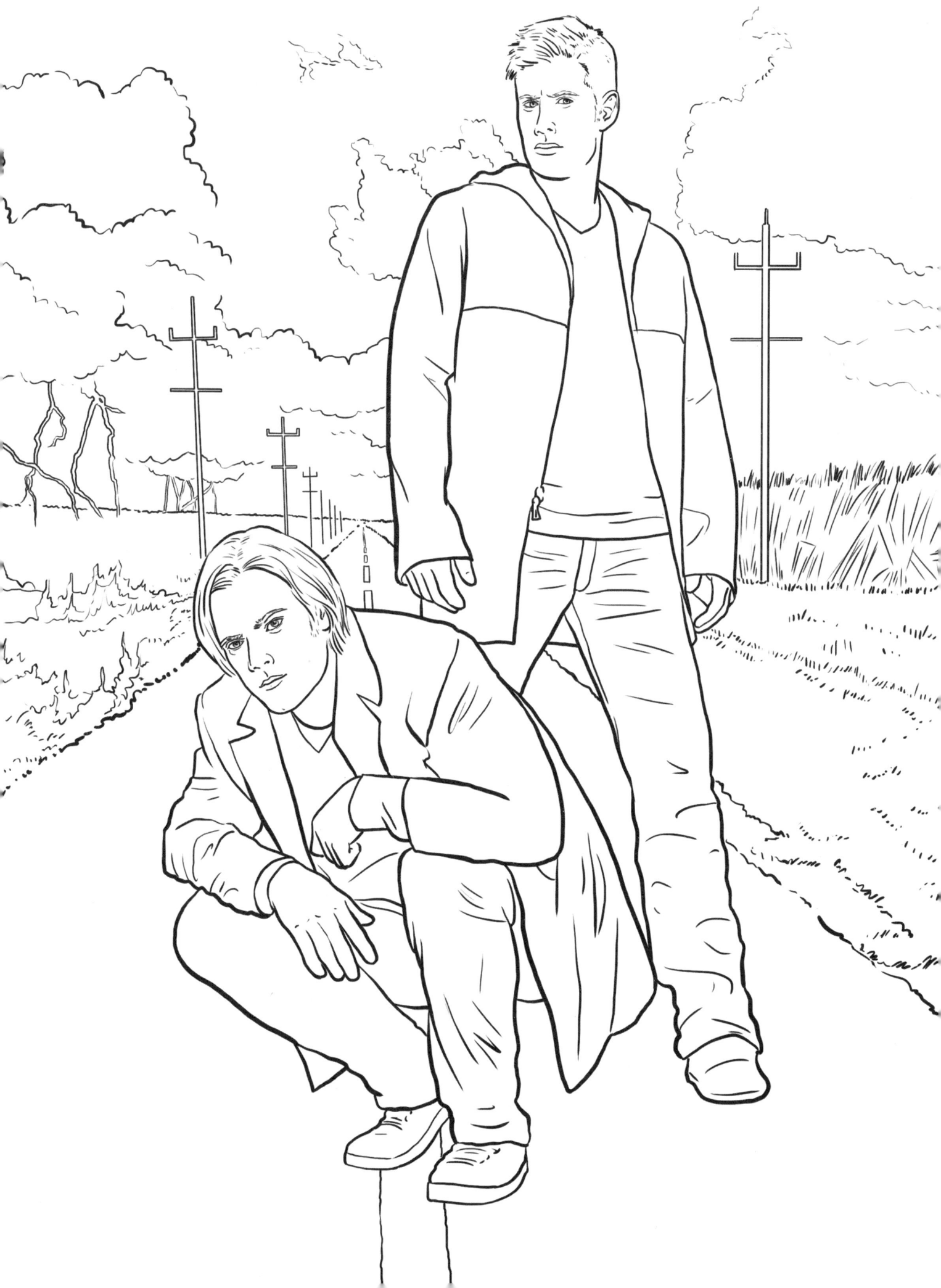

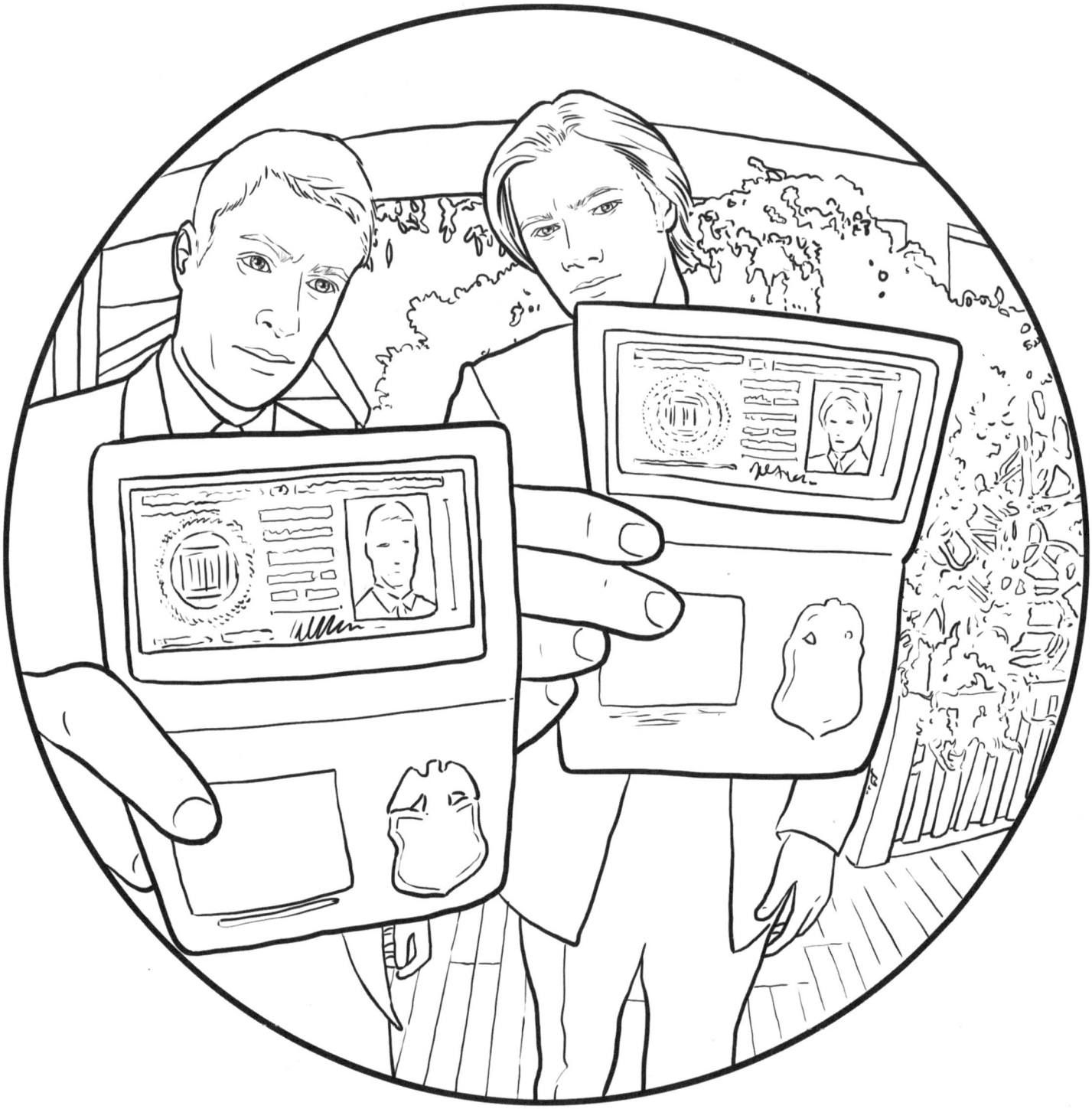

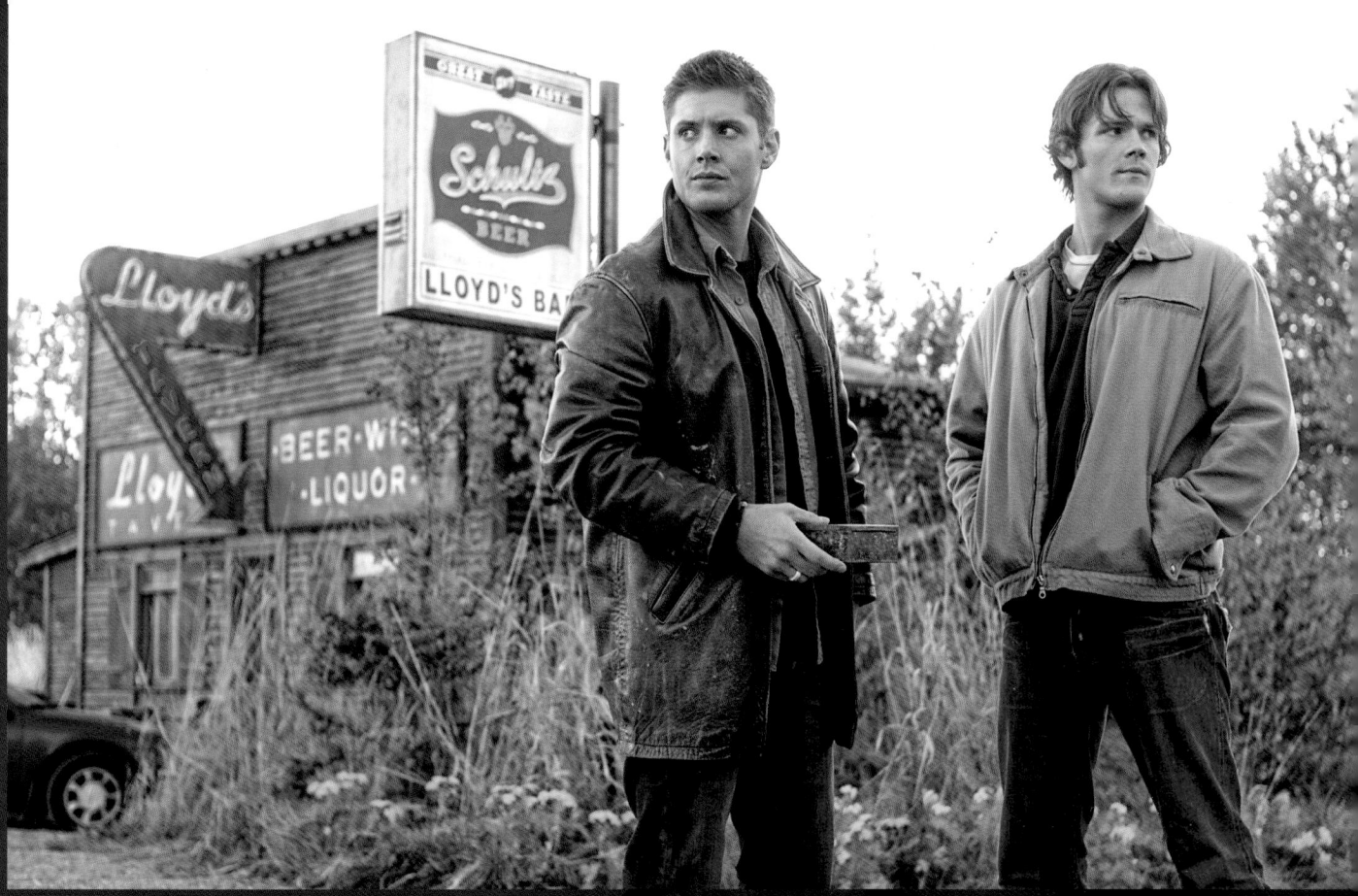
GREAT TASTE
Schaefer
BEER
LLOYD'S BA
Lloyd's
BEER·WI
·LIQUOR·

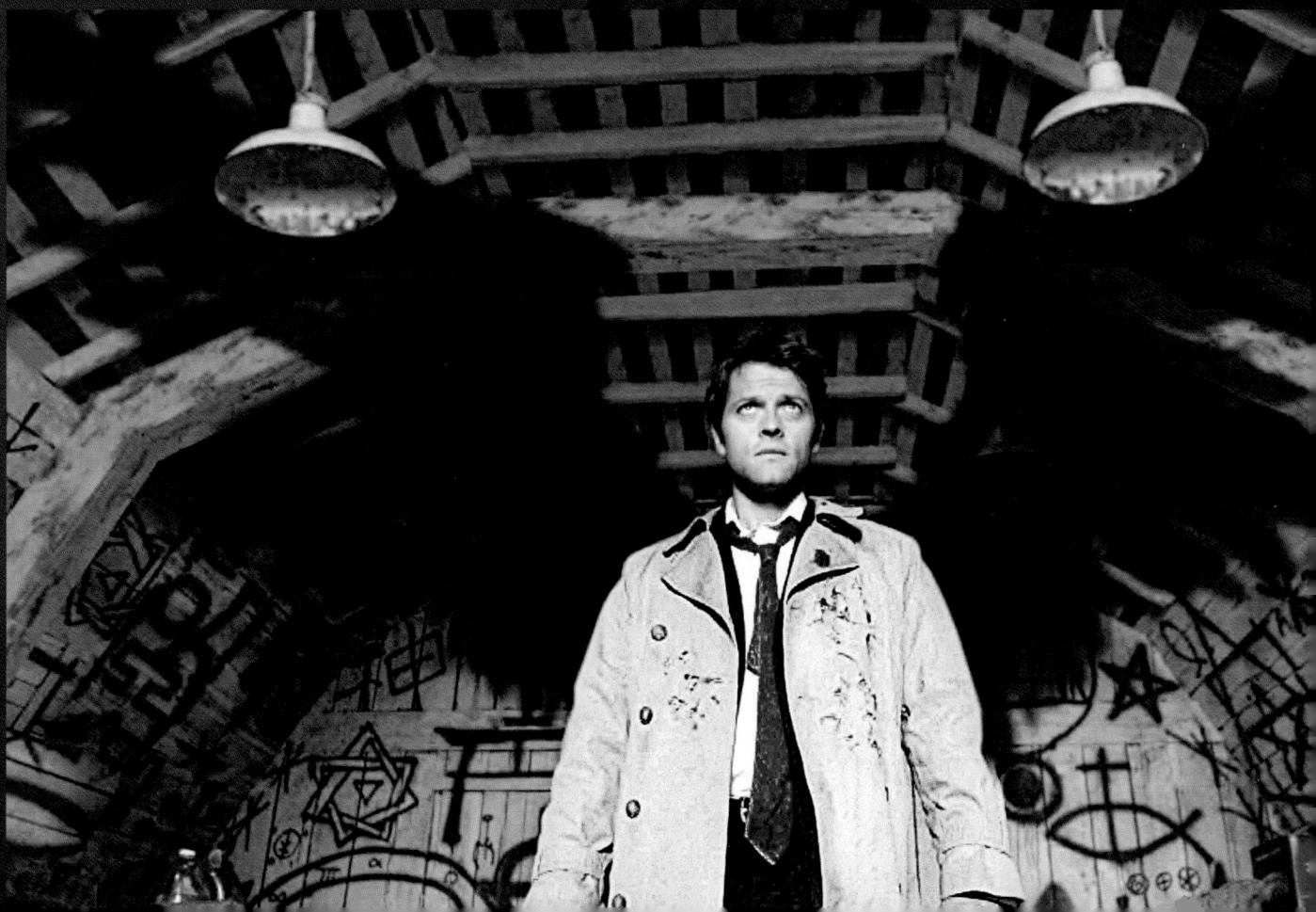

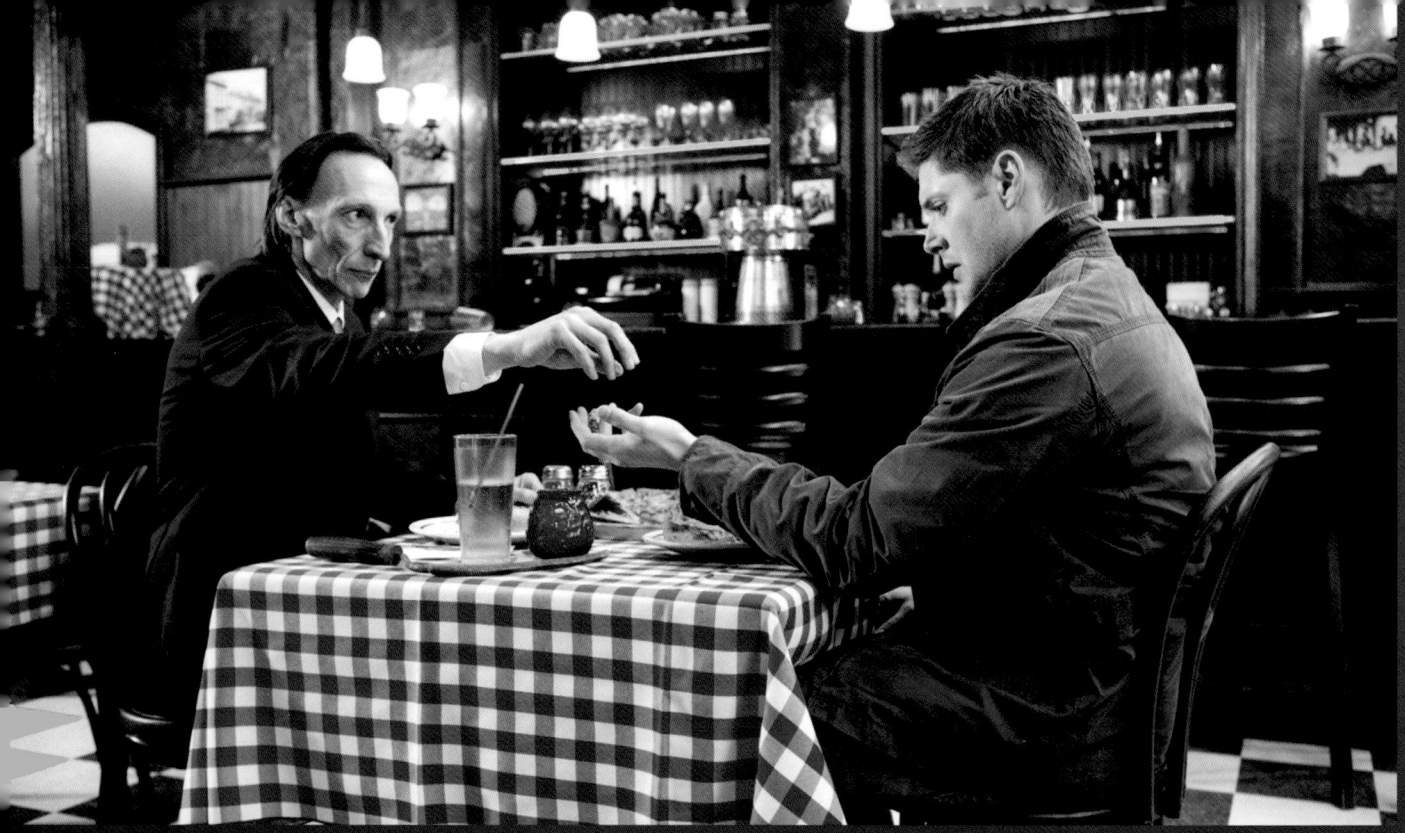

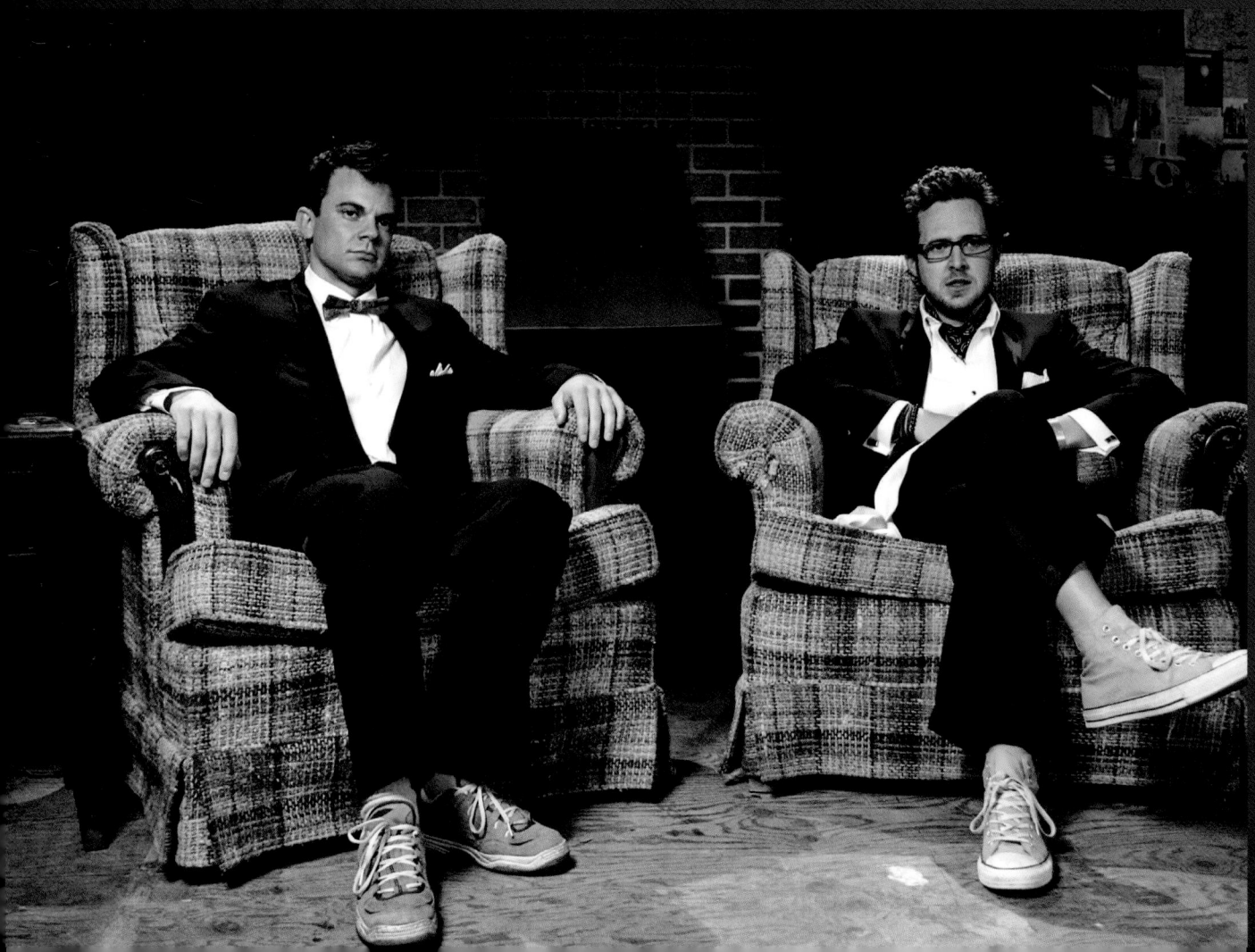

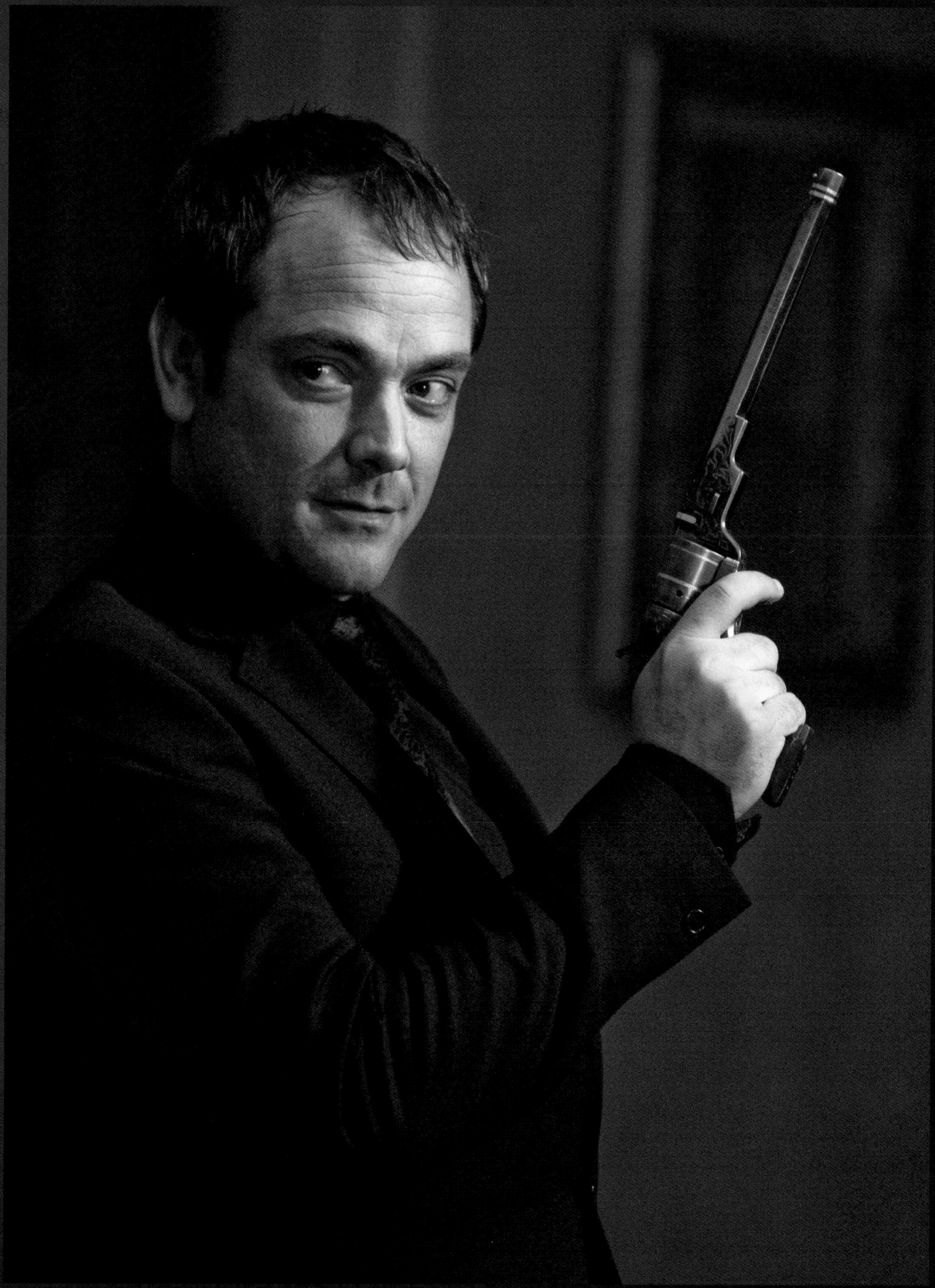

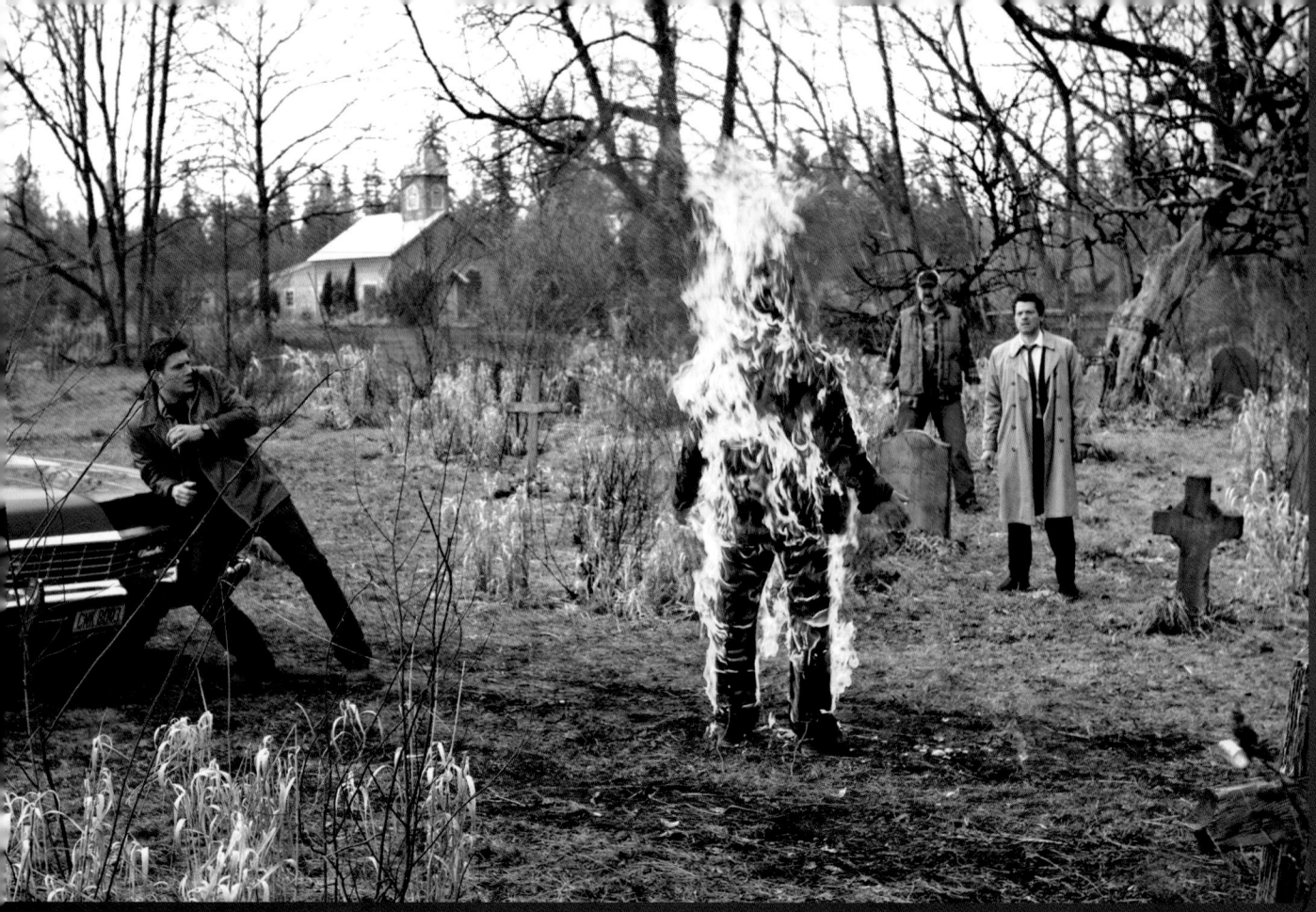

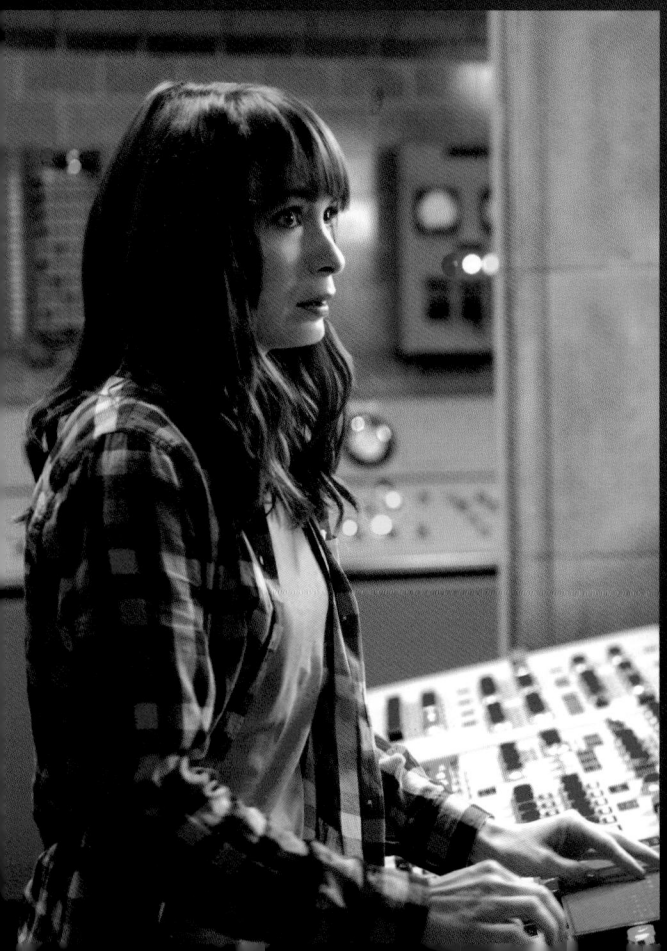

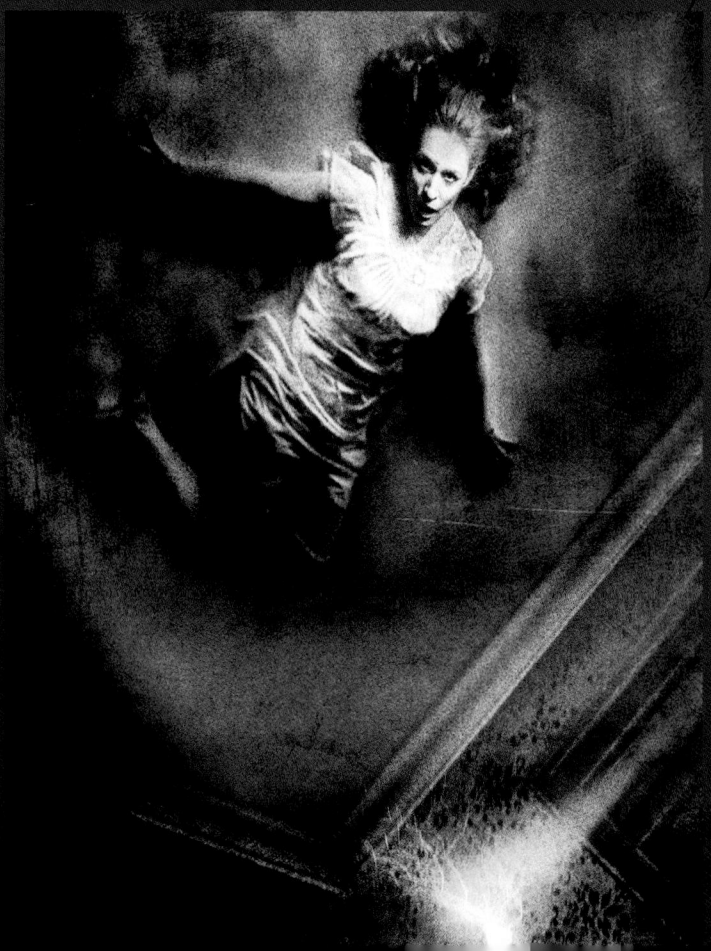

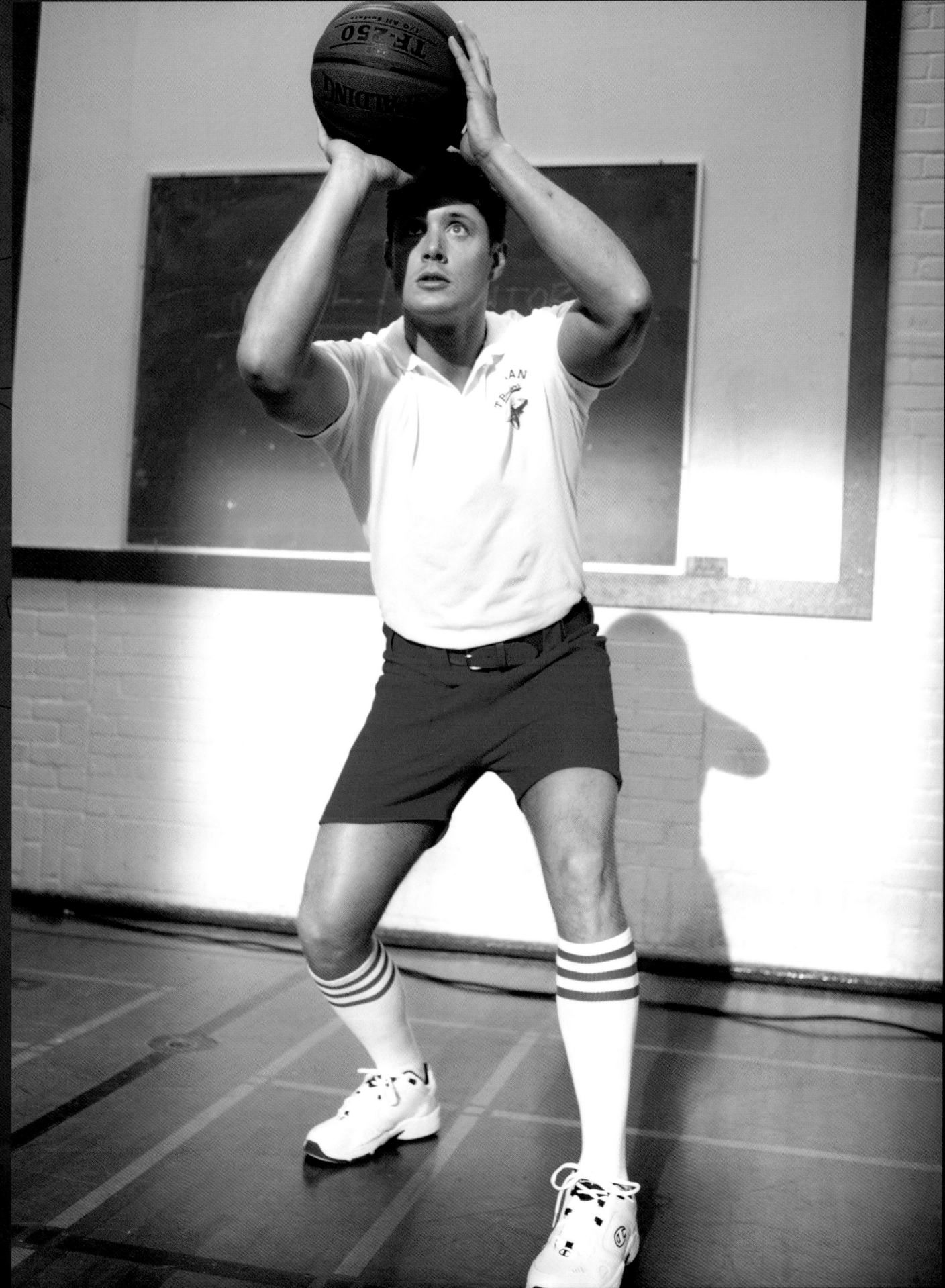

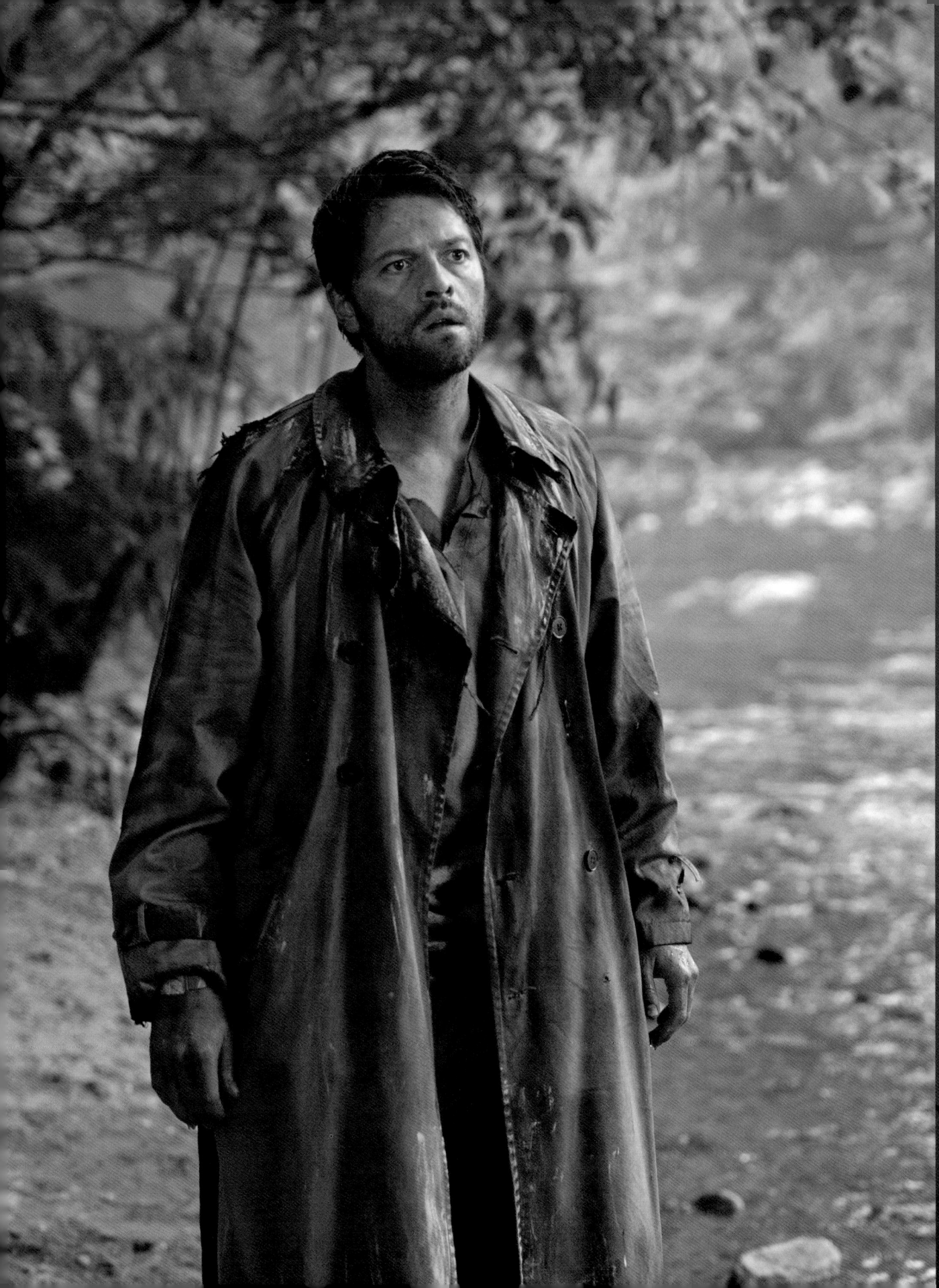

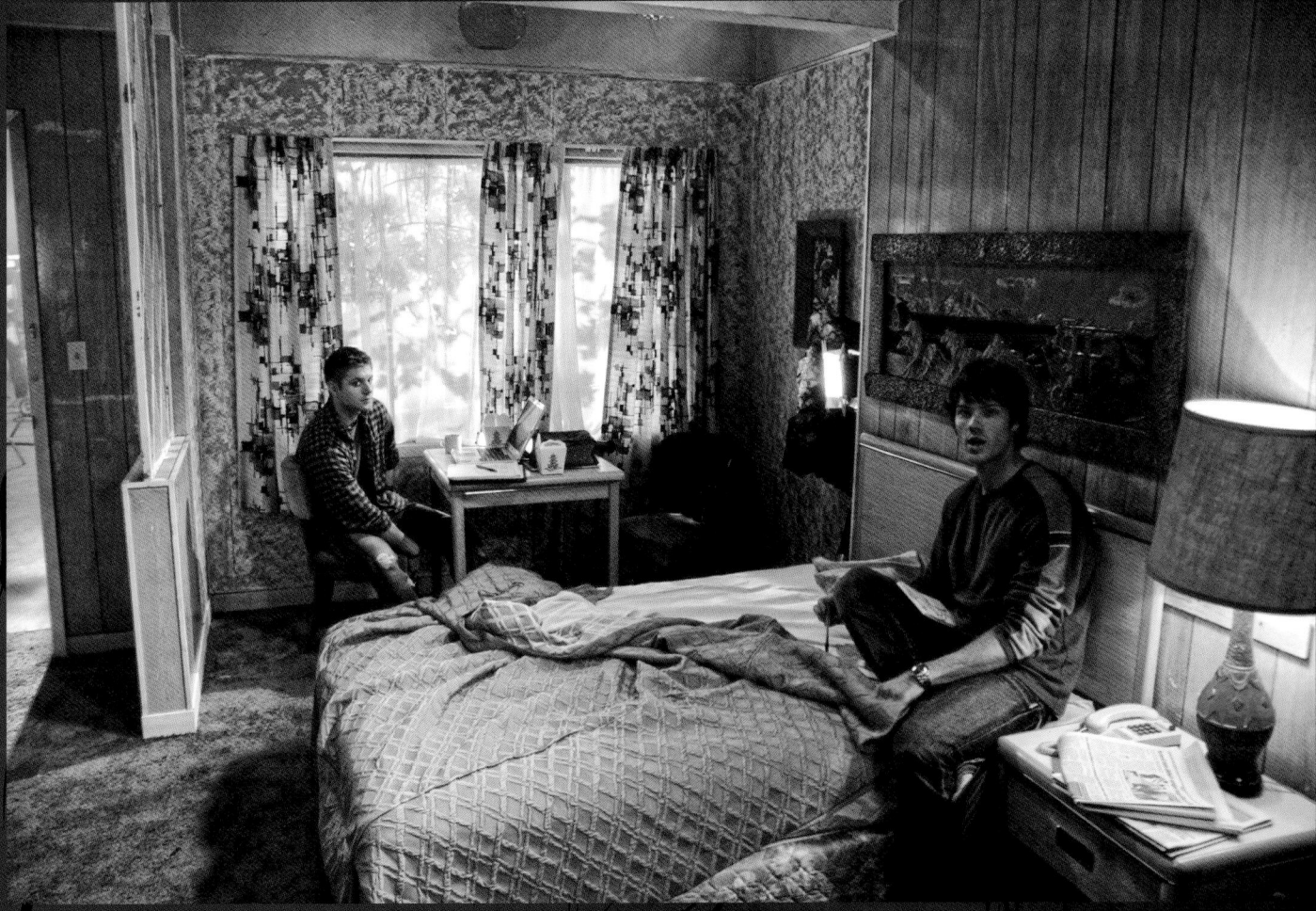

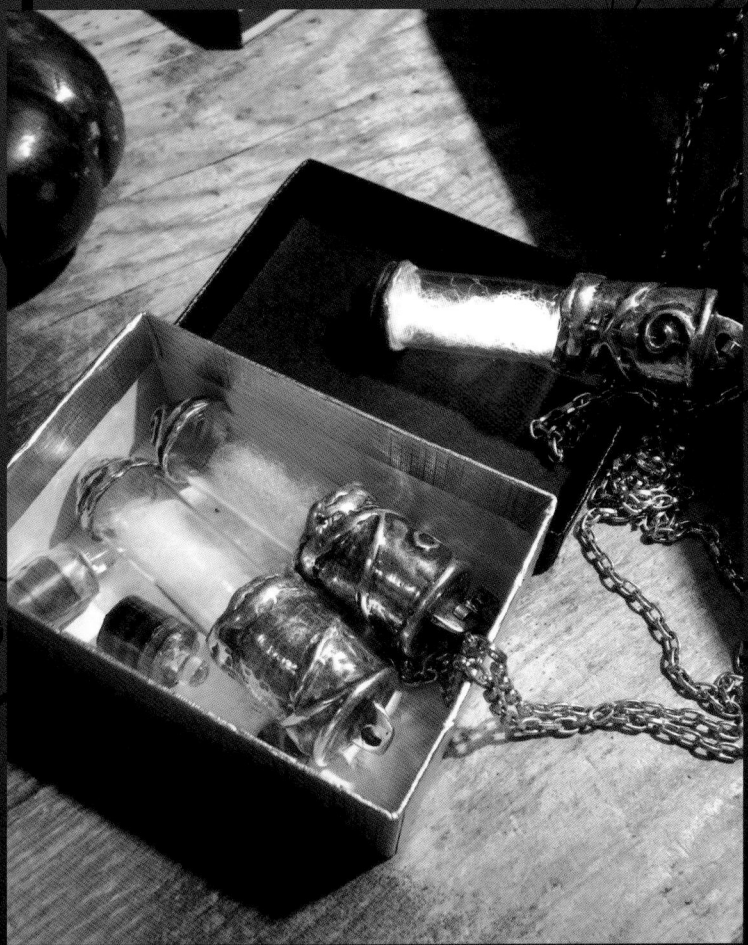

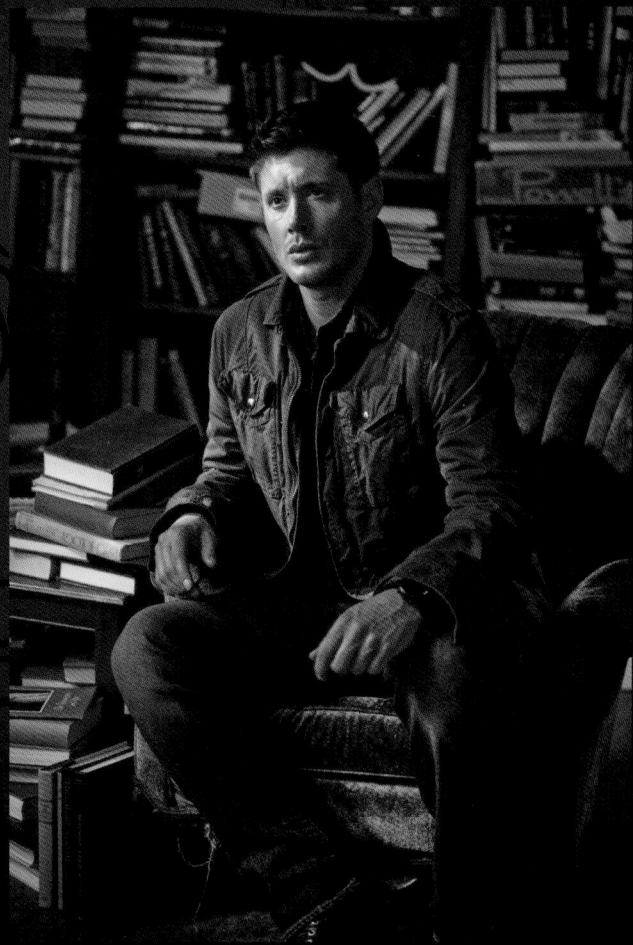

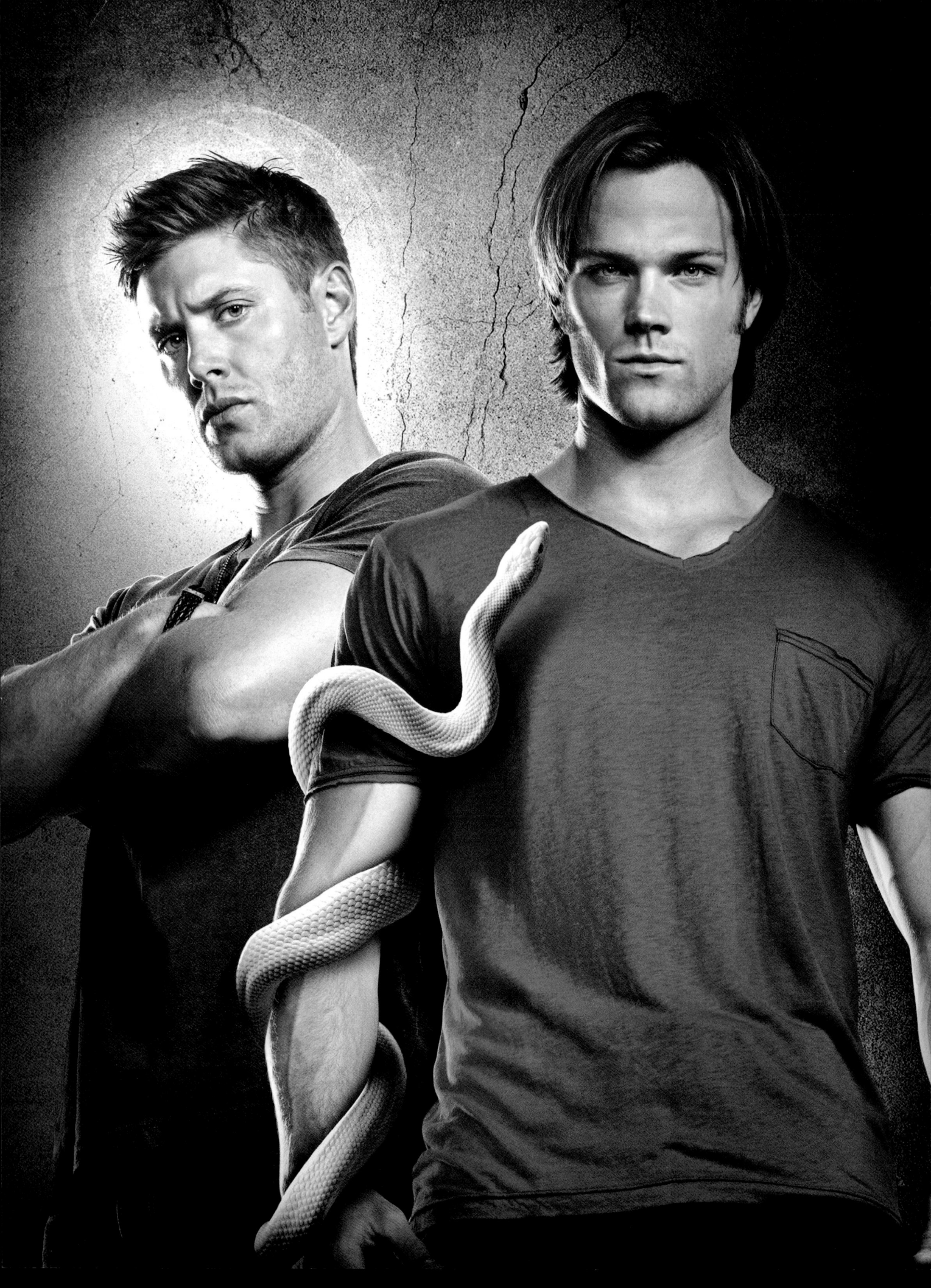

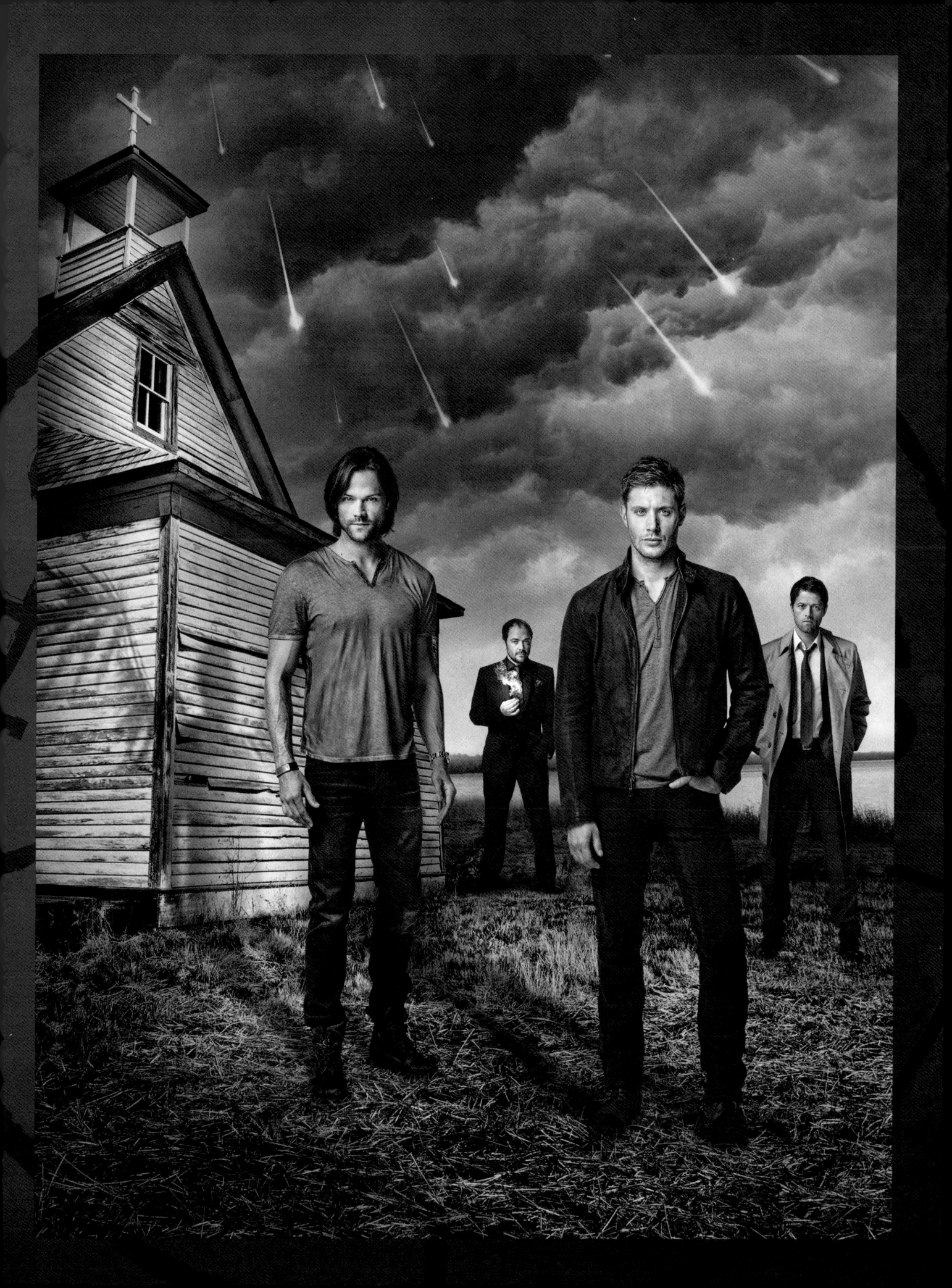

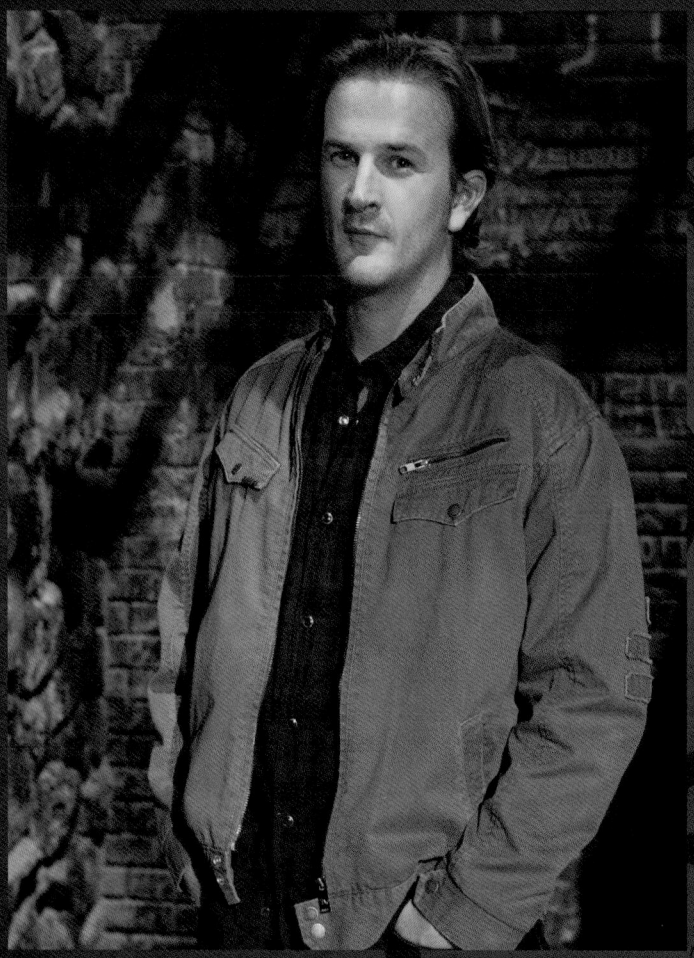

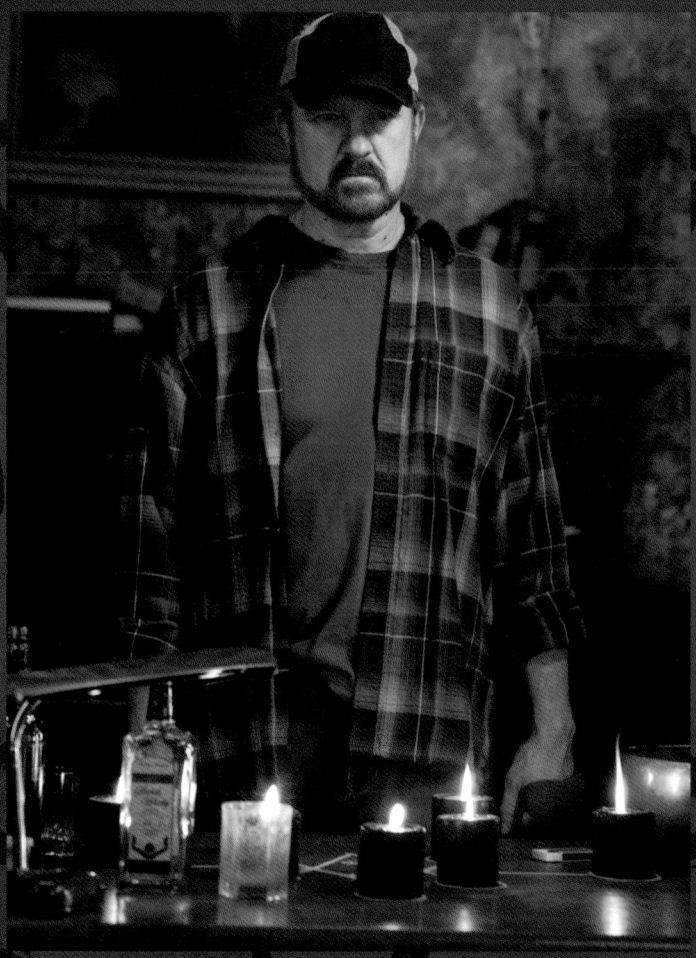

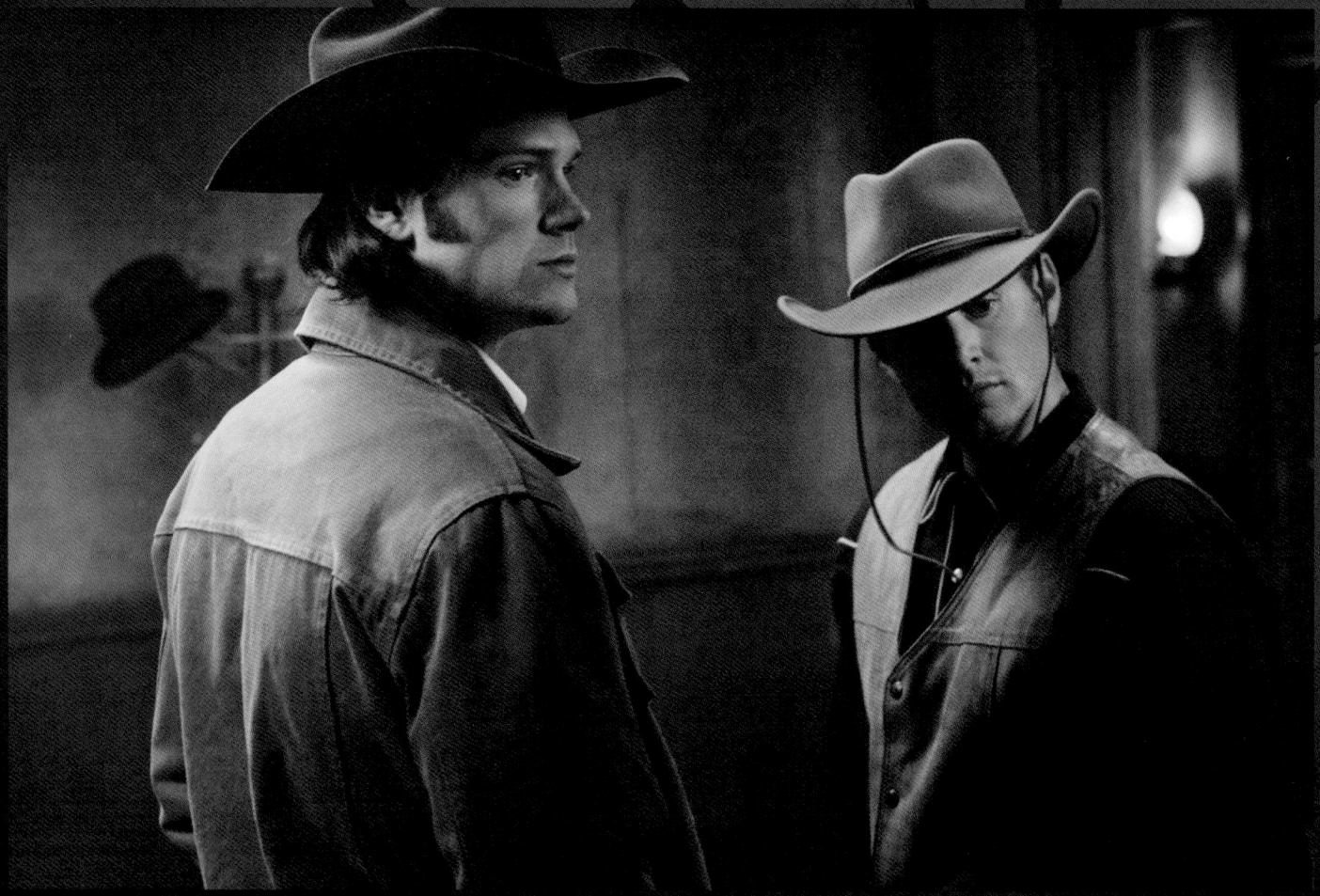

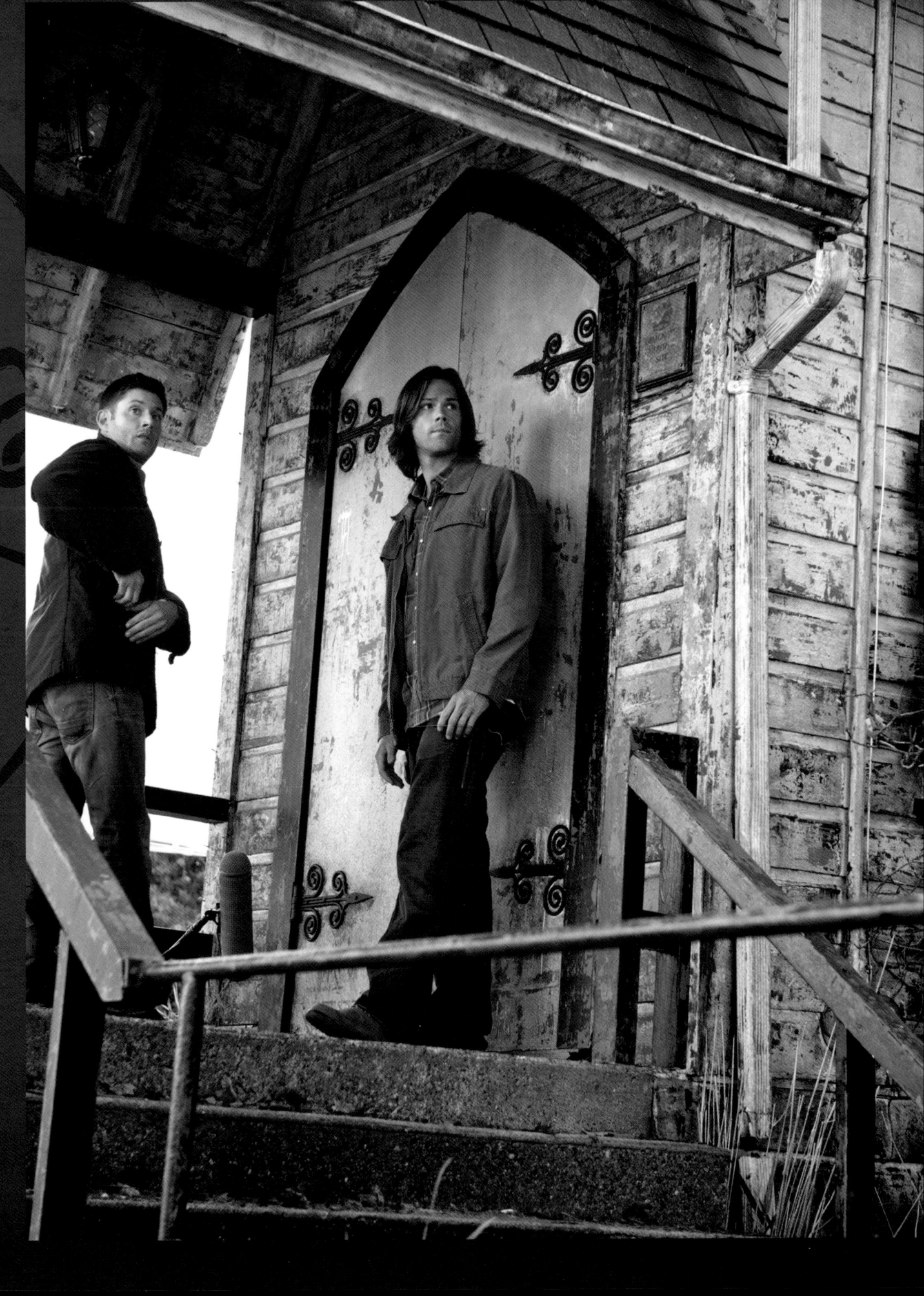

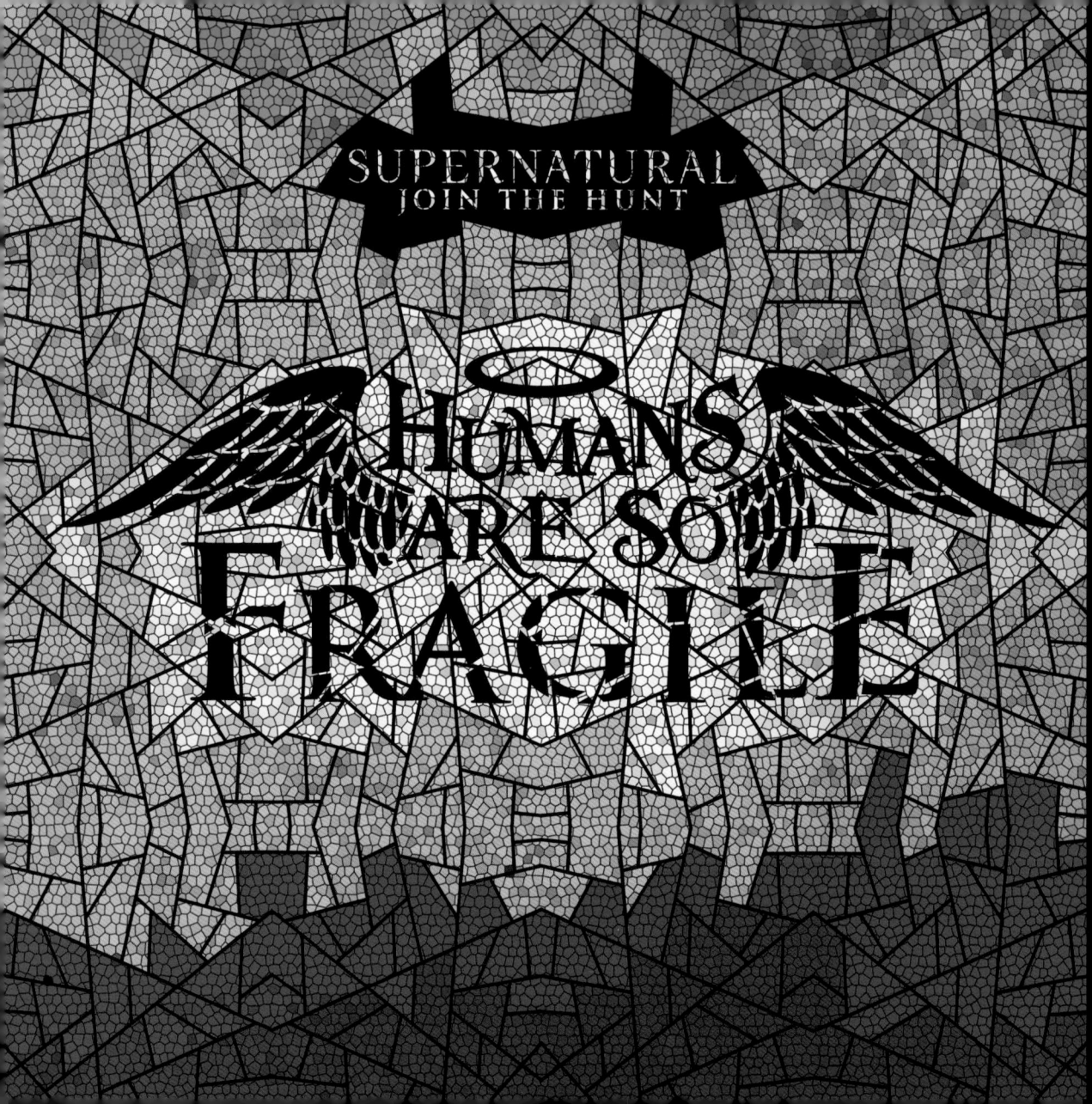
SUPERNATURAL
JOIN THE HUNT
HUMANS
ARE SO
FRAGILE

SUPERNATURAL

by Carver Edlund

SCARECROW

TERROR IN THE CORN FIELD

A visit to Burkitsville, Indiana reveals a terrifying secret in the sleepy rural town. Can Sam and Dean put their differences behind them and stop the next sacrifice?

Flying Wiccan PRESS

"A very scary read, indeed. Hey - that rhymes."
George Neuman, Comic Addicts Monthly

#10

PRINTED IN THE USA

SUPERNATURAL

by Carver Edlund

ROUTE 666

THE HIGHWAY TO HELL

When Dean's old flame needs help, the boys come to the rescue. Our heros investigate a series of racially motivated murders in Missouri. A large black truck with an impressive lift kit is implicated in the crimes.

Flying Wiccan PRESS

"This ain't your average truck, and I'm not just talkin' about the engine."
Jeff Budnick, Comic Universe

#12

PRINTED IN THE USA

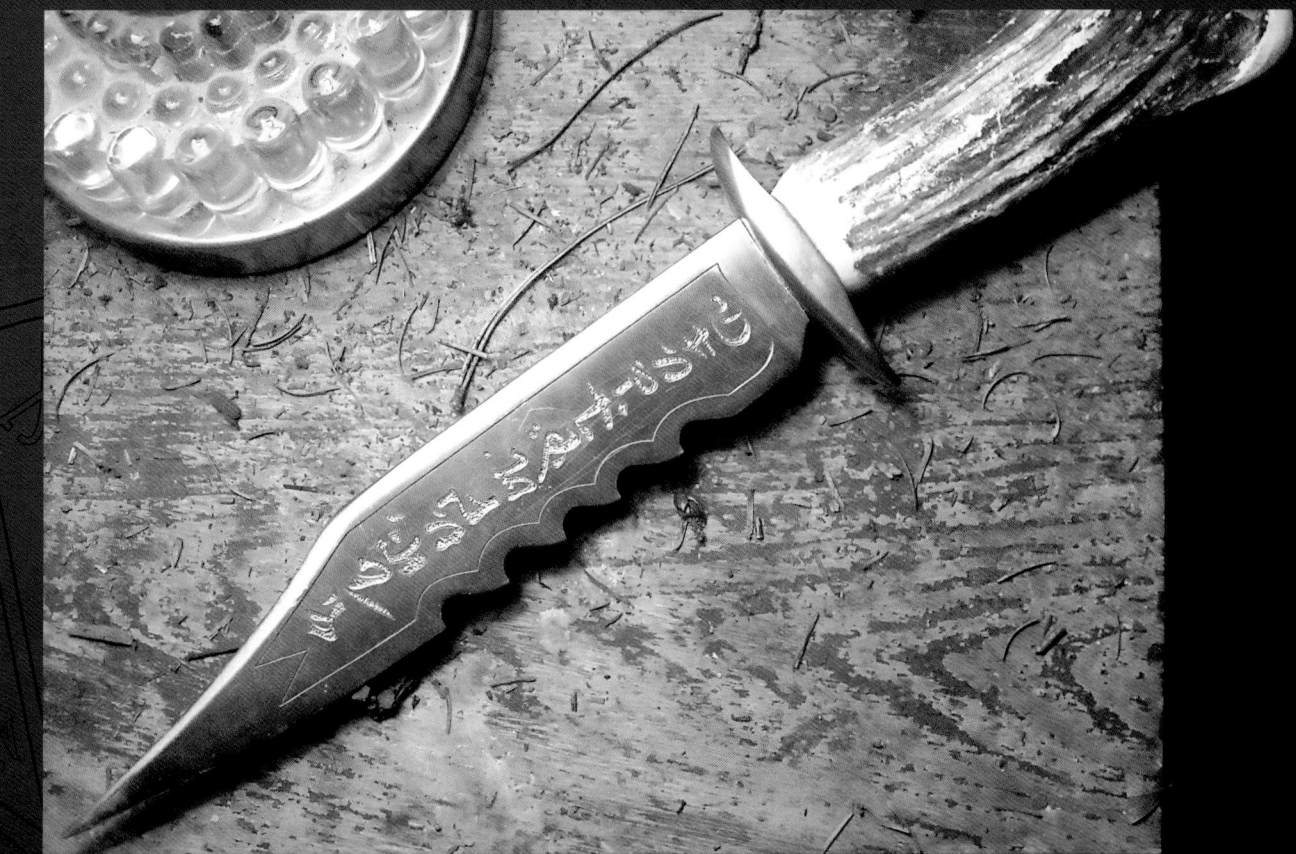

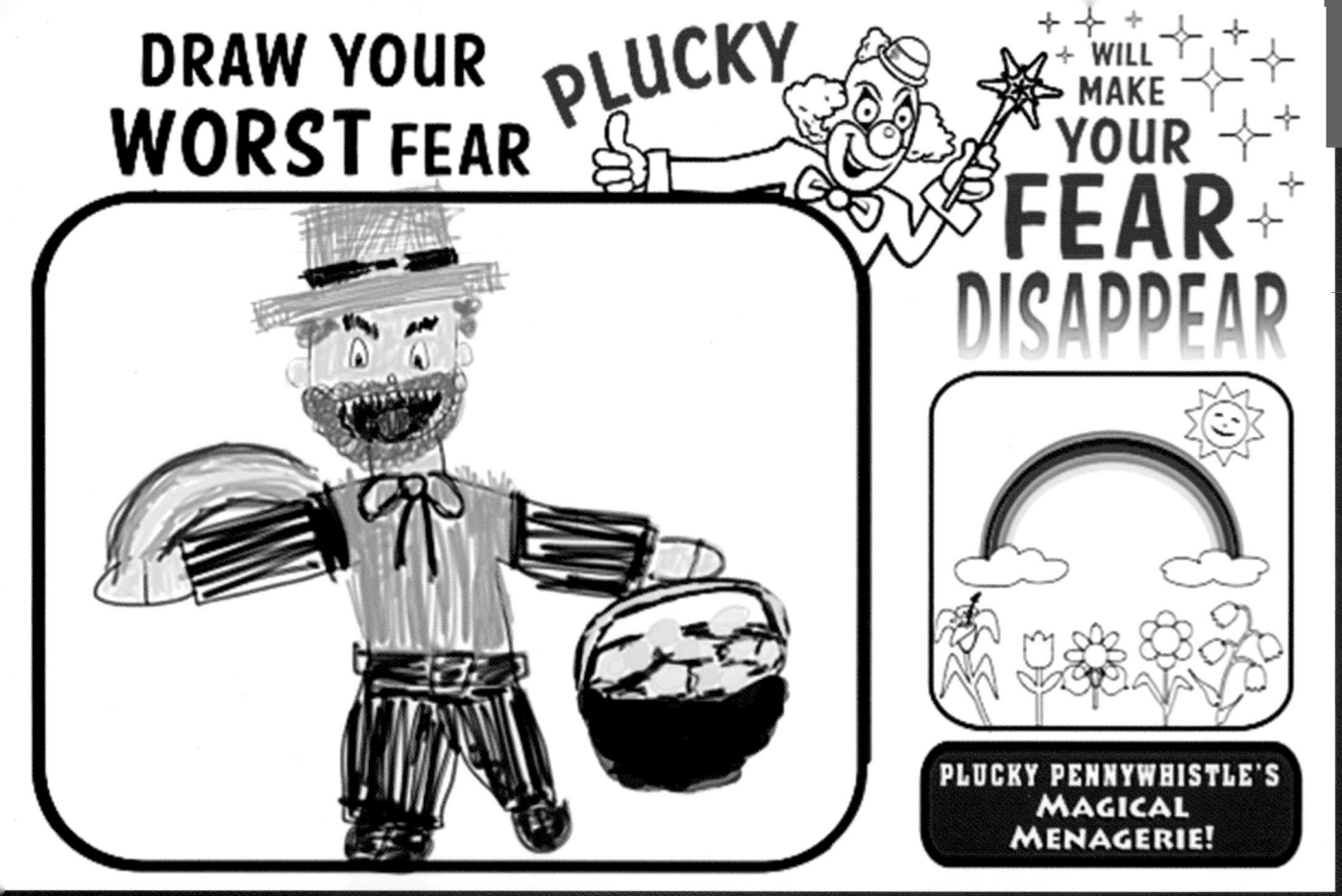
DRAW YOUR
WORST FEAR
PLUCKY
WILL
MAKE
YOUR
FEAR
DISAPPEAR
PLUCKY PENNYWHISTLE'S
MAGICAL
MENAGERIE!

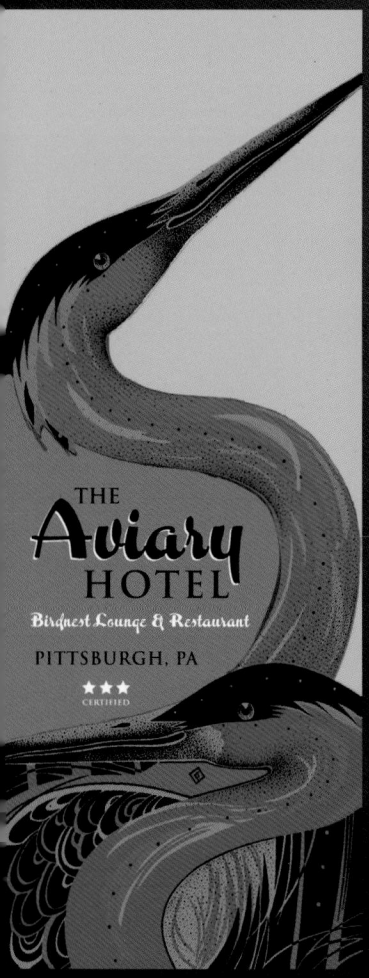
THE
Aviary
HOTEL
Birdnest Lounge & Restaurant
PITTSBURGH, PA
★★★
CERTIFIED

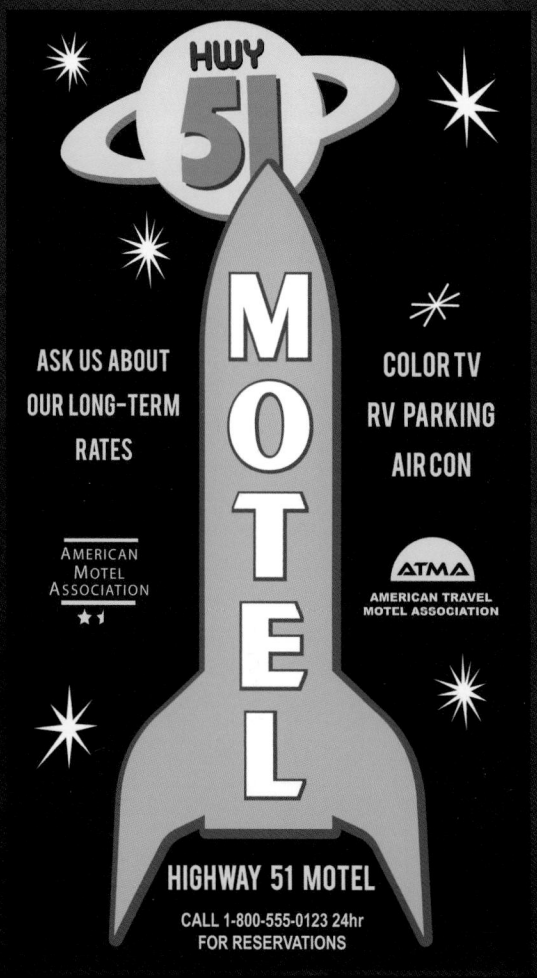
HWY
51
MOTEL
ASK US ABOUT
OUR LONG-TERM
RATES
COLOR TV
RV PARKING
AIR CON
AMERICAN
MOTEL
ASSOCIATION
★1
ATMA
AMERICAN TRAVEL
MOTEL ASSOCIATION
HIGHWAY 51 MOTEL
CALL 1-800-555-0123 24hr
FOR RESERVATIONS

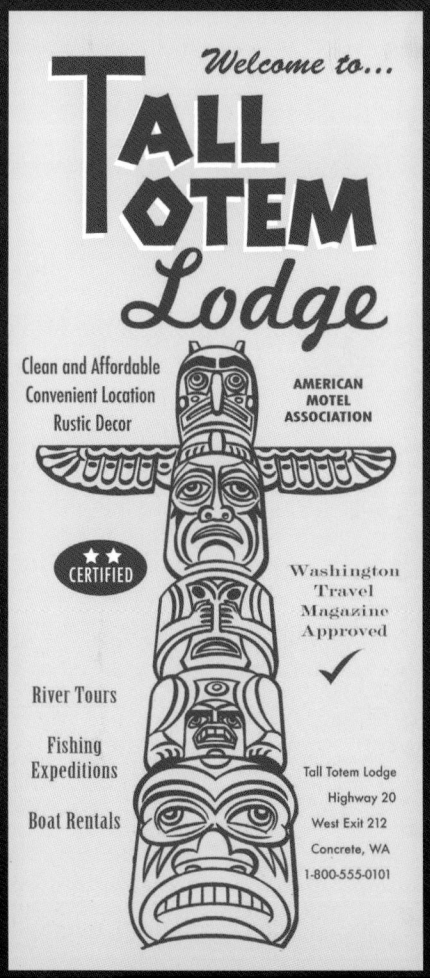
Welcome to...
TALL
TOTEM
Lodge
Clean and Affordable
Convenient Location
Rustic Decor
AMERICAN
MOTEL
ASSOCIATION
★★
CERTIFIED
Washington
Travel
Magazine
Approved
River Tours
Fishing
Expeditions
Boat Rentals
Tall Totem Lodge
Highway 20
West Exit 212
Concrete, WA
1-800-555-0101

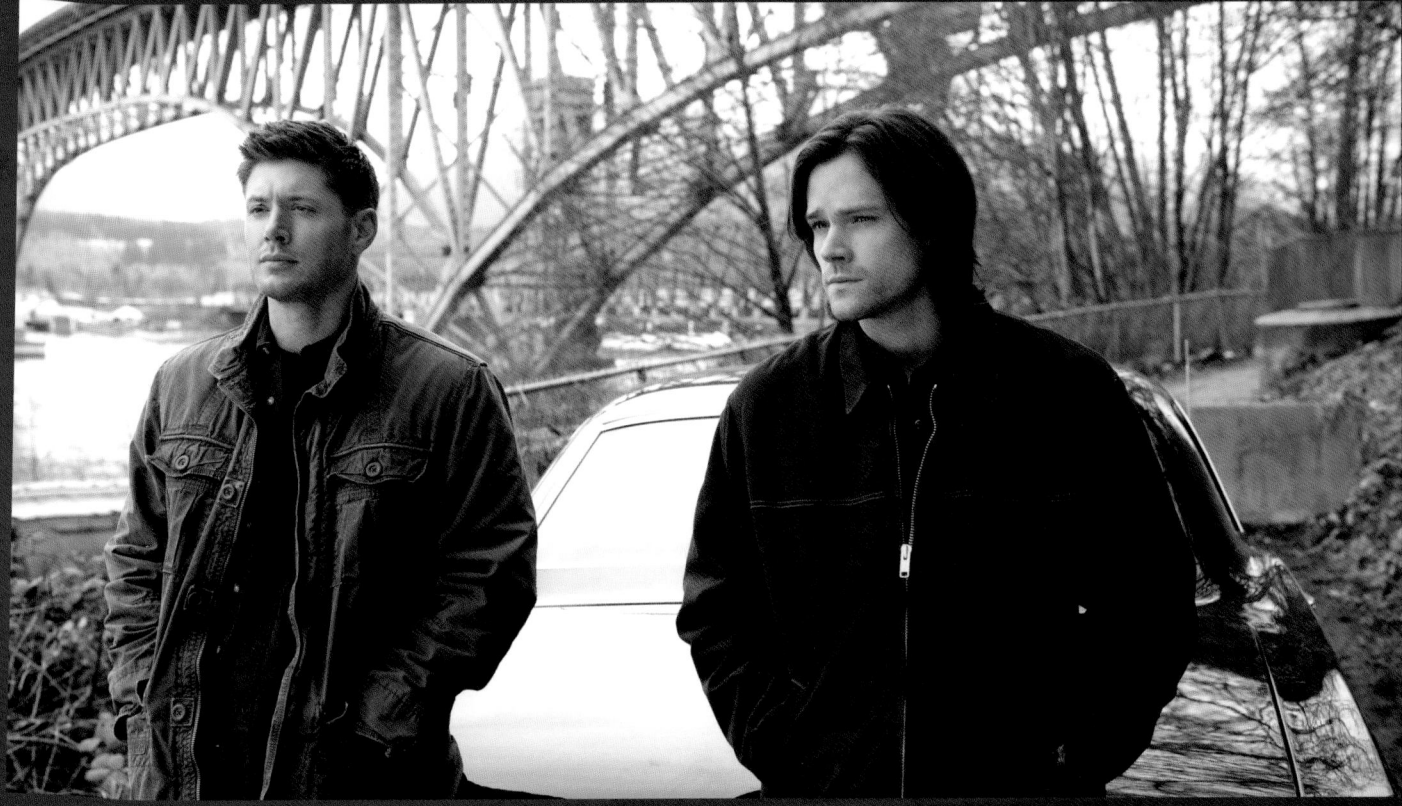

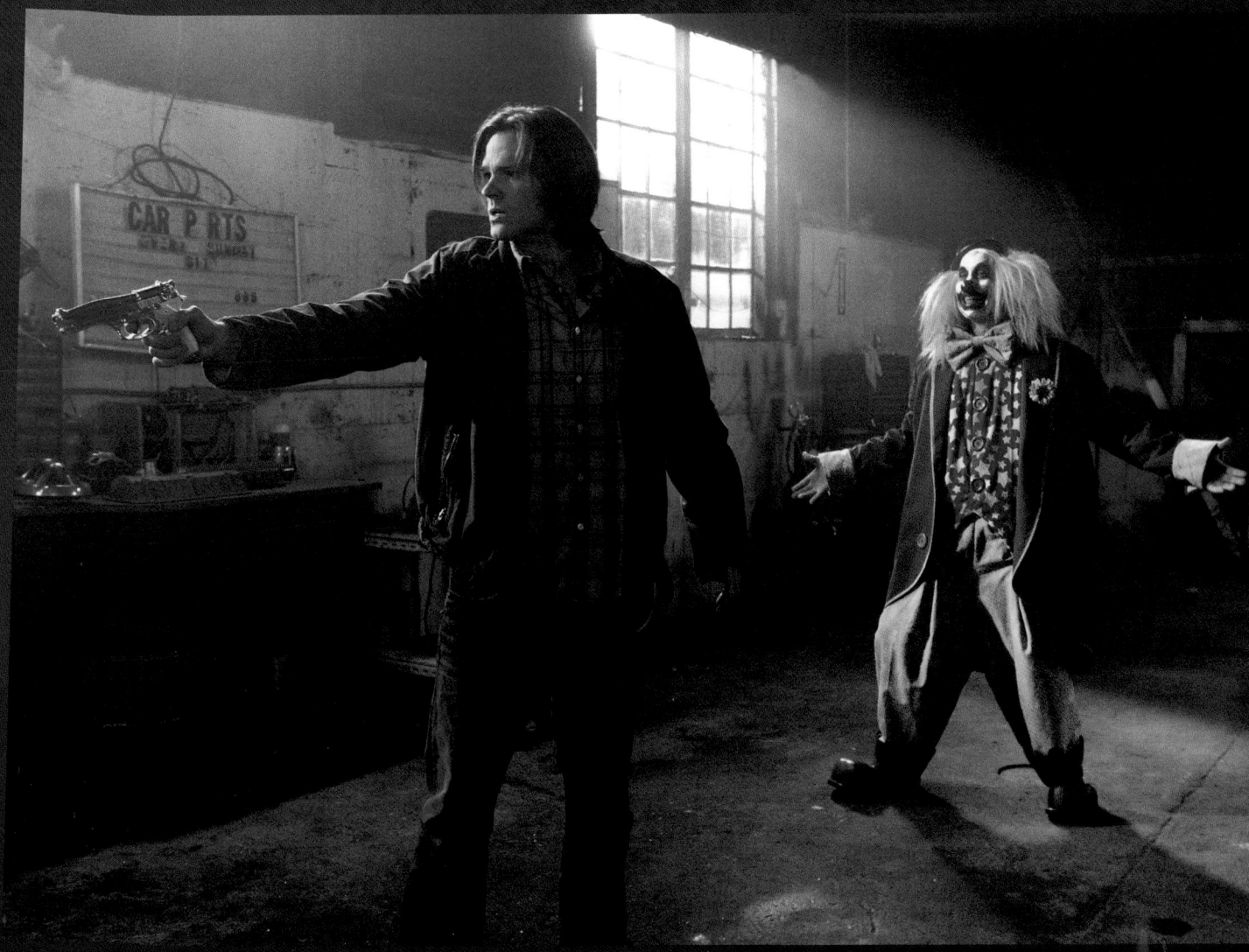
CAR PARTS

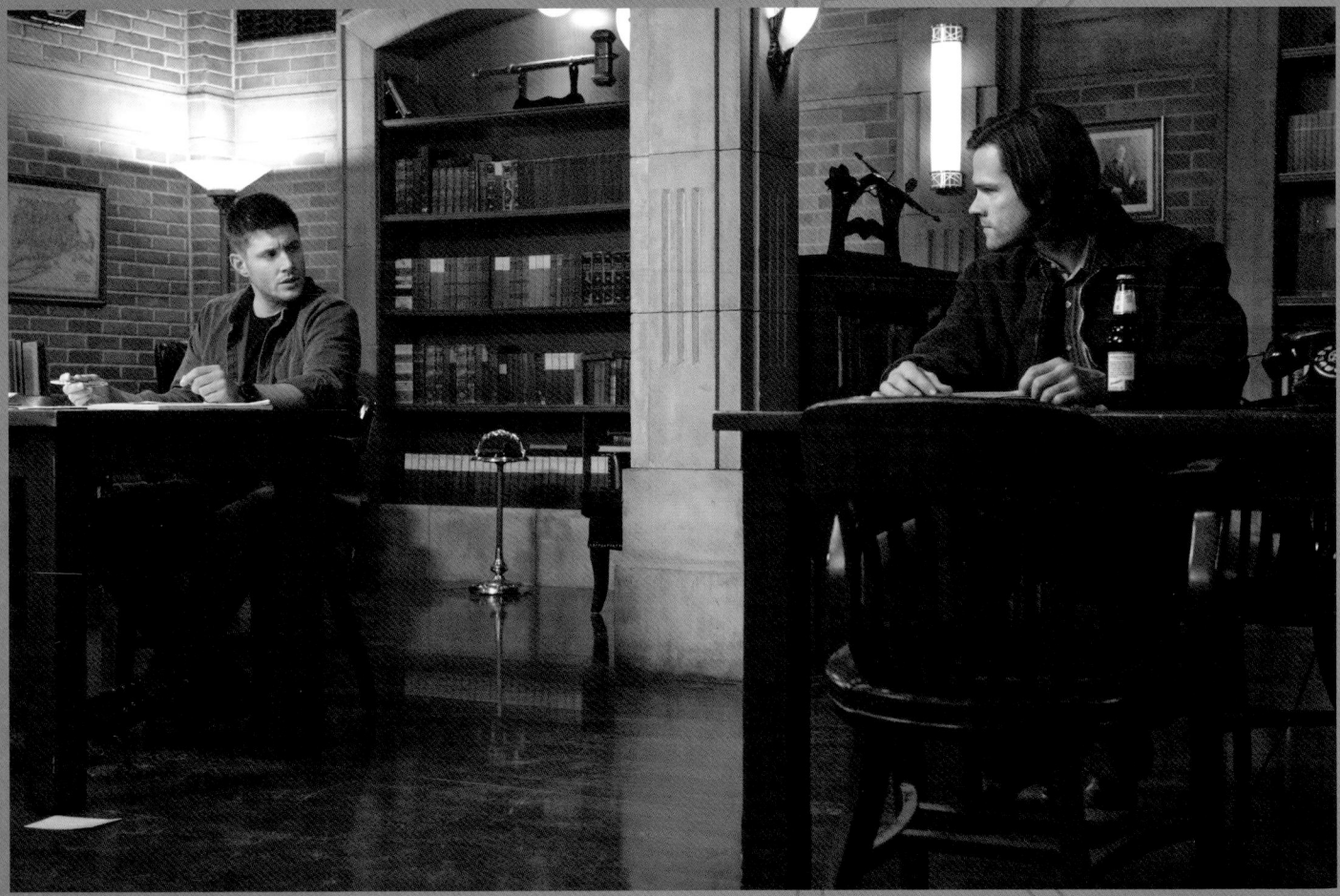

INSIGHT
EDITIONS

PO Box 3088
San Rafael, CA 94912
www.insighteditions.com

Find us on Facebook: www.facebook.com/InsightEditions
Follow us on Twitter: @insighteditions

Copyright © 2016 Warner Bros. Entertainment Inc.
SUPERNATURAL and all related characters and elements are trademarks of and © Warner Bros. Entertainment Inc.

www.cwtv.com/supernatural

Published by Insight Editions, San Rafael, California, in 2016.
All rights reserved. No part of this book may be reproduced in any form without written permission from the publisher.

Library of Congress Cataloging-in-Publication Data available.

ISBN: 978-1-60887-818-5

Publisher: Raoul Goff
Acquisitions Manager: Robbie Schmidt
Art Director: Chrissy Kwasnik
Executive Editor: Vanessa Lopez
Production Editorial Manager: Alan Kaplan
Project Editor: Katie DeSandro
Production Editor: Elaine Ou
Junior Production Manager: Alix Nicholaeff

Illustrations by Robin F. Williams and Adam Raiti

ROOTS OF PEACE REPLANTED PAPER

Insight Editions, in association with Roots of Peace, will plant two trees for each tree used in the manufacturing of this book. Roots of Peace is an internationally renowned humanitarian organization dedicated to eradicating land mines worldwide and converting war-torn lands into productive farms and wildlife habitats. Roots of Peace will plant two million fruit and nut trees in Afghanistan and provide farmers there with the skills and support necessary for sustainable land use.

Manufactured in China by Insight Editions

20 19 18 17 16 15 14 13 12